FALLI

I was hangin[illegible]presso Bar that morning w[illegible]voice I didn't recognize called out my name. When I looked up I saw an old writer, Donald Penn. He was a short, thin man with scared brown eyes and unkempt white hair who came into Madeline's almost every morning wearing the same threadbare gray sport jacket and skinny dark tie. He'd whisper, "Cup of Ethiopian, please," to whoever was behind the counter, then spend the rest of the morning sitting in a corner, scribbling in a dirty old spiral notebook and muttering softly to himself.

Given how quiet he was, and given he and I had never spoken to each other, I was surprised when he came toward me shouting my name.

I was even more surprised when he lurched forward, flinging a small shiny object at me.

And I was most surprised of all when he fell down, dead, at my feet. . . .

"Jacob Burns is a wise-cracking, write-at-home dad with a nose for trouble. . . . Matt Witten is an up-and-coming comic genius in the amateur sleuth game. Watch this guy, but don't spill your coffee!"
—Sujata Massey, Agatha Award-winning author of *The Salaryman's Wife*

BREAKFAST AT MADELINE'S

A Jacob Burns Mystery

Matt Witten

A SIGNET BOOK

SIGNET
Published by the Penguin Group
Penguin Putnam Inc., 375 Hudson Street,
New York, New York 10014, U.S.A.
Penguin Books Ltd, 27 Wrights Lane,
London W8 5TZ, England
Penguin Books Australia Ltd,
Ringwood, Victoria, Australia
Penguin Books Canada Ltd, 10 Alcorn Avenue,
Toronto, Ontario, Canada M4V 3B2
Penguin Books (N.Z.) Ltd, 182–190 Wairau Road,
Auckland 10, New Zealand

Penguin Books Ltd, Registered Offices:
Harmondsworth, Middlesex, England

First published by Signet, an imprint of Dutton NAL,
a member of Penguin Putnam Inc.

First Printing, May, 1999
10 9 8 7 6 5 4 3 2 1

Printed in the United States of America

PUBLISHER'S NOTE
This is a work of fiction. Names, characters, places, and incidents either are the product of the author's imagination or are used fictitiously, and any resemblance to actual persons, living or dead, events, or locales is entirely coincidental.

For Zachary and Jacob

ACKNOWLEDGMENTS

I would like to thank my literary agent, Jimmy Vines; my editor, Joe Pittman; and the folks who helped me along the way: Carmen Beumer, Betsy Blaustein, Nancy Butcher, Gary Goldman, Navorn Johnson, Frances Jalet-Miller, Sujata Massey, Mark T. Phillips, Pam Reed and Malice Domestic, Bonnie Resta-Flarer, Matt Solo, Beth Teitel, Celia and Jesse Witten, and everybody at Madeline's Espresso Bar. Finally, many thanks to Nancy Seid, who is not only one heck of a wife and girlfriend, but also a darn fierce editor.

WARNING: This book is fiction! The people aren't real! Nothing in it ever happened!

One special note: I have been honored to serve on a grants panel for the Saratoga County Arts Council, one of the finest arts organizations around, and never witnessed any of the chicanery depicted herein.

1

I was hanging out at Madeline's Espresso Bar that morning, same as any other morning—except weekends, when I go heavy on the husband and father thing. It still amazes me sometimes, but I'm *forty years old* with a wife, two kids, and three hundred thousand dollars, which I hustled late last fall. The three hundred grand, that is. The wife and kids I've somehow accumulated over the years.

You've seen guys like me sitting in the back corner of every coffeehouse from Podunk to Paris. We're the wild-eyed dreamers scribbling madly in worn notebooks or hunched over coffee-stained old portable computers, muttering to ourselves. People tend to give us lots of room.

In my case, though, I'd become something of a local celeb. Last November it came out in the *Daily Saratogian* how my screenplay sold for a million big ones. Since nothing much happens in Saratoga Springs in November—and since the editor is my wife's best friend—my rather bewildered grin even made the top of page one, right above the winner of the 13th Annual Simulated Deerhunting Competition. The headline screamed, SARATOGA WRITER JACOB BURNS GOES HOLLYWOOD!

So the folks at Madeline's put my mug shot up on their bulletin board, and sometimes I'd hear tourists whispering to each other in hushed reverential tones as they pointed at me. The brave ones would come up and ask for my autograph.

That morning it was already May, and six months had passed since I became a major regional tourist attraction, but I still felt a little stunned. See, I'd spent ten long years—well, to be honest, more like fifteen—writing poignant bittersweet screenplays about migrant farmworkers, homeless Haitians, and others of their downtrodden ilk. To use that infamous *L* word, I'm a *liberal,* a stuck-in-the-60s anachronism, an amusing relic to point out to your grandchildren. After receiving several thousand rejections—at least—I finally figured out that no one in Hollywood would ever in their wildest dreams give a rat's ass about any of this stuff.

But then last year it happened: My old college roommate got the rights to a novel called *GAS,* about deadly fumes seeping out of the earth's core after an earthquake and threatening to destroy the entire population of San Francisco. I guess I must have hit a certain time in my life, because I agreed to do the adaptation. Basically, for a couple of years I'd been wanting to buy myself a pair of hundred-dollar prescription sunglasses. *GAS* seemed like a good way to finally achieve that dream.

So I wrote the thing, in five short weeks. And the rest, as they say, is history. One million buckaroos. Even after the agents, managers, lawyers, producers, accountants, unions, Internal Revenue Service, and other bloodsuckers drank their fill, and even after I treated myself to *two-hundred*-dollar sunglasses, I still wound up with that three hundred K, free and clear.

And not only that, advance word on *The Gas that Ate San Francisco,* which would come out this Christmas, was awesome. So now every studio in Hollywood had a disaster flick they wanted me to work on. Showers of deadly hundred-ton meteors . . . gigantic man-eating weeds . . . a thousand cloned grizzly bears set loose in New York City . . .

Of course, I still had no takers on any of my poignant, bittersweet screenplays.

My agent set up a deal for me to adapt another novel, about a lethal hairy green fungus, transmitted by soap. (I kid you not.) But whenever I sat down to write the darn thing, my brain froze up and all I could think about was eating another handful of Nestlé chocolate bits. I gained twenty pounds without finishing a single page, and eventually realized I'd better take a break from writing before I started looking like Marlon Brando.

Bottom line, I needed a break, period. For fifteen years I'd spent my life anxiously chained to the keyboard, on an endless quest for one perfect word after another. Ever since my kids were born I'd been feeling a wee bit perturbed, to put it mildly, that my better half provided a good two-thirds of our decidedly moderate income. But now, abracadabra, I'd rubbed the magic lamp called Hollywood and woken up wealthy. And like a lifer unexpectedly released on parole, I suddenly didn't know what the heck to do with myself. This strange new freedom was baffling.

For right now, all I wanted to do was sip coffee at Madeline's, read their newspapers, do the crosswords, and chill out. Which is what I was doing on that morning in May when a voice I didn't recognize called out my name. This happened a lot lately; if it wasn't a tourist, then it was some aspiring young writer wanting me to recommend them to my agent.

When I looked up, though, I saw an old writer: Donald Penn. Or as everyone at Madeline's referred to him, The Penn. I'd never heard him speak out loud before. He was a short, thin man with scared brown eyes and long unkempt white hair who came into Madeline's almost every morning wearing the same threadbare gray sport jacket and skinny dark tie. He'd whisper "Cup of Ethiopian, please," to whoever was behind the counter, then spend the rest of the morning sitting in a corner, scribbling in a dirty old spiral notebook and muttering softly to himself.

In short, he acted very much like me, except a lot crazier—or at least, I hoped so. Certainly his beard was scragglier.

Given how quiet he was, and given he and I had never spoken to each other, I was surprised when he came toward me shouting my name.

I was even more surprised when he lurched forward, flinging a small shiny object at me.

And I was most surprised of all when he fell down, dead, at my feet.

2

Not that I knew he was dead. I figured he was drunk, or maybe he'd just tripped on one of Madeline's quasi-Oriental rugs. "Mr. Penn? You okay?" I asked.

But he didn't answer, and he didn't move, either. Everyone in the espresso bar was staring at me. I knew I was supposed to put down the Arts and Leisure section and *do* something. But what? Beyond Band-Aids and kisses, my medical expertise is limited.

I shook The Penn. Nothing. Trying to ignore his rotten fishlike odor, I bent down and felt his neck. No pulse. I put my hand in front of his nose and felt a tickle, but it was just some stray hairs from The Penn's mustache.

"Call an ambulance," I heard someone say, and then realized the croaking voice was mine.

Noise and commotion suddenly burst out behind me, people running around and screaming for a phone. Some guy in a Buffalo Bills jacket raced in from the front room, grabbed The Penn, and started banging his chest and blowing air into his mouth.

As Buffalo Bill pounded away just like the studs on *ER*, I looked down at my shaking left hand. Somehow I was still clutching the shiny object that Penn had flung at me.

It was a key. In fact, a very familiar key—I had one just like it at home.

My hand was holding the key to a safety-deposit box at the Saratoga Trust Bank.

Buffalo Bill wiped sweat off his forehead and frowned. An ambulance roared up and three hyper-efficient EMTs dashed in, zapped and tubed The Penn to no avail, then carried his body out on a stretcher.

Reality suddenly hit me like one of those hundred-ton meteors. Donald Penn was stone cold dead. *And as he was dying, he tossed me the key to his safety-deposit box.*

Why?

There was only one possible explanation I could think of: The crazy bastard knew he was dying . . . and his final dying wish was to have me open his box.

It gave me the shivers.

Three unhappy-looking cops came in and questioned me, followed by a cute young reporter from the *Daily Saratogian.* They all wanted to know exactly what had happened.

I told them what I saw; it looked like a heart attack. But I never mentioned the key. I figured it was nobody's business but mine. Mine and The Penn's.

They didn't probe too hard. Clearly this was just another sad-sack derelict biting the dust from too much booze and too much scrounging for leftover, half-eaten Happy Meals from the McDonald's garbage bin.

So less than five minutes later, the cops let me go. I stepped out of Madeline's and blinked up at the blue May sky. My feet started moving, and before I knew it, I found myself walking up Broadway toward the Saratoga Trust Bank.

I had to sidestep hordes of young mothers idly wheeling their baby carriages as they basked in the sunshine. Saratoga Springs is a tourist town that takes its flowers seriously, so there were tulips, daffodils, and other splashes of color blooming all over the sidewalk. Teenage kids with weird haircuts sat on the benches smooching, and Skidmore College women were out in force wearing ultra-tight tops and ultra short skirts. All of this springtime festiveness made The Penn's death seem even more bizarre.

As I headed up the marble steps of the bank, I wondered what I'd find in his box. Old love letters? Thick stacks of thousand-dollar bills? Dirty socks?

I walked up to the thin-lipped, middle-aged woman who spent her days perched like a withered parrot outside the bank's imposing safety-deposit vault. The way it works at the Saratoga Trust, you give Ms. Thin Lips your key and sign a form, after which she proceeds to open the vault's thick steel doors. Once inside, she hands you your box, and then turns her back to give you some privacy as you put in or take out your valuables. Or if you request it, you get your own small private room.

So I gave The Penn's key to Thin Lips and waited while she got out the form. She looked down at it, then up at me, and frowned. "You're not Donald Penn," she said.

"No, he gave me his key. He wanted me to get something out of his box," I explained.

She eyed her form doubtfully. "He has not authorized you to do that."

"Well, but he gave me the key."

"You are required to obtain his official authorization."

"That'll be a little hard to do. He's dead."

She stared at me, not sure if I was making some kind of sick joke. I decided to give her the works. A tear fell from my eye, a trick I learned from an actress friend once, and I blubbered, "He died right in front of me, thirty minutes ago."

But Thin Lips just constricted her lips even more. I don't know how she managed to get her words out through that tightly zipped mouth. "Unless you're a family member, or you're mentioned in his will, you can't get into his box."

Death to all bureaucrats. *"Ever?"*

"An individual's safety-deposit box is sealed after his or her death. The laws and regulations in this regard are extremely strict."

I thought for a moment, then said, "Oh." Not exactly brilliant, I know, but it was all I could come up with.

Her eyes narrowed suspiciously, until they were even thinner than her lips. "What do you want from Mr. Penn's box, anyway?"

I stood up huffily and threw the woman my snootiest frown. "I'm surprised you would ask. That's a breach of privacy, is it not?"

Thin Lips gave a guilty little start. As I turned and walked away, I could feel her glaring at my back. It was the most fun I'd had all morning.

That night, after our kids were in bed, my wife and I sat on the front porch sipping our almond sunset tea. "What was this guy's story, anyway?" I asked obsessively, for maybe the hundredth time.

"Maybe he was a secret millionaire, the bastard son of Aristotle Onassis," Andrea suggested.

"No, really," I said.

"He's a Venusian spy who faked his own death in order to escape his tyrannical masters."

I shook my head and laughed. Andrea is by nature an upbeat person, and she's also an expert at getting me to lighten up—a skill she was forced to acquire during all those years of being married to a struggling writer.

Andrea looks like a 60s folk singer, with long black hair down to her waist, freckles, and deep brown eyes that reach right into you. Thanks to long hours of working out at the Y, she's in even better shape than she was before her pregnancies.

In short, she's a beautiful woman.

Sometimes when I would sit at Madeline's and think about my life, and how the highlight of my career was some inane B flick about killer gas, I'd get really depressed. But then I'd think about Andrea, Babe Ruth, and Wayne Gretzky, and feel okay again.

Babe Ruth is our five year old, and Gretzky is three. They used to be Daniel and Nathan until they decided to change their names.

After kidding around with Andrea on the front porch, and then kissing my sleeping boys good night, I was able to put The Penn's safety-deposit box out of my mind and get some sleep.

But the next day, while reading the *Daily Saratogian*, all my irritation at being unable to get into his box returned full force. The story on The Penn's death described in moving detail how he had died in my arms. Actually, of course, he'd died at my feet, but why quibble?

The cute young reporter had learned that The Penn's body was examined by the county medical examiner, who declared that the cause of death was indeed a heart attack. But the reporter hadn't succeeded in learning much else about The Penn beyond his age, fifty-three, and his address, 511 Broadway. She mentioned that he was a writer, but said he had no known publications. And no known relatives, no known jobs . . . no known anything.

I sat at the kitchen table wondering if The Penn's friends—assuming he had any—called him Donald or Don, or Donny. Then, thrusting that thought aside, I went out to the driveway with Gretzky to play hockey. His babysitter was sick, and today was Tuesday, one of the three days Andrea teaches at the local community college. So that left me holding the bag—or in this case, the baby.

Gretzky is the more easygoing of our two children, with a knack for relaxing and enjoying the simple pleasures of life, a talent he must have inherited from his mother. The one time he gets really fierce is when he's playing hockey. So he and I battled each other all morning in a hotly contested, no-holds-barred game. I played pretty well, I thought, but the kid is tough, and he beat me 83 to 0.

Then he held his crotch and started dancing. A dead giveaway. "Do you want to make peepee?" I asked.

"Hockey players don't make peepee," Gretzky answered firmly.

"Sure they do."

"No, they don't!"

Normally Gretzky is, as I said, the cheerful, easygoing sort. But not today. After several minutes of attempted rational explanations, followed by several minutes of attempted evenhanded negotiations, I eventually wound up carrying him kicking and screaming to the bathroom, just in the nick of time. He let loose about three gallons.

I figured he was just acting obstinate because he was sleepy, so I said gently, "Honey, time for a nap."

"Hockey players don't take naps," he declared angrily.

Oh, Lord.

Forty-five minutes and several Dr. Seuss books later, I tiptoed out of his bedroom, thrilled that I was about to get some time to myself. But then the door creaked. "Daddy?" Gretzky called out.

I gritted my teeth and tried to keep the desperation out of my voice, because if Gretzky heard it, he'd never let me go. "Yes, sweetheart?"

"Do hockey players die?"

I came back in and sat down on Gretzky's bed. "Only when they get very, very old."

"We've been alive for so long today, maybe we won't ever die."

Maybe we won't ever die. Without warning, The Penn poured into my mind again, lurching forward, flinging me that key. Dying.

And other images flooded in, too. The Penn drinking coffee and writing feverishly in his dirty spiral notebooks. . . . him in one corner muttering and scribbling, me in another corner muttering and scribbling. . . . How many mornings did we spend together like that, a hundred? Two hundred? And what did he do with all those notebooks of his, anyway?

Suddenly the answer shot through me. *They were in his safety-deposit box.*

"Daddy. Answer me."

The Penn wanted me to read his stuff. That was his dying wish.

"Daddy?"

I bent down and kissed him. "You're right, honey. Maybe we won't ever die. Have a nice nap, Mr. Hockey Player."

Goddamn it, I thought as I tiptoed downstairs, I can't let Penn's life work lie in a cold metal vault, unread. What if he turned out to be a secret literary genius? What if he was one of those writers who become famous after they're dead?

But he'd never even have a chance of becoming famous unless I could get into that stupid safety-deposit box. I took The Penn's key from my pocket and restlessly rubbed it between my fingers, then turned it over and read the box number on the back: "2011."

An idea started forming in my head, but suddenly the phone rang loudly. I grabbed it fast, praying it hadn't woken my son. "Hello?"

"Mutant beetles!"

"What?"

"Mutant beetles take over Los Angeles," my agent explained. "Warner Brothers. *Five hundred K.*"

"No." Jesus, what next—satanic gerbils? Carrying the portable phone, I walked into the study and searched my top desk drawer until I found what I was looking for: the key to my own safety-deposit box.

"Will you fucking *listen* to me?!" Andrew was shouting into the phone, furious; after all, ten percent of five hundred is fifty. "It's just a *rewrite.* All you gotta do is add a few commas and exclamation points and shit."

I turned my key over: "2074." I was in luck. With a number so close to The Penn's, my safety-deposit box was probably located right near his—which fit my plan perfectly.

"Baby, this is a hot project," Andrew wheedled. "I'm talking burning. *Sherry Kaplan* is producing."

"Great. Sherry Kaplan is the only Jew in Hollywood who supported Bob Dole."

"Jacob—"

"Look, I'm sorry, Andrew, I'm taking a vacation—"

"Well, isn't that just peachy," Andrew said sarcastically. "Tell me, you *bozo,* how long do you think these offers are gonna last? I hate to inform you, but you're not the world's most brilliant screenwriter." The manipulative creep was on a roll. "You got lucky with that one movie, you better milk it for all it's worth. Don't be a jerk!"

Screw you, pal. "Actually, Andrew, I'm in the middle of a very important project."

"Oh yeah, like what—memorizing the sports section?"

"No. Like robbing a bank." I hung up the phone, turned off the ringer, and went back into the kitchen, where I poured myself a cup of coffee.

Then I sat down and began making my plans.

3

Even if I got caught breaking into The Penn's box, I told myself, they wouldn't really *do* anything to me. Maybe yell a little. I mean, I was pretty much the de facto executor of his estate, so what was the big deal if I cut a few corners?

Besides, I had an airtight plan. Saratoga Springs, being basically a one-horse town, still had banks that used a one-key safety-deposit box system. Clearly they didn't expect devious folks like me to try breaking and entering.

So here's what I'd do: simply give Thin Lips the key to my own box. Then she'd open it, and I'd tell her I didn't need the private room. She'd turn her back, just like always. Except this time . . . *this time,* while her back was turned, I'd quickly open The Penn's box, grab his stuff, close it again real fast, boom boom, and she'd never know.

Piece of cake.

Only one problem: After yesterday, Thin Lips would be suspicious. So I'd wait until she was on break, then hustle somebody else.

I was so revved up about tomorrow's grand adventure I couldn't sleep that night. I decided not to tell Andrea my plan because I knew that, practical person that she is, she'd try to talk me out of it. And I knew I'd never let her. After six months of sudden wealth that had left me shell-shocked, reading endless newspapers in lonely coffee shops, I suddenly felt awake and alive again.

So bright and early the next morning, I put on my dark sunglasses, pulled my Adirondack Lumberjacks cap down low over my eyes, and established my temporary reconnaissance headquarters next to some shrubbery on the post office steps. It was the ideal spot. I could peek around the bushes, across the street, and through a window straight into the Saratoga Trust Bank—in fact, straight into the office of the enemy, Ms. Thin Lips.

So I watched and I waited. And waited some more. Thin Lips turned out to be an extremely dedicated employee—so dedicated, in fact, that for the entire morning she didn't take a single coffee break or go to the bathroom once. Maybe bank employees didn't make peepee.

Meanwhile it seemed like everyone I knew in Saratoga Springs was mailing a letter that morning, and they all felt compelled to come over and chat. I began to feel about as inconspicuous as O.J. Simpson—not a great feeling when you're plotting grand larceny.

I had hardly begun my top-secret spy operation when I was approached by Bonnie Engels, local theater impresario/director/teacher extraordinaire. Bonnie ran the Shoeshine and a Smile Theater School, where she produced an astonishingly large-scale *Christmas Carol* every winter, with a cast that included practically every child in Saratoga County. During the rest of the year she organized a wide array of performances, workshops, and classes, managing by sheer force of personality to eke out a decent living from theater.

Bonnie was also the town's resident woman boxer.

Ever since I hit the Hollywood jackpot, she began hustling me to invest in a boxing video starring herself. She wanted to become the Jane Fonda of women's boxing. Or maybe I should say the Deepak Chopra of women's boxing, since she was always babbling about how boxing is a spiritual experience.

Right now Bonnie came up and hugged me so tight that if this were a boxing match, the referee would have blown his (or her) whistle. The woman had always been a serious hugger, but after taking up her new sport she'd become downright dangerous. Her forearms seemed to have grown three inches thicker since I saw her last, and she almost broke my back. Then she started crying. "Oh God, Jacob, I'm so sorry. I am so sorry!"

"About what?" I asked, genuinely befuddled. I didn't yet realize that the *Daily Saratogian* article would give everyone the mistaken impression that The Penn and I were bosom buddies.

Bonnie gave me a piercing look, then softened. "I mean about Donald. What an amazing *spiritual person.* Such *beautiful positive energy.* I didn't know you knew him so well."

"Actually, I didn't.

She didn't seem to hear me. "I always thought he was an *incredible* writer. So much *passion.* Did he tell you yesterday what he was working on?"

"No, he was too busy dying."

I got another piercing look. Then Bonnie wrapped her arms around me again, refusing to let go until I promised to call her any time—*"any time, day or night"*—if I needed "a friend to talk to, a shoulder to cry on, *whatever.*"

That *"whatever"* made me wonder. Did Bonnie have some kind of special late-night boxing match in mind for me? She was actually a pretty attractive woman, even if she was looking more and more like Popeye with every passing day.

I shook off that thought and tried to hide behind a newspaper so I could do my spying properly. But I must not have held the paper high enough, because I was quickly spotted by Henry Kane, the mayor of Saratoga Springs. Also owner of Kane Construction Company. And owner or part-owner of several other lucrative capitalist enterprises—including the very bank I was keeping within my criminal sight.

Kane did all of the do-gooder things you expect from small-town businessmen/politicians, like serving on the board of the Saratoga Coalition Against Child Abuse, the Literacy Volunteers of Saratoga, and other local charities. My wife, a board member of the Literacy Volunteers, said he donated generously, and I guess I shouldn't have disliked him as much as I instinctively did. He was fifty years old with distinguished silver hair but a youthful face, no doubt helped by the fact he'd never had a day's worth of worry in his life. He came from money, of course, and wore a perfect power tie, perfect capped teeth, and perfect black ribbed socks. Probably saw a barber each week to get his nostril hairs clipped.

Kane shook my hand warmly. "Jacob, I don't know what to say," he intoned.

"Neither do I," I answered truthfully.

"As President of the Saratoga Arts Council, I hate to see one of our most intriguing artists cut down in his prime. My deepest sympathies."

I thought about explaining to the mayor that The Penn and I weren't really close. But the words died on my lips, because it suddenly struck me—maybe I was The Penn's best friend.

Kane cleared his throat. "I hear Donny was making

a"—he paused meaningfully—"a significant writing breakthrough toward the end of his life."

He looked to me for confirmation. I was strangely embarrassed that I, The Penn's best friend, hadn't even known what he was writing. Not wanting to admit my ignorance, I nodded wisely. "Such a terrible thing," I agreed with a sigh. "Who knows what might have happened if he'd lived?"

The mayor gave me a piercing look. Must be my morning for piercing looks. Something passed through his normally complacent face—confusion? Fear?

Then his expression turned bland again. Patting me on the back and murmuring a few more words of comfort, he eased off down the steps.

All morning long, the procession of well-wishers on the post office steps continued unabated. For someone who'd been so obscure his whole life, Penn was sure attracting a lot of attention now.

A little after 12:30, Rob Bassin walked up. He was one of the guys working the counter at Madeline's when Penn died. A twenty-eight-year-old Skidmore film grad with a goatee, Rob bounced around Hollywood for five years after college, then gave up on that dream and came back to Saratoga, where he got a minimum-wage job at Madeline's. But then his luck improved. He got engaged to Madeline herself.

Now that he was happily ensconced in Saratoga, he'd become more sanguine about his California experience. I enjoyed talking movies with him, because whenever he liked a movie, I hated it. We had our own Siskel and Ebert routine going.

Right now I could tell from Rob's sad cocker spaniel face that he was about to offer me his heartfelt condolences. I was getting sick of this preposterous business already, so I tried to distract him by asking how his fire sale was going—engagement sale, actually. Since he was about to move in with Madeline, he was selling his sofa, bed, computer, "and other household items," as his classified ad in the *Daily Saratogian* read.

But Rob didn't let himself get distracted. He put his hand on my arm and gave it a squeeze. "How you feeling, man?"

"Fine," I said irritably.

But then, out of nowhere, a wave of terrible sadness flowed through me. So many people were treating me like I was deeply bereaved, I was starting to actually feel that way.

Or maybe what I really felt was some kind of deep subterranean psychic bond between me and Penn. Between my shell shock and his insanity.

I turned away from Rob, embarrassed by my emotions, as he said, "Madeline's feels so empty without him. I'm thinking we should hold some kind of memorial service—"

But then I stopped listening. I'd just noticed something moving out of the corner of my eye. *Could it be?*

Yes, it was! Thin Lips was actually *standing up.* And actually walking away from her desk, opening the door—

I jumped up. "Rob, I gotta run."

"Listen, Jacob—"

"Later!" Ignoring a DON'T WALK sign and a large fast-moving Bruegger's truck, I dashed across the street and through the bank's back door. No time to lose. Thin Lips was undoubtedly the kind of obsessive corporate lackey who would gobble down a ten-minute lunch and then race back to work. Stuffing my Lumberjacks cap in my day pack so I'd look more respectable, I hustled past the ATM machines to the main lobby.

I strode up to Thin Lips's office and acted dismayed

to see her empty chair. "She's not here?" I said aloud. "Oh, boy!"

When you're in a bank—a small-town bank, at least—a loud "Oh, boy!" qualifies as a major cuss-word. Banks have zero tolerance for strong emotion; I guess when you've got that much cash money lying around, you try to keep things as calm as possible. So my "Oh, boy!" got immediate results, in the form of a short, pudgy young woman hurrying toward me with a nervous smile plastered to her face, asking, "May I help you, sir?"

"Absolutely. I need something from my safety-deposit box, and Ms. Thin L—I mean, Ms. Reingold—isn't here."

"Don't worry, sir, I'm sure she'll be back soon. She never takes long lunches."

"But I'm late for my plane and I need it *immediately.* It's absolutely *essential.*"

"I'm sorry, sir, but Ms. Reingold is the only one who's authorized—"

"Oh no, this is terrible!" I raised my voice so the customers in the lobby could hear me. "I'm on my way to Hollywood to meet with Steven Spielberg and I desperately *need* my computer disk, but it's in my safety-deposit box. You've probably heard of me. I'm Jacob Burns, I wrote *The Gas that Ate San Francisco,* which is about to become a major motion picture—"

"Mr. Burns, I'm sure it won't be long—"

"One o'clock in the freaking afternoon, and I can't even get into my own safety-deposit box?!" I yelled. *"What the hell kind of bank is this?!"*

The poor young woman stood there openmouthed. The entire bank was watching us now.

A skinny, frightened guy wearing a gray suit, even younger than the young woman but evidently her superior, rushed toward us. "Maybe I can help you, Mr. Burns."

"I certainly hope so," I growled, brusquely handing him my safety-deposit key.

Young Gray Suit started to say something, but instead just nodded. The paperwork went down smoothly, and in less then three minutes we were inside the vault.

He unlocked my safety-deposit box and handed it over. He offered me the private room, and I turned it down. So far, so good.

But then, to my dismay, he watched me as I put my box on a metal shelf and pretended to look inside it for my computer disk. *Come on, birdbrain, turn around already,* I implored silently. But he stayed put.

"So what's on this disk, anyway?" he asked conversationally.

"Hey, aren't you supposed to turn around?"

Young Gray Suit just laughed, thinking I was joking. Apparently some sloppy bank official—someone other than Thin Lips—had trained him insufficiently in bank-vault etiquette. Or maybe he was just being young and rebellious. Because now, safe from the watchful eyes of his colleagues, he was loosening up and turning positively friendly. Exactly what I didn't need. "So you're really meeting with Spielberg?"

"I'm serious; Ms. Reingold always turns her back."

At the mention of her name, Young Gray Suit instantly tightened up. No surprise there; the woman had the same effect on me. Young Gray Suit frowned. "You're not trying to pull anything, are you?"

"Of course not," I said with a chuckle.

He chuckled too. And, thank God, finally turned his back.

I whipped out The Penn's key and found box number 2011. The key turned easily enough in the lock. But when I started to take out the box it made a horrifying rasping sound—metal scraping metal—*scree-eek!*

I froze, expecting Young Gray Suit to turn back around. Suddenly that whole rationale about just cutting a few corners wasn't so reassuring anymore. If this guy caught me redhanded with two safety-deposit boxes open in front of me, I was in deep shit. How deep I didn't know, but I suspected Thin Lips would get a thrill out of making my life truly miserable.

And no way in hell would I ever get another shot at The Penn's box.

But amazingly, so far the bank guy hadn't moved. Either that *scree-eek!* wasn't really as loud as it sounded to my insanely terrified ears, or else he just assumed the noise came from my metal box being jostled on the metal shelf as I searched for a disk. In any case, I took a deep breath and looked down at The Penn's box. I'd pulled it out two inches, which meant thirteen more inches of metallic rasping left to go.

My adrenaline was pumping so fast it didn't even occur to me to just shove the box back in and give up. Instead I pulled the box out more, and the *scree-eek!* got even worse. Desperate to cover up the sound, I started babbling fast and loud. "Actually, I'm gonna tell Spielberg about this new movie idea I have. It's about a—" *Scree-eek!* I noisily cleared my throat and blathered on rapidly, "This movie, it's about a guy like you in his twenties—picture Leonardo DiCaprio, okay?—who's working at some dead-end job, like a bank or something, and all of a sudden—*all of a sudden!*" I yelled, as I yanked The Penn's box the rest of the way out.

"All of a sudden what?" asked Young Gray Suit, and he started turning around.

I quickly shielded The Penn's box from his sight. "Hey, watch it, or I'll tell Ms. Reingold."

The guy still couldn't tell if I was joking or not, but he decided not to take any chances. He turned away.

"So what happens?" he asked.

I didn't answer. I barely even heard him. At last, I had Donald Penn's mysterious safety-deposit box right there in front of me, ripe for the plucking. But what if there was nothing in it after all but dirty socks? I reached out and opened it.

And stood there in awe.

The Penn's entire life work was staring up at me. The 10 x 12 x 15–inch box was crammed to overflowing with spiral notebooks, looseleaf notebooks, old-fashioned composition notebooks, white scrap paper, pink scrap paper, toilet paper, old menus, paper bags, torn milk cartons. . . .

And every single one of these motley surfaces was filled from top to bottom with Donald Penn's very small, very neat handwriting.

Behind me Young Gray Suit tapped his feet restlessly.

"So here's what happens," I said, opening my day pack and frantically stuffing it with The Penn's papers. "One day Leonardo is out walking in the park and there's this odd-looking little bug. A mutant beetle."

"A mutant beetle?"

I reached down and grabbed a couple of heavily scribbled-on paper towels that had fluttered to the floor. "Exactly. And this mutant beetle *jumps* onto Leonardo." I checked The Penn's box—empty. His life's work was now inside my day pack. All I had to do was get his safety-deposit box back into its slot, and I'd be home free.

"So here's the twist," I announced loudly, to cover that damn *scree-eek!* as I shoved in the box as hard as I could—

But it got stuck halfway.

"Here's the twist!" I called out even louder, as I desperately tried to twist the box back onto its tray. I yanked and rattled and shoved—***"Here's the twist!"*** I shouted—and finally, *finally,* the box slid in. Just in time too, because that final shout turned Young Gray Suit around to look at me.

I heaved a huge sigh of relief. "Okay, we're all set," I said to Young Gray Suit.

"So what's the twist?" he asked.

I thought about it for a moment. "I don't know yet. We'll have to leave that to Spielberg."

Young Gray Suit shot me a disappointed look as he led me out of the bank vault—

—and straight into Thin Lips, who was carrying her takeout lunch—salad and plain no-fat yogurt, no doubt—back to her desk. She stopped and glowered at me suspiciously. "What are *you* doing here?" she snarled.

"Mutant beetles," I said briskly, and pointed a thumb at Young Gray Suit. "Ask him. Long story. Got a plane to catch."

Then I hustled off as fast as I could without running, expecting at any moment now to hear her yell for the bank guard to stop me. I could already feel the handcuffs tightening around my wrists.

But I guess Ms. Thin Lips was too hungry to pursue the issue.

Or maybe I was just plain lucky that day.

And like my agent always tells me: It's better to be lucky than smart.

4

I jumped on my bike and dashed off, eager to examine what I hoped would be a masterpiece. Some seemingly poverty-stricken derelicts squirrel away millions of dollars. Had The Penn squirreled away millions of precious words?

I needed to find someplace quiet and solemn, where I could let the dead man's thoughts envelop my soul. A church or synagogue would be perfect, except that places of worship always gave me the heebie jeebies, so I went to the next best place.

Madeline's.

Early afternoon is their slowest time and the front room was deserted except for Rob, my ex–film major friend, and the one and only Madeline herself. Madeline is a slightly plump but attractive young dynamo who used to work at the mall. Like most people who work at malls, she hated it. Unlike most people, though, she figured out a way to do something about it. She opened up her very own espresso bar.

Madeline's was a classy joint with marble tabletops, comfortable sofas and easy chairs, and esoteric magazines. At first, we Saratogians just shook our heads. We already had one bagel place and one upscale coffee shop, and we figured there was no way our little town could support an espresso bar, too, for goodness sake. But Madeline proved us wrong, and now, at age twenty-nine, she was one of Saratoga's most impressive, successful young citizens. Almost enough to make you believe in capitalism.

Madeline and Rob were behind the counter leafing through a bridal magazine when I walked in. She was exuberantly pushing the merits of baked salmon as a main wedding dish, and he was indulgently nodding his head. I smiled. They made a cute couple: the bubbly outgoing type and the quiet artistic type. Kind of like my marriage with Andrea.

They looked up as I came over to the counter. "Hey man, where'd you run off to this morning?" asked Rob.

I knew if I told him the truth he wouldn't believe me any more than my agent had, so I went ahead. "I was robbing a bank," I said.

"Yeah, right," he snorted, as Madeline came around the counter and gave me a hug. "Oh, Jacob, we're gonna miss that guy," she said.

I nodded. "So what do you know about him, anyway? What was his shtick?"

Madeline furrowed her eyebrows. "All I really know is he liked Ethiopian. I used to make it just for him—hardly anyone else ever drank it."

Rob smiled wryly. "I guess people don't like eating or drinking stuff from a country where everyone's always starving to death. It's bad karma."

Madeline sighed. "I made a pot of Ethiopian this morning, and it's just sitting there. Makes me sad."

"I'll have some," I told her. She looked at me and nodded gratefully.

Rob took her arm. "Hey, you know what would be really cool? When we do our memorial ceremony for The Penn, we should give everyone a cup of Ethiopian."

"Yeah, that'll bring people in for sure," I teased Rob. He looked a little hurt, so I added, "Just kidding. That's a real nice touch."

I paid for my coffee and headed for the corner table in the back room, my favorite spot. But unfortunately, Madeline had just hung a new exhibit, and right above my head was a bizarre pointillist painting of a grossly overweight, naked man sunning himself on the beach. The kind of thing that can ruin your digestion.

I angled my chair so I wouldn't be facing Pointillist Fat Man, but the walls were covered by other obese nudes, and no matter how I angled my chair I couldn't escape them. I muttered "Oh phooey," or words to that effect, and just then Rob came up behind me. "You know," he said, "the way you sit back here muttering to yourself, you'd make a fabulous character in a low-budget art film."

"An anarchist? Plotting to blow up the Statue of Liberty?"

"No, I was thinking comic relief. Crazy old Uncle Fred."

Is that how he saw me? Shoot, I really must be getting old. I was tempted to tell him I truly *did* rob a bank.

Instead I opened up my day pack and brought out a fistful of pages. "Check this out. The Penn's masterpiece."

Rob's eyes widened, and he reached out his hand. "Let me see."

"No, they're mine," I said.

Rob laughed. "Yo, come on." Then he picked up a few pages from the table and started reading.

I snatched the pages away from him. I knew I was being unreasonable, but I couldn't stop myself. Rob eyed me, annoyed, and I shrugged apologetically. "I'm sorry, Rob, The Penn wanted me to have it. I'll let you read it after I finish."

"You're a nut, you know that? So why'd he want you to have it, anyway?"

"How the hell should I know?"

"Hey, I got it!" Rob snapped his fingers, excited. "We should, like, *cover* the walls with these pages. As a tribute to The Penn. Be an awesome exhibit—better than this garbage, anyway," he added, pointing up at a portrait of a gargantuan Asian woman who looked like she was leering at me.

I turned away from her. "That's a beautiful idea, Rob. I think The Penn would really have appreciated that."

Rob nodded. "I'll clear it with the boss lady."

As if she'd heard him talking about her, Madeline called out from the other room, "Or chicken if you want. We can always go with that, if you don't want salmon."

"Either one is fine, honey," Rob called back, then whispered to me, "I'll thank God when this wedding is over."

I laughed. "Don't worry, it won't be half as bad as going to the dentist."

"Yeah, but at least when you go to the dentist, you don't have to wear a tux." He stood up. "Well, happy reading, dude. Let me know if it's the next *Ulysses*."

"I hope not. *Ulysses* is junk. James Joyce is the worst famous writer that ever lived."

He threw me a disgusted look. "I don't know why we even let you into a high-class eatery like this."

As Rob walked away, I spread Penn's writings on the table in front of me. It was a huge jumble. None of the notebooks, loose pages or scribbled-on envelopes were numbered. No way of knowing where to start.

I decided to try a green spiral notebook that looked relatively recent. It was bought at Staples, which only opened up in this area about four years ago. I turned to page one.

At the top of the page was the word *Preface*.

I sipped my Ethiopian and dove in.

* * *

It was a dark and delirious day in December, I read, *when I first learned that my mother and father did not love each other.*

If only Bob Dylan and Joan Baez had stayed together. He was righteous anger and she was kindness. But how to harness the two? How to combine Tupac Shakur with Liberace?

They say no two snowflakes are ever alike. But then they say a lot of things, and where's the proof? In my mother's case, 151 proof, the result of much research: The Cheapest Way to Ingest Alcohol. Studies show 151 Clear Sky beats MD 20 20, which has it over the generic no-name beers hands down.

Myself, I go for Ethiopian, zero cents a cup where possible, until death do me part. Never touch clear sky or anything else, since the snow came down that day.

Of course, all would have transpired otherwise in these days of waxless skis. No more carefully stored containers of red, blue, and purple wax, to say nothing of glisters and clisters, which were at issue that cold winter morning. All my father wanted was a simple little ski, but where was the clister? A man has a day off, just one day, and does he want to spend it looking around the whole frigging—frigging, *not* fucking, *because they were simpler days then, and yet harder—house for his glister, or clister, memory fades, but stays with this thought: A man wants a substance, a substance to put on his skis, so his skis can glide, so he can fly, so the air rushes by, so the whish of the wind and the snow enters his soul, and the factory disappears and so does his wife and even his child—yes, I must say from this vantage point of time, yes, even his child.*

But Dylan will never marry Baez, and Tupac will never marry Liberace, except in heaven perhaps though studies show that heaven probably does not exist. For if they did marry, it would be like my father and mother, in contravention of the natural order. Do gorillas marry? Or baboons? And if they did, would the male work in a shoe factory all day? Highly unlikely, and this is what we must remember when we evaluate the actions of mere mortals for whom the merest act of love brings unbearable responsibility. And this is why we, all of us, choose to live our deepest lives in isolation—in clear sky, in Ethiopian, in newspapers. And if you choose to interrupt our lonesome glide, you do so at your peril, for one man's Ethiopian may be another man's clister, and he will fight for that ion of deepest life with every weapon at his command.

And this is why I am entitling this tome "The History of Western Civilization Careening, as Seen through the Eyes of One of Its Primary Practitioners." Volume 1, as you shall see, is History. Volume 2 is Careening. And Volume 3 is Practicing.

Pretty darn weird, I thought to myself, but intriguing. Not really my cup of tea, but then again, neither is Joyce.

I took another sip of Ethiopian and turned the page.

Preface, I read. *It was a dark and dreamy night when I first learned that O.J. Simpson and Paula Barbieri did not love each other. To those who would say, no, O.J. was at this time a mere child with rickets, and it was your own progenitors at issue, I would reply: All life is metaphor, and one man's clister is another man's Ethiopian.*

Indeed, all might have transpired otherwise in these days of waxless skis. The years of red, green, and blue wax are no more, and you can travel the streets for many years, as I have, without meeting a man who knows whether it's clister or glister . . .

I skimmed the rest of the page long enough to determine this was a reworking of the same preface. Again, there seemed to be some indication that his father had been searching for clister, or glister, one snowy morning so he could put it on his cross-country skis. Beyond that, the narrative once again twisted, turned, and ended with the now-familiar announcement that this was a preface to a three-volume *"History of Western Civilization Careening, as Seen through the Eyes of One of Its Primary Practitioners."*

I turned the page.

Preface, I read. *Snoopy might have said it was a dark and lonely night, and he would have been correct, the most common and even comical clichés being the truest. Here, of course, the wrinkle was clister, or as some would have it, glister.*

I flipped the page.

Preface, I read. *Beware of clister; or as it may be, Ethiopian.*

I flipped again.

Preface, I read.

I flipped. *Preface.* I flipped again, and again, and again. *Preface. Preface. Preface.*

I put the notebook down and picked up another one. A red one, with a date on the cover: *June, 1983.* Beneath that Penn had written: *Civ Careening: Vol. 2.*

Volume 2. Okay, here we go. I opened up the notebook. *Preface,* I read. *Every man has a clister, or glister, as I learned one dark and snowy night . . .*

I quickly turned the page. *Preface.* Shit. I flipped the pages faster and faster, reading that ugly word *Preface* over and over, getting more and more frantic.

I flung the notebook down, snatched another one and opened it. My heart sank.

I threw open every single notebook. They went back thirty years, to 1968, and with every goddamn one it was the same. I shook all of The Penn's restaurant menus, Kleenexes, and cereal boxes out of my day pack. Each and every available writing surface had the word *Preface* at the top.

I threw the whole mess on the floor and sat there. Donald Penn.

His whole life had been one big preface.

And that was all.

Finis.

5

I sat there gloomily puzzling over the clister—or glister—of life, when suddenly a cheerful voice interrupted me. "Writing the Great American Screenplay?" said the voice.

It belonged to Gretchen Lang, the one and only executive director of the Saratoga Arts Council for the past fifteen years. If all arts administrators were as top-notch as Gretchen, then art galleries would be as crowded as Knicks games, theater would still be alive, and ballet dancers would be so famous they'd get their own shoe commercials.

Sweet as Adirondack maple syrup on the outside but tough as a Mamet play inside, Gretchen had almost singlehandedly transformed the Arts Council from a genteel coffee klatch of lady landscape painters to a powerhouse quasi-public nonprofit corporation with a yearly budget of $200,000. Which was huge, by Saratoga standards. Gretchen's Arts Council was involved in financing just about every theater opening, gallery exhibit, or other cultural event in the entire Saratoga County area. If you were a Saratoga Springs artist, you definitely wanted Gretchen Lang on your side.

Gretchen's biggest coup came last year when, after a decade of ardent lobbying, she convinced the mayor and city council that what Saratoga needed to attract more tourists and keep business away from the malls was a glamorous new Cultural Arts Center right in the heart of downtown, which would be run, of course, by Gretchen herself. The city fathers voted to lease the old library building on Broadway to Gretchen and her Arts Council for the grand sum of *one dollar a year* for the next twenty-five years. Not bad. Especially since the building was in a great location, solidly built, and probably worth close to a million bucks.

The Cultural Arts Center as envisioned by Gretchen would feature a grand, high-ceilinged gallery on the main floor for showcasing Saratoga painters and sculptors to the rich summer tourists; a plush three-hundred-seat theater with state-of-the-art lighting and sound equipment; plentiful studio, darkroom, and classroom space; and a host of other goodies. For the past month and a half downtown traffic had been snarled by all the construction and renovation work that was being done to turn Gretchen's glorious vision into reality.

Like a mother duck with her ducklings, Gretchen generally had artists in tow whenever I saw her. Today her flock included Bonnie Engels, the boxer/theater impressario, and four other artists who fell into the "struggling" category, like most artists in Saratoga (and everywhere else). I knew everyone in today's entourage, and except for Bonnie, some of whose shows I had truly enjoyed, I didn't think any of them was particularly talented. But maybe I was just being overly hard on them because they reminded me of myself, of who I used to be. And you certainly had to give them credit for trying. Who knows, maybe one of them would even break through one day.

In any case, I was glad to see them. It gave me a break from contemplating Donald Penn's wasted life. "You guys having a party?" I asked.

"You better believe it." Gretchen smiled, waving to her crew. "This is my trusty grant panel. We just finished giving out the NYFA grants."

NYFA grants. Pronounced "knife-a." For starving New York artists, thar's gold in them thar words.

For those of you who have the good sense not to be starving New York artists, let me explain. Every year the state-funded New York Foundation for the Arts distributes grant money to arts councils sprinkled throughout the state, which in turn dole out the money to local artists. The Saratoga Arts Council gets twenty-five grand a year, and has the highly sensitive job of divvying up the dough among the eighty or so desperate local "emerging artists" who apply. The council can only say yes to about twenty of them. The losing applicants then go into deep depressions, take jobs at the post office, or both.

It may not sound like there's a lot of money at stake, but these NYFA grants are prestigious and can kick-start an artist's career. Putting that NYFA imprimatur of respectability on your résumé can help you hustle larger grants, fellowships, and artist-in-residence gigs. And it's something to tell your parents when they ask you how come you're not going to law school already.

Also, in Saratoga Springs, even one or two thousand dollars goes a long way. You can still rent a perfectly decent apartment for $350 a month up here.

So I could see why Gretchen and her grant panelists would want to celebrate getting their task over with. All of the artists in town know each other, and it must be embarrassing to have to reject applications from people you'll be running into at Madeline's the next morning.

"Congratulations, guys," I greeted them as they headed for a nearby table. "So did you give me any money?"

"You should give *us* money, you Hollywood sell-out," Antoinette Carlson shot back with a petulant toss of her long dreadlocks, but then softened it with a smile. She was looking flamboyant as always in her dreads and African nationalist earrings.

Antoinette was a video producer/director who, so far as I could tell, had never actually produced or directed any videos. However, that minor detail didn't prevent her from receiving an astonishing amount of grant money from all kinds of sources. Once you get onto the grant circuit you can ride that wave for quite a while, and if you're lucky, ease on from there to a cushy teaching job.

As soon as Antoinette sat down, a pale young guy named Steve Something-or-Other scurried over to make sure he got a seat right beside her. Something-or-Other absolutely idolized Antoinette, maybe because she had so much exuberant vitality and he had so little. She was also a good six inches taller than he was, and they made an odd but sweet pair: the Queen of Sheba and her faithful Caucasian sidekick.

Something-or-Other had been rewriting the same eighty-page novella for the past two years. Having once labored for almost that long on a hopelessly uncommercial screenplay about elderly Cambodians in a garment factory, I was tempted to identify with him. But the fact that he had a rather large trust fund made me keep my empathy for Mr. Novella to myself.

Sitting down next to him was a folk musician with a long, droopy, hairy face named Mike Pardou. Pardou's biggest claim to fame was that he played the spoons on a Jim Kweskin Jug Band album thirty-some years ago, back in the fabled 60s. His other claim to fame was that he once had a torrid affair with Maria Muldaur—or so he said. Every time he got high, he'd start singing her hit song "Midnight at the Oasis," and burst into tears.

Behind Mr. Novella and the King of Spoons came Bonnie, who gave me one of her killer hugs before heading over to join the others. She seemed to have acquired several new muscles on her neck since I saw her this morning. Was I sexist for thinking all those huge muscles of hers were starting to make her look a little weird? "If you want to make money," she informed me, "you better invest in my boxing video now before it's too late. I've got investors lining up."

George Hosey, the last artist in the flock, stroked his white goatee, pointed a finger at me, and declared sternly, "Uncle Sam, and Aunt Bonnie, want *you*."

They all erupted into huge gales of laughter at Hosey's sally, acting punchy as hell. Hosey was a retired chemist from Finch Pruyn who grew a mustache and long white goatee just for kicks, and suddenly everyone started telling him he was the spitting image of Uncle Sam. It's true, he was. So now he went around playing Uncle Sam at parades and conventions.

I saw his act once and hated it. I may not be the fairest critic, because I think patriotism is for the birds and the fascists, but it sure looked to me like the only artistic talent the guy had going for him was his facial hair. Nevertheless, Hosey was making more money doing his inane routine than he ever made as senior vice president of research and development.

I tired to shake these negative thoughts out of my mind and just enjoy the happy mood at the table. Even Mike Pardou, who usually looked about as cheerful as a dead basset hound, was smiling and beating an upbeat rhythm with a couple of soup spoons.

"So how about you guys?" I kidded them. "Did you give yourselves any grants?"

I have a long-standing knack for putting my foot in

my mouth. I meant it as lighthearted teasing, but instantly everyone at their table stopped laughing and beating their spoons, and fell silent.

Theoretically it's a great idea, giving local communities the power to decide which of their artists to support. But there's a flaw. The grant panelists are often artists themselves, applying for the same grants they're giving out. When this happens, the interested party is supposed to leave the room while his or her application is discussed, but obviously there's great potential for conflict of interest.

Gretchen broke the uncomfortable silence, declaring stiffly, "Some of them did receive grants, but of course we followed all the proper procedures, and—"

"I know, Gretchen, I was just kidding."

But everyone was still glowering at me. Fortunately Gretchen stepped in again and changed the subject. "Interesting way of working you've got there," she said, pointing at the plethora of notebooks, flattened milk cartons, and toilet paper piled high on the table in front of me.

"Actually, this stuff isn't mine. It's Donald Penn's life work," I said, eager to keep the social ball rolling.

Instead, the social ball screeched to a complete halt. If before I had put my foot in my mouth, this time I'd put my whole leg in. As for *their* mouths, they were all hanging open.

Bonnie was the first to speak. *"Really,"* she said, treating me to one of her piercing looks.

"Huh," said Ersatz Uncle Sam, scratching at his mustache.

"How interesting," Pardou said, then started playing the spoons with an angry vigor, off on some emotional tangent of his own.

"Yeah," drawled Novella Man. He wasn't a great

conversationalist, but small verbal tasks like this he could handle.

"Well, well," Gretchen intoned. I waited for her to say more, but all she said was, once again, "Well, well."

And then they all went back to their coffee and soup-sipping and studiously ignored me.

Somehow, I wasn't sure how, I had ruined their party.

6

I stuffed Penn's notebooks and assorted junk back into my pack and headed out of Madeline's back room, waving good-bye to my fellow artists. I must say, they didn't act like they'd miss me much. Why had they all reacted with such distaste when I showed them Penn's magnum opus? You'd think I was showing them John Wayne Bobbitt videos or photographs of Jesse Helms or something.

Madeline was gone from the front room when I came through, but Rob was still there, working behind the counter with Marcie.

Marcie. Don't get me started. May God have mercy, Marcie was a young woman that I simply could not look at without picturing her naked. It wasn't just the long blond hair and the low-cut dresses—well, okay, maybe it *was* just the long blond hair and the low-cut dresses.

No, there was something else, too. A sly gleam in her eyes that made you suspect she was picturing *you* naked. A smoky scent that snaked across the room and pulled you forward like some primeval mating call. I'm usually very olfactorily challenged, but Marcie sure brought out the nose in me.

She smiled as I came in from the back room. I ducked my head and smiled back vaguely, without looking at her straight on. I get embarrassed when gorgeous women can see on my face that I'd love to go to bed with them.

I'm happily married with two great children. But still. For six months, ever since that three hundred K gave me both freedom and a midlife crisis simultaneously, I'd been wondering if I would suddenly start doing something totally out of character, like going scuba diving, or becoming a born-again Christian, or sleeping around. So far I hadn't. But I knew that, unchained from the constant demands of eight hours a day at the computer, anything was possible.

And since anything was possible, I carefully avoided Marcie's sparkling eyes as I walked past her. But Rob stopped me. "So how's The Penn's stuff? Any good?"

"It's, uh . . ." I hesitated.

Should I tell the truth? But that would turn the dead man into a laughingstock—and what right did I have to do that? Penn had trusted me. "It's . . . extremely interesting," I said.

"No shit?"

"*Absolutely* no shit. I mean, *wow.*" I pumped my fist with fake enthusiasm.

Rob laughed and high-fived me, looking every bit as excited as I was pretending to be. "Far fuckin' out! Hurray for my man Penn!" I just stood there smiling nervously, bobbing my head up and down. "So what did the guy write about?" Rob continued.

"Man, what *didn't* he write about? I'll give you the whole scoop after I finish reading."

"Okay, dude, but hurry up. We gotta turn his stuff into an exhibit already, get rid of all this crap," Rob said, waving at the pointillist monstrosities on the walls.

"I think fat people are sexy," Marcie said, turning to

me. She was wearing a thin white muscle shirt that showed her nipples off nicely. "Don't you?"

It was hard to answer her with my tongue hanging out.

"Seriously," Rob broke in, "Madeline gave it the okay. And since we want to hold the memorial on Sunday, and we'd like to have The Penn's stuff up on the wall by then, we'll even do the work. You know, read it and decide what to put up."

Sure, I could just picture it. A hundred different versions of that frigging preface lining the wall. What a horrible mockery of a man's life.

"I'll think about it," I lied, and got the hell out of there.

But even after I made it outside, Marcie's scent stayed with me—so much so that when Judy Demarest waved to me, I felt guilty. Besides being the editor of the *Daily Saratogian*, Judy is also my wife's best buddy and my children's favorite babysitter. "Hey, Judy, how's it going?" I chirped.

"Big story." Judy always spoke in short clipped phrases, trying to sound like a tough, hard-boiled editor. But anyone who knew about her babysitting prowess, as well as her passionate involvement in the Literacy Volunteers of Saratoga—she was their chief fundraiser and chairperson of their executive board—knew that in reality Judy had only been boiled for three minutes, at most. "Guy stole forty-six cans of whipped cream from Price Chopper. Sniffed the gas to get high."

"Well now, that *is* a big story. Definitely page one."

She shrugged. "Best we got so far. Unless you have something better."

I started to give her a return shrug, but then my shoulders froze. I *did* have something better.

A hundred versions of that preface on Madeline's walls would be grotesque . . . but how about publishing just *one* version in the *Daily Saratogian?*

And then, *boom,* it finally hit me. *That's what this is all about. This is why Donald Penn threw me his key!*

He knew his heart was attacking him and he sensed he was about to die. So with his last living breath and his last desperate lurch toward my feet, he was begging me to *please for God's sake* get him published. Because like myself and every other poor sucker of a writer who ever picked up a pen or sat down at a keyboard, he believed that if he was published, he would never really die.

He'd be immortal.

If I could get Judy to go for it, Donald Penn would finally, after thirty long hard years of writing, become what he had always dreamed of: a real honest to God *published writer.* Right there in the same ballpark with Shakespeare and all the rest of the big guys.

No wonder Penn came to me when he was dying. I was undoubtedly his best contact in the publishing world. Hell, his only contact.

His only hope.

Nervously, my breath getting shallow, I asked Judy if she'd like to publish an excerpt of Penn's work. I offered her exclusive first rights, trying to make it sound like I was doing her a big favor.

To my astonishment, she jumped at the chance. "Sure. Let's do it," she agreed.

I was so thrilled and relieved at how easy it had been, I could hardly hear her as she continued on. I was flashing back to the first time I was published (a "Letter to the Editor" for McGovern in my high school paper).

"After all," Judy was saying, "man was a celeb.

They even gave him free coffee at City Hall every morning."

I tried to act casual, afraid that if I jumped up and down with joy Judy might get second thoughts. "Free coffee, huh? I didn't know that."

"Sure, Mayor's orders. Cup of Ethiopian."

Weird. "You have any idea why he was so into Ethiopian?"

"Maybe he owned stock. So when you gonna get me Penn's stuff?"

As soon as I can cut and paste together a couple of pages that don't sound like the man was totally insane. "As soon as I can. He wrote so much terrific material, I'll have to, you know, pick out the best."

"Just give me the whole shebang. I'm the editor, I'll edit."

First Rob, now Judy. Nice of everyone to be so darn helpful. But no way was I going to let Judy Demarest find out that Penn's entire oeuvre consisted of ten trillion versions of a one-page preface. Two pages at most. "No, the handwriting's, like, totally illegible."

"Not for me. Why I became an editor. Never yet met handwriting I couldn't handle."

I smiled but held my ground. "Thanks, I'm happy to just do it myself."

"Look, it'll be quicker if I do it. Guy died two days ago, I gotta get this in the paper by Sunday at the latest."

"I'll give it to you before then."

Judy argued for a while longer, but finally shrugged her shoulders and gave up.

"So," she said, "guy was a diamond in the rough, huh?"

I gave a knowing nod.

"You could say that," I answered.

7

"You did *what?!*" Andrea screeched, her voice rising. It was several hours later. The kids were in the backyard playing while Andrea and I fixed dinner; I hoped they couldn't hear us fighting. "You robbed a *safety-deposit vault?* Isn't that, like, a *federal crime?*"

"Honey, I had to. It was the only way I could get in." I'd already decided to leave out the part about the *scree-eeks*, so I added, "There was no risk at all. I was in and out of there in about two seconds."

Andrea pointed a chopping knife at me. "What is the matter with you? You're wacko! You hardly even knew this guy, and now you risk going to jail for him?!"

I kept right on setting the table, playing nonchalant. "I'm telling you, it was no big deal. Besides, even if they caught me, they wouldn't have done anything—"

Andrea grabbed the plates out of my hand and stared me down. "Don't you ever do something like that again without talking to me first! You've got a wife and two kids, you can't act like this!"

I sighed. "Okay, okay, don't worry. No more funny stuff."

"There's nothing funny about it."

Dinner that night was a decidedly tense experience. Even the eggplant parmesan, usually one of my faves, tasted flavorless somehow. Babe Ruth spent the entire meal loudly complaining that in his T-ball league, you're not allowed to get doubles or triples or homers, only singles. "I could get a homer every time, if they let me!" he declared.

It's true: The Babe is a darn good little baseball player. We're happy about that, because he's shown signs of being intellectually gifted—he can already add and subtract better than most politicians—and we figure the baseball playing will help keep him well balanced. Also, he seems to have inherited some of my sensitive *artiste* tendencies, and exercise is the best way for guys like us to mellow out.

But Andrea and I weren't in the mood to talk baseball with the Babe that night. On top of being angry at me, Andrea got mad at Gretzky for his hockey-players-don't-make-peepee routine, which was showing no signs of abating. Meanwhile, I was still preoccupied with how I was going to put together a good version of The Penn's preface for the newspaper.

So later that night, as I set Penn's magnum opus down on my bedside table and lay back in bed watching Andrea undress, I still felt a residue of our earlier quarrel. Which was unfortunate, because lying back in bed watching Andrea undress was usually one of my favorite pastimes. To hell with Marcie. Like Paul Newman says, Why go out for hamburger when you can have steak at home? Right now Andrea was shaking her hair free from her barrette. I began to get that old familiar tightening in my thighs.

The Sultan of Swat and the Great One were sound asleep in their room, and maybe Andrea and I could make up with some good loving. I held out my arms for Andrea to slide into. But she sat down on the edge of the bed, looking fretful.

"We've got to do something about this, we really do," she said.

"I got it all squared away," I reassured her.

She stared at me blankly. "What?"

"I picked out the best three versions of the preface I could find. I'll edit them together, then give it to Judy tomorrow."

Andrea impatiently tossed her underwear to the floor, and I tingled all over. To hell with Marcie. Definitely.

"I was talking about *Gretzky,*" Andrea said. "He was whiny all afternoon, and I'm sure it's because he was holding in his peepee. That can't be healthy, going a whole eight hours without peeing."

"Maybe this is just some kind of stage they go through," I said hopefully.

"Babe Ruth never went through it."

"Well, look at the bright side. At least Gretzky doesn't walk in his sleep. Speaking of which, did you put the newspaper down?" Two weeks ago, Babe Ruth sleepwalked right into the middle of a seriously X-rated scene in our bedroom. Ever since then we've been putting crumpled newspaper in front of our bedroom door at night, so we'll get advance warning before the Babe stumbles in and makes it a kinky threesome.

Andrea sighed. "The newspaper's downstairs. I forgot about it." She turned away from me in the bed. "I have to get final grades in tomorrow. I'm really tired."

"Don't worry, gorgeous," I said softly, then bent down and licked the back of her knee. "I'll take care of it."

And I did.

"Jacob. *Jacob,*" my wife said.

Andrea and I were sitting in a crowded library auditorium, listening to Steve Something-or-Other read from his novella. After fifteen minutes of this torture, I still had no clue what the cursed thing was about, except he used the word "ubiquitous" a lot. Everyone around me was asleep. I wished I was, too.

"Hey, Jacob," Andrea repeated.

"Shh," I whispered.

Now Antoinette Carlson, looking stunning in a green, yellow, and black dashiki, came onstage and began lecturing about the future of video in this country. As she explained it, video's future depended on increased government funding for artists with true integrity and vision.

Artists like herself.

The audience applauded. Then Andrea shook my shoulder. "It's your turn to get up."

Everyone turned around. I was supposed to go onstage and pontificate about "Is Art Possible in Hollywood?" or some such topic.

"Hell, no, I won't go," I mumbled.

"Come on. What if Babe Ruth bumps into something?"

Now I was thoroughly confused.

Andrea shook my shoulder again. "Honey, don't make me get up. I did it last time."

I opened my eyes. I was still in bed. But apparently Babe Ruth was not, since there were noises downstairs.

I stood up wearily. "Yeah, okay, okay. Batman to the rescue." I found my pajama bottoms on the floor and put them on. To protect my eyes I left the hall light off as I felt my way down the stairs. When I got to the first floor I heard Babe Ruth call out, "Daddy."

"Coming," I said. Usually the Babe is silent when he does his midnight rambling, but every now and then he comes out with interesting comments. Like once, while still sound asleep, he asked me, "Why do people make poop, and why did the Red Sox trade Babe Ruth?"

Questions I've been wondering about for years.

This time, my son asked, "Daddy, how come you're wearing a mask?"

It sounded like he was in the study. As I turned the corner from the dark dining room into the even darker study, I said, "Babe, I'm not wearing a—"

I froze. Somebody was crouching in the shadows by my desk, wearing a mask.

Whoever it was suddenly sprang out at me and Babe Ruth, knocking my son hard to the ground and swinging something at my face.

I jumped back and threw up my arms to ward off the blow. Luckily it turned out to be something soft, a bag maybe. The intruder started dashing around me, but without even thinking I kicked out with my foot and tripped him, sending him sprawling into the wall. Or maybe her; bulky sweaters and darkness hid the intruder's shape. I moved forward to attack. But then Babe Ruth screamed.

I glanced back at my kid, and in that instant the person dove away, still holding the bag or whatever it was. I took a wild swipe at it, caught a strap, and held on. My day pack, I realized. The intruder yanked at the pack, pulling me forward. I landed on the floor, my forehead smashing into a dining room chair.

I could hear Andrea running down the stairs shouting. Somehow I was still gripping the strap, even though the person kept trying to yank my pack out of my hands. Babe Ruth screamed again. I suddenly let go of the strap, surprising the intruder, who tumbled backward onto the kitchen floor. "Babe, go to Mommy!" I yelled, and charged.

But the intruder was up again, jumping to the other side of the kitchen table. "You motherfucker!" I screamed, and shoved the table in his gut. It hit him hard. He doubled over in pain. I dashed around the table to rip that mask off his face and finish him off.

But there was a big metal pressure cooker on top of the stove. Andrea is always telling me to put the pots away in the cabinet, and I guess this time I really should have listened. Because the intruder grabbed that pressure cooker by the handle and swung it at my head full force. *Ka-boom.* I went down, my skull bursting with fiery agony, and screamed. Behind me Babe Ruth screamed too, and also Andrea.

Ahead of me the intruder was dashing out the door. I fought the furious red jolts pulsing through me and ran outside.

The bastard was racing up the street. I jumped down the steps and chased him.

For about ten feet. Then I stopped and threw up. My cranium was pounding and my ears rang like a four-alarm fire. Andrea ran up to me.

"Jacob," she said.

"Goddamn pressure cooker," I groaned.

Then I threw up again.

8

Gretzky was still asleep. Thank God for small favors.

The Sultan of Swat was in the living room cuddling with Andrea and whimpering softly.

I was sitting on the floor in my study, praying for the aspirin and Jack Daniels to kick in.

"You should go to the hospital," Dave repeated yet again. Dave is the cop from across the street, nice guy, snowblows our driveway in the winter just to be neighborly. Andrea had run over to get him as soon as she dragged me back home. Now he sat there watching me, drumming his fingers on my desktop. "You might have a concussion."

"Don't touch anything." It was painful moving my face enough to get the words out. "Fingerprints."

"I thought you said he was wearing gloves."

"I'm not sure. I told you, I'm not even sure it was a he."

"Listen, Jacob, the department doesn't take fingerprints on a simple burglary."

"Simple burglary?! That assassin practically ripped my head open! He assaulted my five-year-old son!"

Dave thought about it, then took his hands off the desktop. "Okay, we'll get someone in here to dust the place. Special favor."

"Thanks. Remind me to mow your lawn this summer." I tried to smile, but it didn't work.

"You really should go to the hospital—"

"I hate hospitals. What did Andrea say?"

"About what?"

"The guy."

"So your gut feeling is it was a guy."

"My gut feeling is it wasn't Dolly Parton. But it could've been a woman who was less endowed, if you know what I mean."

Dave nodded. "Andrea said pretty much the same thing you did, though she left out the Dolly Parton part. Between five and a half and six feet, not too fat, not too skinny."

I waited for more, but there wasn't any. "That's all she saw?"

"Yeah."

"Great." I closed my eyes. Even that small gesture was painful.

Dave stood up. "Come on, I'll drive you to the hospital."

I shook my head, instantly regretting the sudden motion. Then I gingerly leaned back against the wall and tried to think.

It was easy to figure out how the burglar got into our house. He or she had no problem there; this being safe, small-town America, or so we'd thought, we often didn't even bother to lock our doors at night.

The burglar's other activities were harder to fathom, though. My desk drawers had been thrown open, and my papers were strewn around; but other than that, the burglar hadn't touched anything in the whole house. Not even Andrea's purse, which was lying in plain view on the kitchen table. The only thing he'd stolen, so far as I could tell, was my day pack.

Why in the world would the burglar want my day pack?

I considered the bizarre possibility that someone

stole the pack because they'd seen me carrying Penn's magnum opus inside it. But if that's what they were after, why didn't they just open the pack, see there was nothing in it anymore but a couple of Disney videos, and then toss it aside?

Unless . . .

What if Babe Ruth enters the study just at the exact moment when the burglar finds my pack—but before he's had a chance to look inside it?

Highly unlikely.

But wait a minute. I gritted my teeth against the pain in my head. What if the burglar heard Ruth coming, dove behind my desk to hide . . . and that's when he suddenly sees my pack, or hell, even lands right on top of it. Because last night, like most nights, I'd left my pack on the floor at the far end of the desk, by the wall. Which meant it was partially hidden, I realized. So the burglar dives on top of my pack, figures out what it is, and grabs hold of it as Ruth enters . . .

Okay, maybe. I guess it was *possible.* But *why?* Who would want Donald Penn's literary oeuvre badly enough to burglarize my house, terrorize my child, and bust my head open?

I considered all the people who'd shown an interest, positive or otherwise, in The Penn's writing: the Mayor, Judy, Rob, maybe Madeline, Gretchen, Bonnie and her fellow artists. Could the burglar have been Steve the Novella Man, hoping to find some good stuff written by The Penn that he could pass off as his own work? Or Rob, in a fit of insane artistic mania, desperate to set up that exhibit at Madeline's? Maybe Judy Demarest, wanting to make sure I didn't double-cross her and give The Penn's literary pearls to a downstate newspaper? Or some overly dedicated editor from Simon & Schuster, up in Saratoga on vacation, who'd overheard me talking to Judy on the street and thought maybe she could steal herself a bestseller?

Frankly, it seemed equally likely that the burglar had opened my pack, found our rented copy of *Mighty Ducks 2*, and decided he must have that video at all costs.

My increasingly deranged musings were interrupted when the telephone rang. I jumped. So did Dave. It was three a.m. I grabbed the phone.

Before I could speak, a voice boomed out at me, "Seven fifty! *Seven fucking fifty!*"

What the hell—? I was so scared and pissed off, I started shaking. "What do you want?! *Who are you?!*"

"I'm your guardian angel, kid! I just got you an extra two-fifty grand!"

My mind reeled. By now I'd figured out it was Andrew, my agent, but I hadn't the foggiest what he was saying to me. It was like he was speaking Swahili. Maybe I really did have a concussion. "Andrew, what in heaven's name are you talking about?"

"Mutant beetles, kid! They're hot!"

Mutant beetles. It all came back to me with a rush. I groaned. "Look, do you have any idea what time it is?"

"Hell yeah, I've been working on this deal all day, baby! Awesome, huh? So you gonna thank me or what?"

I hung up the phone and poured myself another shot of Jack Daniel's.

The next morning, or rather, later that same morning, I woke up with a splitting headache, whether from concussion or hangover I didn't know. But I figured either way a cup of coffee couldn't hurt.

I stepped carefully downstairs, avoiding sudden movements, and came upon Gretzky in the living room putting on knee pads. "Daddy, let's play hockey!" he crowed, delighted to see me.

Hockey. My aching body cringed at the thought. "Not right now, sweetie."

He shot me an outraged look. "Why not, Daddy?"

"Later." I headed toward the kitchen as fast as the old bod could carry me. If Gretzky started crying, my skull would crack into little tiny pieces.

I heard noises from the study and went in. Dave was with another cop, collecting prints from my desk. The purplish-gray powder they were using made me sneeze, which made my head feel even worse. Dave and his partner looked up. "Let me see your thumb," Dave said.

I held it up, and he examined it under the lamp and compared it to a thumbprint they'd taken off the top drawer. "Yup, it's a match," he said.

"You find any others?"

"Sure. Andrea's."

I watched for a while until it became apparent they weren't getting anywhere, then went to the kitchen. Andrea and Babe Ruth were in there reading a baseball book. I looked up at the clock: 10:35. "Hey, how come you guys are still at home?"

Babe Ruth ran and jumped into my arms, hugging me tight around the neck. It jarred my head painfully but I didn't complain. Babe Ruth isn't a kid who hugs too often, so when he does hug me, I treasure it.

Andrea kissed my forehead as her eyes searched mine. "We wanted to make sure you're okay. How are you feeling?"

"Nothing a cup of coffee and another hug wouldn't cure."

But the Sultan of Swat pulled away from me. Enough of this hugging stuff; now for the important business of the morning. "Daddy! Who won the Mets game?"

So we settled into our usual routine of checking the box scores and discussing the Mets bullpen. How had my son, at such a tender age, already turned into a guy who wasn't comfortable giving hugs, but would talk sports with you ad infinitum? Was it something I did? Something he picked up from watching men in general? Or is there really something defective about that Y chromosome?

All of this speculating wasn't doing my head any good, especially with Gretzky running in and demanding to know if it was "later" yet, because if it was, then we should be playing hockey already.

I reached out for the coffee that Andrea had placed on the table for me. And that's when I noticed, on the obituary page placed for some reason at the back of the sports section, the small item about Donald Penn. His viewing was scheduled at Otis Funeral Home from 10:00 to 11:00 this morning. "Damn," I said. I got out of my chair.

"What's wrong?" Andrea asked.

"I gotta hit the funeral home. The showing's almost over." I threw on my jacket.

"But you promised you'd play hockey with me!" Gretzky screamed.

"How about the Devil Rays?" Babe Ruth shouted. "Who won the Devil Rays game?"

"Honey, are you feeling well enough to drive?" Andrea asked.

"The Brewers, three to two," I told Babe Ruth, and headed out the door.

"Jacob, my grades are due today. When will you be back to take care of the kids?"

But I was gone. And so was my headache, driven off by adrenaline. Because I had a strong intuition.

A strong intuition that whoever cared enough about The Penn to break into my house looking for his masterpiece would also care enough about him to be at Otis Funeral Home, viewing his body.

By God, I was going to find out who had walloped me and terrorized my kid.

And I was going to make the bastard pay.

9

Well, I guess I should leave intuition to the feminine half of the species, because whoever had busted my head was definitely not at the funeral home. There were only two people there: Virgil Otis, who owned the joint and had to be there, and his nineteen-year-old daughter Molly. The father was too fat to have been my burglar, and the daughter was too short.

It was odd that we were the only people at the viewing. I mean, it seemed like the entire population of Saratoga Springs was intrigued by this guy, so how come nobody came?

Before I ventured into the room where Penn's body lay, I stopped and chatted with Virgil for a while. I knew him from before, had interviewed him while researching corpses for my killer gas movie. Virgil was a friendly guy, an easy interview. My guess is that funeral home directors have such a ghoulish reputation that Virgil tried to be extra friendly in order to overcome it.

"So who's paying for Donald Penn's funeral?" I asked.

"The county. They couldn't find any next of kin."

I looked through the open door to the viewing room and shivered inside. I wasn't ready to go in there yet.

Virgil was still talking. "Happens every year or so. They'll find some guy, froze to death on the street, had a heart attack in the library bathroom, whatever, and he's got no relatives, no friends, nobody. Nobody but us, that is."

Looking at Penn's corpse couldn't be any more depressing than listening to this. I went into the viewing room.

Hidden track lights were giving off dim lighting, and hidden speakers were giving off dim classical music. When I die I want them to play Frank Zappa at my funeral. At the front of the room was Donald Penn's casket. I walked up to it.

I was pleasantly surprised. I'd expected his casket to be some kind of splintery plywood thing, but it actually looked respectable. And not just because of the lighting. The wood was a rich, dark brown, and draped over it was an embossed cloth that even had some style to it.

I looked down at Donald Penn's face.

Again I was surprised. He looked good—much better than when he was alive. They'd trimmed his beard and hair, and they must have put on some kind of makeup because his face had lost its gray pallor. He looked pleasantly tanned, like he'd just come back from a beach vacation.

His eyes were closed. Hell, maybe he was just taking a nap. Maybe when he woke up, he wouldn't be a crazy, lonely, blocked writer anymore. Instead he'd be what he looked like now: a wise man, a thoughtful man, a man you'd be glad to have as your grandfather.

"Donald," I whispered, and got all teary-eyed. I stood there for a moment, then tried again. "Donald, it's a great preface," I lied. "Really. Very Joycean."

Had Penn read Joyce? Had he rooted for the Mets? Had he ever loved anyone?

"Listen, Donald, I'm getting it published, just like

you wanted. I hope you'll be happy with my editing job. I'll do my best."

Over the hidden speakers Beethoven came in soft and sweet, not sounding dim anymore, but more like a bunch of angels jamming. I continued on.

"Hey, Donald, one more thing. There's somebody out there who's so interested in what you wrote, they burglarized my house and attacked me and my son, trying to find it. Do you have any idea who that might be?"

Was it my imagination?

Or did I really hear Donald Penn chuckle?

I rode to the county cemetery in the hearse, along with Virgil, Molly, and Penn's casket.

"What religion was he, do you know?" Virgil asked, as we turned onto Route 50 and the casket rattled in the back.

"No, I don't."

"Well, we'll give him the standard nondenominational funeral. I've got a Presbyterian minister meeting us at the cemetery. The money the county gives us barely covers our expenses, but it's important to us to do an honorable job."

It must be a drag, working at a funeral home and always having to convince people you're really a nice guy, not some sicko that gets off on dead bodies. Virgil droned on, detailing all of the many preparations that go into an honorable funeral job. I glanced over at Molly, who was staring out the window, her face a blank. Molly was one of those five-foot-two, eyes-of-blue types, but without the perkiness I would have associated with her cute-as-a-button looks. Was she naturally unperky, or was her perkiness just temporarily missing in action? I wondered what it was like to be a teenage girl, eager to embark on life's grand adventures, but always surrounded by death. Your dad comes home every day smelling of formaldehyde. Do you become sullen and withdrawn, lying around playing solitaire? Or do you get really into kinky sex, sneaking into the funeral home with your boyfriend at midnight and making love inside the caskets?

I felt guilty having such fantasies about this young girl who was just minding her own business, looking out at the gloomy day. It had started to rain and the sky was an endless dirty gray. The windshield wipers were relentless, and so was Virgil's voice. I interrupted him. "So, Molly," I said conversationally, "you help out your dad with the business?"

"You kidding?" Virgil answered for her. "She hates the business. Always has, ever since she was a little kid. Now she's studying arts administration over at Skidmore. Any money in that?"

The truthful answer would have been no, but I didn't want to get in the middle of any father-daughter arguments. "Sometimes. God knows the world needs good arts administrators." That part, at least, was true.

Molly looked away, clearly not in the mood to chat. But I was curious. "So how come you're going to this funeral?"

She turned and spoke to me for the first time that whole day. "I knew him," she said.

"Really? How?"

Her eyes went back to the window, looking far away again. "I made him a cup of coffee every morning."

I was puzzled for a moment, but then it came to me. "Oh, you work at City Hall in the mornings."

Now it was her turn to be puzzled. "No, the Arts Council."

Huh? "The Arts Council?"

She nodded, getting a little more animated now. "I intern there from nine to eleven, and he always came downstairs for free coffee. He lives right above there. I mean, used to live."

Amazing. This guy seemed to get free coffee everywhere. I wondered if it was free at Madeline's too.

"Did you make him Ethiopian?" I asked.

She eyed me curiously. "How'd you know?"

"Wild guess."

After that we rode in silence for a while, thinking about the dead man. Saratoga's suburbs gave way to a dark spruce forest, which turned into a series of video rental stores and fast-food outlets that somehow managed to look glum despite their garish colors. The windshield wipers beat out their lonely rhythm. Ahead of us was the cemetery.

Then Molly spoke again. There was something different in her voice this time, a kind of quaver. "Did you hear about his application?"

"Molly," her father said warningly.

"What application?" I asked.

"The one where he said someone was threatening to kill him."

10

"No, I hadn't heard about that," I said, when I could get my mouth working again.

"Molly, *enough.* Let the man rest in peace."

I put my hand on the girl's shoulder. "Who was threatening to kill him?"

She bit her lip. "Dad's right. I shouldn't talk about it."

"About *what*?"

"Jacob, forget it—" Virgil began, but I stopped him.

"Damn it, Virgil, come on. I was the man's only friend in the world. Except maybe for you," I added, turning to Molly.

Virgil was driving fast and angry. "Who cares what the guy thought? Face it, he only had one oar in the water."

That was true, of course. Probably no one had ever threatened to kill Penn—and certainly no one had actually done it. He died of a heart attack, right?

But still, something strange was going on here. I tried another tack. "What kind of application are you talking about, Molly?"

"Nothing," she said nervously, "just a NYFA grant. He applied every year." Virgil caught her eye in the rearview mirror, and she clutched at her hair with a fist. "I promised I wouldn't say anything."

"Who did you promise?"

Suddenly Virgil turned the wheel sharply. We veered into the cemetery, tires squealing on the wet road, and the car fishtailed. Penn's casket banged into the side of the hearse, and the casket lid sprang upward. Molly looked back there and gave an earsplitting scream.

Donald Penn's eyes had been jarred open and he was staring straight at us.

My heart stopped. Molly screamed even louder.

Virgil jumped from the hearse, opened the rear door, and slammed the lid back down. He shot me a hate-filled look—probably picturing me naked and full of embalming fluid.

I'm sure he would have preferred for someone else to help him carry the casket instead of me. But the gravediggers were on lunch break, the ninety-year-old Presbyterian minister wasn't exactly up to the job, and nobody else had showed up for Donald Penn's funeral.

Nobody.

So Virgil and I lugged the casket up a hill to the gravesite, with Virgil in the rear giving laconic directions and me in front walking backward. The rain had turned into a sad little drizzle, just enough to fog up our glasses and add that extra dollop of misery. We trudged past several rows of graves marked only by small aluminum gravestones. Molly was ahead of us, out of hearing range.

I lifted the casket higher, trying to get comfortable, and took a deep breath. "Virgil, I'm not trying to get your daughter riled up or anything, I just want to find out—"

"Look, Penn had a vivid imagination, that's all. And unfortunately, so does my daughter."

"Why don't you tell me about it yourself? Then I won't bug her anymore."

Virgil suddenly sped up. Since I was going backward, his quick movement shoved the casket into my hips, knocking me off balance. I fell in the mud. The casket fell too, landing with a hard thud about an inch from my knee.

Virgil stood over me, furious. "Are you making me some kind of threat?"

I scrambled to my feet, equally furious. Fighting a fat man in the cemetery in the rain is not my idea of a good time, but still. "Did you just knock me down on purpose?"

He jabbed a finger at me. "Look, this internship is an important career opportunity for Molly. You better not screw it up."

I got in his face. "How could I screw it up? What are you so scared of?"

But Virgil just gave me a disgusted grunt and wouldn't say any more. We picked the casket back up and slogged silently up the muddy hill. We had to stop a couple of times to rest. Virgil was sweating profusely, and my headache was back.

I read the names and dates on the small aluminum gravestones. MERYL RENÉE DANVERS, 1998. RAOUL CISNEROS, 1997. UNKNOWN, 1996. I found names going back to 1993. Older than that, though, the aluminum had corroded and the names were illegible. I resolved to dip into my *Gas that Ate San Francisco* nest egg and buy The Penn a proper gravestone.

When the funeral service finally began, I feared the worst. The nonagenarian Presbyterian minister was so frail he looked like he might keel over any minute himself. But he had a surprisingly powerful voice, and it cut through the rain right into the heart of our loneliness. He told us that the least among us are known intimately to God, just as if they were presidents or kings instead of derelicts. God was waiting with open arms to receive Donald Penn.

I haven't figured out yet if I believe in God, and I guess I never will. But despite my doubts, a good funeral speech always hits the spot.

When he was finished, the minister asked me if I would like to say a few words. I wanted to say no, but of course I couldn't, so I cleared my throat and began.

"Donald Penn," I said, "was an artist. A true artist. He devoted his whole life to his art."

Then I got stuck. I didn't know what else to say about the man, except that a couple of people seemed to like him or at least pity him enough to give him free coffee.

What I said out loud was, "God bless him."

Then I stepped down, the minister said amen, and that was that. The gravediggers lowered The Penn into his grave and covered him up, and the rest of us walked back through the rain to our cars.

Figuring I'd worn out my welcome with Virgil and Molly, I hit up the minister for a lift home. But first I went over to tell them good-bye. Virgil nodded gruffly and got in the hearse, leaving Molly and me alone for a moment.

She looked up at me anxiously. "Please don't tell Gretchen I mentioned the application."

Gretchen? "Why not?"

"She said it could really get the Arts Council in trouble."

I was dying for details, but Virgil rolled his window down and yelled at Molly to hurry. She got in the hearse, and they sped off.

The minister tottered up. "She's too young for you," he said with a lewd wink that looked odd coming from his wizened old face.

What was Gretchen Lang trying to hide? Could sweet, middle-aged Gretchen be the one that Penn said was threatening to kill him?

And what was in that NYFA application, anyway—and was it somehow connected to my burglary?

As we got into the minister's white Cadillac—"a dying man's last car," he told me—the minister began expounding on his sex-and-young-girls theme. " 'Course, folks in the Bible never used to worry about a girl being too young," he said, as he locked the doors and zoomed off down the highway. "You know how old Rachel was when Isaac fell in love with her at the well?"

And then I saw it. A face, peering furtively at us from behind the McDonald's sign across the highway. Not a whole face, though, more like a pair of sunglasses and a baseball cap. Just as effective as last night's mask.

The face ducked behind the sign. "Stop the car!" I shouted at the minister.

"Three. Rachel was *three,*" the minister continued.

"Let me out!" I yanked frantically at the door handle. But it was locked—luckily for me, since we were now doing fifty.

The minister chuckled. "And Isaac gets all pissed off because Rachel's father won't let him marry her until she's *ten!*"

"Please let me out!" I screamed.

"Sorry. Forgot to put in my hearing aid." The minister proceeded to put it in while driving sixty miles an hour. "Hate the darn thing, gets more feedback than a rock 'n' roll concert. Now what were you saying?"

I watched the McDonald's sign go out of sight around the bend. We were at least half a mile away by now, and back in the spruce forest. The next place to turn around wouldn't be for another mile at least. I shook my head, frustrated. "Never mind."

The minister patted my arm. "Don't sweat it, kid. Funerals are tough, you never know how you're gonna react. Like one time a few years back I was doing this funeral, and afterward the widow asked if she could ride in the car with me. Well, of course I said yes, not thinking anything about it. But as soon as she got in the car, oh boy, let me tell you . . ."

Who the hell was that behind the McDonald's sign? The same person who bashed my head open last night? Was someone following me?

Or following Molly?

Or watching the funeral from a distance, out of morbid fascination? But why? Because he was Donald Penn's killer?

Wait a minute, that was insane. My head started to spin. I needed some damn aspirin.

Heck, as fuzzy as I felt, maybe I just hallucinated that face.

11

As the minister and I drove down Route 50 back to Saratoga, he described in picturesque detail exactly what happened on his car ride home with the widow. Even in my distracted state, I had to admit the man knew how to tell a good story. Though personally, I felt the part about what the widow was wearing underneath her black mourning dress was a tad tasteless. I mean, there's a time and a place for crotchless Minnie Mouse underwear.

He went on to regale me with tales about the marriage counseling he'd done during his long and illustrious career. Apparently, some of the couples he'd counseled had asked him to assist them in rather surprising ways.

Listening to his tales made me nostalgic for the old days when I used to write every morning, and everything that happened in the great wide world was fodder for my creative juices. In this hyper-aware state, which was sometimes so intense it was like being high, I would have carefully recorded every detail of the minister's wild yarns in my mind, then jotted them down verbatim as soon as I got home so I could use them later in a screenplay.

Maybe I should try writing again. Go home and do up the minister's stories, turn them into a movie. A warm-hearted comedy about a sexy old preacher, starring Walter Matthau. That face behind the McDonald's sign could belong to a romantic rival, part of a humorous subplot.

Sure, dream on, I told myself harshly. By the time Hollywood got done with your script, they'd scratch Matthau for Keanu. Your sexy old preacher would be turned into a coldblooded young action hero battling renegade Uzbeks or some shit like that. Or more likely, if the script was any good it would never get produced. Instead it would sit on a shelf somewhere for twenty years, then get tossed out.

I hated myself when I got all bitter like this. Every screenwriter I've ever met, even ones who make seven figures per year, have that streak of bitterness inside them. There's so much dumb luck involved, to say nothing of dumb *people.* That was the main reason I'd decided to take a hiatus from writing—I didn't like what it was turning me into. I could feel the bitterness growing inside me like a tumor, and I wanted to cut it out.

Though to be honest, I reflected, as we turned off Route 50 onto Broadway, it wasn't so much a question of *deciding* to take a hiatus; my writing urge just plain up and left me. Half a year ago already. When would it return . . . and what if it never did? If I wasn't a writer anymore, then what was I?

One day, forty-some years from now, a lonely group of people would be standing in the rain at some suburban cemetery. A tired old rabbi would mouth a few final words, and then I'd be lowered into the ground. And what would those people be saying about me? What would I say about myself, in the final moment of my life? What would God say, if there was a God?

Lately Andrea had been after me to try volunteer work, maybe some tutoring with the Literacy Volunteers like she did, but I seemed to be just too darn lazy these days. I was staying away from the Nestlé chocolate bits now, but I was still five or ten pounds overweight; I should exercise more. Hey, I should exercise, period.

I gazed moodily out the window. We were stuck behind a cement truck that was laboriously positioning itself in front of the new Arts Center. Even in the rain, the work never stopped; they just rigged up tarps overhead and kept on going. Gretchen was determined to get the place up and running in time for the summer tourists, and what Gretchen Lang wanted, Gretchen Lang generally got.

Speak of the devil, there she was. On the sidewalk, sharing the mayor's umbrella. A quick jolt went through me; by jiminy, I had some questions for the woman. This time I found the door lock on my first try, and jumped out of the car.

"Hey!" the minister called out.

"Thanks for the lift! You should write a book!" I called back as I walked up to Gretchen, interrupting her tête-à-tête with Mayor Kane. He looked perfect as always, totally dry and not an eyebrow out of place, as though mere rain couldn't affect a great man like him. Gretchen was her usual self too, her arms flying excitedly all over the place as she talked. She was fifty-five if she was a day, maybe sixty, but the woman hadn't lost a step.

"Hi, Gretchen," I said.

Her arms stopped in mid-air. A shadow passed across her features, quickly replaced by a big welcoming smile. "Jacob, how are you? Want to watch them pour the wheelchair ramp?"

"No. I want to talk to you about Donald Penn."

The Mayor gave a quick start, but Gretchen just smiled at me even more warmly. It was like she'd been expecting me.

"Sure, I'd love to talk about Donny. Such a sweet,

wonderful little man. Let's just watch this first." Her arms started flying again. "See, this ramp is a symbol of what our whole project is all about: making the arts accessible to *everyone,* not just the Mary Lou Whitneys and the rich summer tourists but the women who work the checkout counter at Wal-Mart, the men who work at International Paper their whole lives, and the kids, especially the kids, that's my passion, I want to start a children's theater here . . ."

She went on and on. I tried to stop her, but it was like trying to stop some radio talk show host. I got the feeling she realized she was under an umbrella and I wasn't, and she hoped if she kept on yakking, I'd eventually get tired of being rained on and go away.

My attention wandered from her monologue. I noticed the words HUDSON FALLS BUILDING AND RENOVATION on the side of the cement truck, and was reminded that the mayor owned a similar company, Kane Construction. "So how's the construction business, Mayor?" I asked him.

I was only making conversation, trying to shut off Gretchen's flow of words. But for some reason the mayor didn't seem to take it that way. He tensed his jaw and narrowed his photogenic blue eyes at me suspiciously.

Gretchen quickly stepped in. "You know, I'm getting tired of standing in the rain," she said. "Why don't we go to Madeline's? That'll be the perfect place to talk about Donny."

Meanwhile the mayor had recovered his cheerful equanimity. "I wish I could join you guys, but business calls," he said, waving a friendly good-bye and then striding off purposefully down Broadway.

Gretchen and I headed off in the other direction. But when we came to the stoplight, I turned around and took a look back at the mayor.

As it happened, the mayor had turned around too. And he was standing there, watching me.

As soon as Gretchen and I stepped into Madeline's, she began working the room. First she glad-handed a city councilman named Walsh. After that she collared Linda Olive, who owns Saratoga's *premier* video production company—in fact, Saratoga's only video production company—and sweet-talked her into saying she would produce, *gratis* of course, a video promoting the new Arts Center. Then Gretchen stopped to speak with someone else, a big man with a big tie whose name I didn't know. Gretchen, however, knew absolutely *everybody*. The woman was a wonder.

She was also driven as hell. Why? I realized I knew almost nothing about her personal life. She was married, but I'd never met her husband. Or her kids, if she had any.

I wiped the rain off my face with a jacket sleeve and went up to the counter, where Madeline and Marcie were doing the honors. There was a long line, since Madeline's tends to get busy on rainy afternoons, so I had plenty of time to study the two women. It was like watching a ballet, the way they were able to move fluidly and quickly in the narrow space behind the counter without ever bumping into each other. One woman would ring up the other woman's sales if it happened to be more convenient. Seeing them work so well together reminded me that they were cousins; Madeline had once mentioned they were just like sisters growing up.

They were both very attractive, but in different ways: Marcie was totally out there with her sexuality, while Madeline was more demure. Most men, if given the opportunity, would probably choose Marcie for a one-night stand, but they'd feel safer marrying Madeline. Rob was a lucky guy.

Marcie broke into my thoughts. "May I help you?" she asked. She must have been out in the rain, because her T-shirt was clinging to her. Tearing my eyes away from her curves, I looked up at Marcie's face. Her eyes twinkled. I wondered, for the thousandth time, if she knew what kind of effect she had on me.

Gretchen came up behind me and broke the spell. "What'll you have, Jacob? My treat."

Madeline turned away from the espresso machine and gave me a bittersweet smile. "I made a pot of Ethiopian."

I gave the smile back to her. "Then that's what I'll have. By the way," I added, "did you used to give The Penn free coffee?"

Madeline shook her head. "No. Matter of fact, he always paid with exact change. I used to wonder how he managed to get ninety-seven cents' worth of change every single day."

Since I didn't have an answer to that, I took the coffee and headed for the back room, while Gretchen got involved in yet another shmoozing exercise. There was an empty table way at the rear, near the back stairs to the basement. As I sat down, I remembered that this was where The Penn always used to sit. My brain swam a little, the events of the last forty-eight hours catching up to me. To say nothing of that blow to my head.

I greedily guzzled my java, trying to get rid of the dizziness so I could interrogate Gretchen properly about Penn's NYFA application. But when she finally arrived at the table, before I could even open my mouth she immediately began filibustering. "*Stunning work,*" she exclaimed, gesturing at the pointillist obese people defacing the walls. "By Joanne Clemson—do you know her? Such a *fabulous artist*. I'm featuring her in our very first exhibit at the new Arts Center. I just know the tourists who come up for the ballet in July will *love* Joanne. It could really put her on the map!"

Joanne Clemson wasn't the only starving artist Gretchen hoped to put "on the map" this summer, as she went on to explain. She had thought things out very carefully. Offbeat types like Clemson would be exhibited in July, when the New York City Ballet did its thing at the Saratoga Performing Arts Center, a huge but elegant amphitheater in the state park right outside of town. Gretchen would exhibit more mainstream artists in August, when the middlebrows came to Saratoga for the horse races. I watched Gretchen, no longer listening to her words exactly, just mesmerized by the constant exuberant gesticulations of her arms. This woman was so totally *dedicated* to helping starving artists. I personally knew two painters and one sculptor who had been catapulted to nationwide prominence, and economic solvency, by Gretchen's Herculean efforts. And soon, with the help of her new Arts Center, Gretchen would be leading even more starving artists to that promised land.

And this was the woman that I suspected of . . . of what? Some kind of chicanery with Penn's NYFA application? Something that might help explain my burglary? And what about that crazy business about threats to Penn's life? I tried to remember what Molly had said about Gretchen, but my thoughts were somehow echoing strangely all over my head. I poured some more Ethiopian down my throat, but it didn't help. What exactly did I . . .

"So what exactly did you want to talk to me about?" asked Gretchen.

Damned if I knew. The coffee cup was getting awfully heavy. It fell from my hands.

"Jacob? *Jake?*"

And everything went black.

12

I truly hate hospitals. I can't even watch *ER*, have to leave the room when Andrea turns it on. So I'll spare you the details. Let's just say that when I woke up later that day, I was in some crummy bed with flimsy sheets, there were plastic tubes attached to various parts of me, and some doctor type in a white jacket was blabbing at some other doctor type in a white jacket about "delayed concussion syndrome." Apparently my nerves, coffee, Jack Daniel's, aspirin, and adrenaline all wore down at the same time, and my body finally decided to close up shop for a while. Fortunately the prognosis was good, as long as I steered clear of any pressure cookers in the near future, and stayed in the hospital long enough for them to rack up some exorbitant fees.

Andrea bopped in around dinnertime with Gretzky, Babe Ruth, and a bunch of daisies, and I smiled bravely and we did that scene as best we could. But the Sultan of Swat started to cry and the Great One peed in his pants. So let's just do a quick Cut To, as they say in the biz.

Speaking of the biz, when Andrea came to visit by herself later that night, she brought me a FedEx package from L.A. I opened it. Inside was a contract full of fancy legal language which boiled down to this: By

June 15—one month from today, I noted—I would complete a rewrite of *The Night of the Mutant Beetles.*

For which I would be paid $750,000.

I looked at Andrea. Andrea looked at me.

It's one thing to turn down huge amounts of money when it's just talk on the phone. After all, most Hollywood deals fall through anyway. But it's another thing to turn down huge amounts of money when they've been typed into an honest-to-God binding legal contract complete with "henceforth"s and "whereas"s, and all of those beautiful zeroes are staring up at you. Four of them, in fact. With that cute little "75" in front.

"So what do you think?" Andrea asked me.

"I think it's a hell of a lot of bucks."

"It sure is." She grinned.

"Yeah, but mutant beetles. I mean, Jesus, what a dumb-ass idea," I grumbled petulantly. We both knew full well I was going to sign that deal with the Hollywood devil, but I didn't want to admit it right away.

"You don't have to do it if you don't want," Andrea said, but that was just words. Of course I had to. Of course I *wanted* to. Didn't I? I knew I should be happy, but my head hurt. I rubbed it, and Andrea eyed me, worried. "Jacob, how are you feeling?"

I couldn't tell her the truth—in fact I could barely tell *myself* the truth—which was that after six months of being unable to write, I was afraid I'd fail miserably and pathetically at this mutant beetles script. Maybe that *Gas* screenplay was a one-shot deal, a freak, and if I tried to write this mutant beetles thing, everyone would find out I was a total fraud.

"I'm fine," I told Andrea. "I'm just sick of this stupid hospital." I flicked my fingers at the contract. "Can you believe this? For fifteen years, I practically have to *pay* people to read my stuff. Now all of a sudden people I've never even met throw money at me like it's some kind of carnival game. To rewrite some script I haven't even read yet, for God's sake."

"You deserve it. You're a good writer," Andrea said soothingly, as usual understanding my deepest fears. She's the perfect wife. Irritates me sometimes.

I leaned back against the bed, tired, wishing I could forget my self-doubts, and wishing I could forget about all the noble aspirations I'd had during my fifteen years of writing serious movies. Come on, I told myself, just enjoy all those zeroes. I pulled Gretzky and Babe Ruth's daisies over to me, hoping to revive myself by sniffing them. But I couldn't smell a thing, maybe some weird side effect of delayed concussion syndrome. Of course, my nostrils had never been my best feature.

Andrea got her worried look again. "Are you sure you're well enough to start working? Maybe we should talk to the doctor before you sign anything."

"I'm well enough," I said, putting the daisy vase down, "and even if I'm not, so what? Let's say I do a lousy half-ass job, no one ever hires me again, and my career is ruined." I gave a cheerful shrug. "No problem. Because after taxes and shit, we'll have ourselves another two-fifty grand. It'll be our 'fuck you' money."

"Our what?"

"We'll have so much money we can say 'fuck you' to anyone we want."

Andrea laughed. "Sounds good. And it'll totally pay for the kids' college."

"Only problem is, what if I *don't* do a lousy job?" She looked at me blankly. "Then I'll be back in the game. And I'll never be able to get out. The zeroes will have me by the balls. I'll spend my next ten years writing about mutant beetles and their equivalents, forgetting all my youthful ideals, and end up a terminally cynical middle-aged man drinking Scotch around the clock and wondering where the hell my soul went." I rubbed my eyes. "Of course, on the other hand, I'll be incredibly fucking rich. Where do I sign?"

"You don't have to." Andrea took my hand. "We have enough money already. It's okay with me if you say no. It really is."

I looked into her eyes. The amazing thing is, she truly meant it.

"I love you, sweetheart. Hand me a pen."

As I signed the contract, all four copies, a siren began blaring outside. I looked out the window at the ambulance, and it took my mind back to the ambulance that carted away Donald Penn's body. It sure was odd how the man and his magnum opus seemed to make an awful lot of people awfully nervous. In fact, I reflected as I signed the final copy, someone had been nervous enough to break into our house and—

I stopped. "Andrea, where are the kids?"

"Spending the night at Judy's. I got them the new *Mighty Ducks* video, so they should be fine—"

"Honey, call Dave. The cop. Tell him to get over to our house *now.*"

Andrea understood immediately what I was getting at and grabbed the phone book. "What's his last name?"

Damn. "Bass? Trout?"

"Pickerel?"

It was some kind of fish, but which? Tuna? Haddock? "The hell with it. Call nine-one-one."

She started to dial, then stopped. "And tell them what?"

"Tell them there's a burglary in progress at one-oh-nine Elm Street!"

"But we don't know that."

I grabbed her shoulders. "No, we don't. But whoever broke in last night didn't get what he wanted. This is his first good chance to try again."

"Come on, Jacob, you're being—"

I swung my feet out of the bed and stood up. Fortunately all of my tubes had been removed. "Let's go."

"But—"

"Hurry, before they try to feed me any more Jell-O."

"Are you sure you're well enough to—"

"Sweetheart, let's blow this joint."

I threw on my clothes and we snuck out to the hallway, where two nurses were deep in discussion about how unfair it is that Sean Connery is still considered sexy at sixty-eight, whereas a beautiful woman like Angela Lansbury is considered over the hill. Knowing how passionate women get when talking about this subject, I was confident they'd never notice Andrea and me even if we walked out right in front of them. And I was right. Easiest getaway since Nixon got pardoned.

Andrea took the wheel in deference to my questionable medical status, but we didn't lose any speed because of it. She grew up in Brooklyn and can run red lights with the best of them. And despite her protestations she must have been feeling as anxious as I was, because we made it home from the hospital in five minutes flat, and jumped out of the car.

But there were no signs of weirdness. No suspicious vehicles out front, and no house lights turned on. False alarm.

"That's too bad," Andrea said as we walked up the driveway. "I was kind of looking forward to doing my Geena Davis female action hero imitation."

I laughed. "As long as you don't expect me to do a Bruce Willis—"

She stopped suddenly and I bumped into her. "Whoa," I said.

And then I saw it: a dark shadowy figure. Our house seemed to be full of them these days. This one was outside our side door and slinking away. "Hey!" I shouted.

The shadow immediately stopped slinking and started running. It dashed into our backyard, with Andrea and me in hot pursuit.

Her pursuit was hotter than mine, I must confess. I slipped in the wet grass—the rain had continued intermittently all day—and fell down. When I got up, the shadow had already vaulted over our back fence. But Andrea was vaulting right behind it. *Go, Geena.*

I was about to do some vaulting myself when I noticed a glittery object sticking out of the mud in our back garden. I reached down and grabbed it, then went over the fence, yelling, "Andrea!"

"Over here!" I saw her in the distance, racing up Western Alley. I darted after her, looking all around for that shadowy figure.

Andrea stopped at the top of the alley and I stopped beside her, breathless, my head pounding. She put her finger to her lips and we stood there listening. It was a quiet small-town night, with crickets, a dog barking . . . and a car starting up nearby. Oak Street probably. We dashed toward the sound.

We turned the corner just in time to see a dark midsize car speeding away into the night.

"Oh, God," Andrea groaned. "I was so close."

I put my arm around her. "Hey, even Geena has her bad hair days. Look at *Cutthroat Island.* Besides, we have a clue."

She eyed me doubtfully. "A clue?"

"You betcha." I held up the glittery object I had found in our back garden.

It was a shoe.

A spiked, silver-colored, high-heel shoe.

13

"What must have happened," I said as we headed for home, "she took off her shoes so she could run faster. And then she dropped a shoe when she was jumping over the fence."

Andrea examined it. "Size eight. She has medium-size feet."

Andrea is sensitive about her own size ten and a halfs. "Big feet are sexy," I told her.

She ignored me. "This shoe is stylish. Whoever it is, she has class."

"Unless it's a he."

"If it's a he, he definitely has class. But why would anyone wear high-heeled shoes to do a burglary?"

"I guess if she got caught, she wanted to look her best."

"Or maybe the burglary was just a spur of the moment thing."

I nodded. That sounded logical. We were walking up the driveway, but then I halted suddenly and stared. "What's wrong?" Andrea whispered in alarm.

I pointed. The windowpane on our side door was smashed open, and the door was ajar. Ms. High Heels must have broken in and been inside already when we drove up; then she panicked and tried to sneak back out the door. For the second night in a row, someone had invaded our home.

"This isn't funny," Andrea said.

"No," I agreed. I ran inside, crunching glass shards under my feet, and rushed up the stairs, then opened the drawer of my bedside table, looking for The Penn's magnum opus.

It was still there. We'd come home just in time to save it.

I sat down on the bed, holding one of The Penn's yellowed old notebooks in my hand. Who wanted this pathetic excuse for a book badly enough to burglarize for it? Gretchen? But surely a fifty-five-, maybe sixty-year-old lady would never be able to run that fast—or would she? Gretchen wasn't exactly a fat matronly type, far from it. But still . . .

How about Bonnie Engels, the boxer/theater impressario? Or maybe Antoinette Carlson, the Grant Queen? The two of them had certainly seemed disturbed when I showed them Penn's magnum opus at Madeline's. But disturbed enough to burglarize my house?

Was it the same burglar tonight as last night? Both times Andrea and I got the sense it was someone five six or taller, average weight, wearing something loose. Beyond that we couldn't be sure. It was hard to tell how tall a person was when they were always either crouching, running in the darkness, or bopping you on the head with pressure cookers.

After Andrea swept up the broken glass, we sat down at the kitchen table eating bowls of chocolate ice cream—we were both ravenous. We were going to call up Dave about the break-in, but despite the heavy infusion of chocolate and sugar we were both so worn out we could hardly think straight, let alone remember what kind of fish he was. So we decided it could wait until morning, especially since Andrea was worried about my health and wanted to make sure I got a decent night's sleep.

We found out later that getting a decent night's sleep is about the worst thing you can do after a concussion, because you can slip right into a coma. But at the time we didn't know that. Fortunately, tired though I was, I didn't fall asleep. Instead I lay awake obsessing. Over and over again, like an endless series of television replays, I saw The Penn lunging toward my feet. Even when I closed my eyes I saw it.

Finally I grabbed a handful of The Penn's magnum opus, got out of bed, and slipped downstairs. I made myself some coffee and took another look at the umpteen gazillion different versions of the preface. I didn't know what I was looking for, but what the hell, it beat counting sheep.

I carefully unfolded a long sheet of toilet paper on which The Penn had written a preface that began, *"It was the kind of night Snoopy made famous . . ."* This toilet paper probably dated from the 60s or early 70s, when Peanuts was at its height, before Doonesbury or Calvin and Hobbes.

I picked up a Marlboro box that had been opened up and flattened out and scribbled on in tiny letters. *"It was a cold night, and in the distance Paula Barbieri and Paula Jones were howling . . ."* began this preface. Definitely mid-90s.

"It was so cold that night, God would have frozen His balls off, if He had any . . ." began a third. Hmm. The cynical 80s?

Well, I wasn't coming up with any amazing Holmesian inspirations, but at least I was getting a nice tour of American history. Or as The Penn would have put it, "the history of Western civilization careening." My reading had another benefit too: It was making me finally feel sleepy.

"The clister, or glister, glistened, or perhaps clistened, in the snow . . ."

"Every man has his clister, his 151 proof, his dreams . . ."

I yawned. Why this decades-long obsession with clister? I remembered, as a student at a small New England college, putting clister on my cross-country skis when the snow was so crunchy that regular wax wouldn't work. Clister was certainly nice to have around on days like those, but I couldn't picture spending thirty years writing about the stuff.

"Only now, with his supply of Ethiopian threatened, did he understand his father's feelings for the glistening clister . . ."

I was about to toss this preface aside—it was written on some kind of menu—when the next sentence grabbed me. *"Like his father many years before, he would protect his clister/Ethiopian by any means necessary . . . and they knew it."*

Strange, that sounded ominous. I was eager to read more, but there was nothing else on the page but a list of muffins: pumpkin raisin, cappuccino walnut . . . This was the menu from Madeline's. I turned it over, and above the beverage selections, Penn had continued:

"No, you don't fuck with a man's coffee. Especially when he needs it to create, to write, to exist. If humankind has constructed civilization in such a way that a man cannot easily obtain the small metallic and paper objects that have arbitrarily been defined as money, then he must find a way to secure his precious fluid, his beloved life force, for free. Fortunately, civilization has been so constructed that blackmail is a simple alternative."

My eyes popped wide open. "Blackmail?"

"Yes, no one is a saint, and no one is immune. A man can get free Ethiopian anywhere, if he knows what cards to play."

There was nothing else on the page but price lists for exotic coffees. I sat there and reread Penn's last three sentences. Then I reread them again.

If I understood them right, The Penn had gotten his free Ethiopian by *blackmailing* people.

Suddenly that crazy idea of mine, that Penn had been murdered, came back to me. But this time it didn't seem so crazy.

Two burglaries, alleged death threats, and now, for icing on the muffin, blackmail.

I got up and paced the kitchen floor. Where had The Penn drunk free Ethiopian? City Hall, the Arts Council, and maybe Madeline's too, if she had lied to me about him paying for his coffee.

Had blackmailing these people led to The Penn's death?

Had one of them, say, poisoned his coffee?

But wait a minute. The county medical examiner had already checked the body out and ruled it a heart attack.

On the other hand, though, how carefully would the local medical examiner check a corpse from the town bum, a guy with no money and no family? He probably wouldn't bother to check for poison or anything like that. Sure, the dead man was only fifty-three, relatively young for a heart attack, but no doubt the M.E. would figure that Donald Penn's lifestyle aged a man quickly.

I got some milk from the refrigerator to calm my nerves. Then, all of a sudden, I began to laugh at myself. What was I doing here? Who did I think I was, Columbo?

Then the telephone rang.

The kitchen clock said 2:00 A.M. At first I had the wild feeling it must be the murderer himself, or herself. But then I realized that made no sense. It had to be my agent; no one else would be rude enough to call me this late.

As I rushed to get the phone before it woke up Andrea, my mind fast-forwarded to all the stuff I'd be doing in the next few days. First I'd FedEx the contract to Andrew—to his house, since it was Friday already. Then the producer would FedEx me the script and call me up to tell me how terrific I was and how ecstatic she was to be working with me. I'd tell her how terrific *she* was and how ecstatic *I* was to be working with *her.* Then we'd have a marathon three-way phone conversation with the director to make sure we all shared the same *artistic vision* about mutant beetles. Good old mutant beetles—soon they'd rule my life. Soon I'd be working twenty-four/seven, and I'd have no time for anything else.

Including playing Columbo.

"Hi, Andrew," I sighed into the phone.

"You told someone, didn't you?"

Whoa. Definitely not Andrew—it was a woman. But who? I was mystified. "Told someone what?" I tried.

"About the application, damn it," the woman sputtered furiously, but her voice sounded girlish, and I figured it out—Molly Otis, the funeral home daughter. "It had to be you. I didn't talk to anyone else. Now you got me in trouble!"

"What kind of trouble? Who's bothering you?"

"I don't know. *Nobody.*" Molly's anger turned into a whine. "Just don't ever say my name again, okay? Please?"

"Molly, I have got to know what the hell—"

"I'm not talking to you anymore!"

And she slammed down the phone.

I looked in the phone book. Molly wasn't listed, so maybe she still lived at home, but I doubted it. Any girl who grows up in a funeral director's house is going to get her ass out of there as fast as she can.

I called the Skidmore operator, an uptight-sounding, middle-aged woman who confirmed that Molly did indeed live in the dorms and had her own phone number. But she wouldn't give it up to me. "I'm not authorized," she said. Her voice sounded familiar—was Ms. Thin Lips moonlighting as an operator?

"Look, I need to talk to her. It's imperative."

"If you'd like to leave a message, I can connect you to her voice mail."

I racked my brain. Sick uncle? Dead grandmother? No, this was the 90s, I needed something fresh. "The thing is, I'm afraid she won't call me back, and I really must talk to her *immediately*. See, I'm her ex-boyfriend, and I just tested positive for HIV. Not the kind of message you can leave on voice mail."

There was a moment's silence. I had her. I smiled to myself.

"I'm sorry, sir. I can't help you."

How aggravating. What would Hercule Poirot do now? I borrowed an idea from the movie *Kids*. "Ma'am, this is literally life or death. I just heard that Molly went out with my cousin Pete tonight, and I better reach her before she sleeps with him. Pete is a real mover, you know what I mean? I need to get in touch with them before it's too late."

"Sir, would you like to leave a voice mail message?"

Screw you, lady. "Yeah. Tell her to use a condom." I hung up in disgust. No doubt old Hercule would have already solved the murder—assuming there *was* one. Maybe I should just take some aspirin, go to sleep, and call Dave the Fish in the morning.

But then I had an incredibly, amazingly brilliant idea. I called Information.

And got Molly's phone number.

When I dialed it, either she was gone or she was screening my call, because her machine picked up. It was one of those cutesy messages you get from college students, with people giggling in the background and Molly saying, "Hello, if you believe in sex before marriage, please leave a message at the beep."

I pictured her father listening to that message. Thank God I don't have daughters. *Beep!* I lowered my voice, trying to sound menacing. "Molly," I growled at her machine, "something very fucked up is going on, and I plan to find out what. If you don't tell me the truth, and I mean the whole truth, I will call the cops immediately. I will use your name and tell them everything you've told me—"

"You bastard!" Molly shouted. "You lousy creep!" And then she started to cry. I certainly *felt* like a lousy creep, blackmailing a scared little college girl. So now The Penn and I had yet another thing in common: We were both blackmailers.

Finally, after I did some more cajoling and haranguing, Molly poured out her story. About half an hour previously, while she lay in bed asleep, someone had heaved a brick through her window. The brick landed right on her forehead, bruising it painfully. And she had bad gashes on her arms, hands and knees from when she jumped out of bed, terrified, and fell on some shattered window glass.

She would have gone to the hospital, except she didn't want to have to tell anyone what had happened. The brick had a typewritten note taped to it which read, quite succinctly, "You talk any more, bitch, we'll kill you."

"Who do you think did it, Molly?"

"I don't know."

Exasperating. This girl knew a lot more than she was admitting. I understood she was traumatized, so I tried to sound patient. "Listen, Molly, you can trust me. I never told anyone you talked to me. Nobody knew about it except your dad."

"Well, *somebody* must have known, otherwise why would they do this to me?"

"Molly, help me get to the bottom of this. You told me at the funeral, you promised someone you wouldn't say anything about the application. Who did you make that promise to? Was it Gretchen?"

"I don't want to get in any more trouble," Molly whimpered.

I couldn't say I blamed her, but that didn't stop me from pushing even harder. "Look, I know The Penn was blackmailing somebody. You've got to tell me who it was."

"I told you, I don't know anything about it!" Molly shouted.

Like heck she didn't. "For God's sake, Molly, what did Penn write on that application? Why is someone so desperate to hush it up?"

"I just want to go back to sleep!" Molly screeched hysterically. "I want everyone to leave me alone!"

She was about to hang up on me again. I backed off. "Look, I'll make you a deal: Just tell me one thing, and I'll leave you alone. Where can I find this grant application?"

For a few moments there was no answer. I thought maybe she'd hung up. But finally she said, "At the Arts Council. In the NYFA file. But don't tell anyone I told you."

Jeez, enough already. I sympathized with the girl, but I was getting sick of her. "Hey, I get the message. Your secret is safe with me."

I hung up the phone. The puzzling part was, I really *hadn't* said a word about Molly, or Penn's application, to anybody. So why did someone throw a brick through her window with a warning not to "talk any more"? How did someone know she had talked to me in the first place?

Had Virgil, for some obscure reason, thrown a brick at his own daughter? Or did that mysterious person lurking behind the McDonald's sign see Molly and me talking together in the cemetery parking lot? Or did Gretchen—or the Mayor—somehow guess that Molly must have told me something, and that's why I'd confronted Gretchen about The Penn?

Too many questions, and not a single goddamn answer. Totally infuriating. And beginning about forty-eight hours from now, I'd be too busy dealing with mutant beetles to find out what the fuck this was all about.

I looked up from the kitchen table, my eyes fastening on the broken windowpane to our side door. I sat there, my anger building, then stood up and threw on my jacket. I stuck my trusty Adirondack Lumberjacks cap on my head and pulled it down low, then grabbed work gloves and a hammer from my tool box. I left Andrea a note on the kitchen table—"A, Gone fishing. Back soon, J." Then I headed outside.

I mean, heck, everybody else in town seemed to be into burglarizing these days. Maybe I should try it myself.

14

The building that had housed the Arts Council office for the past fifteen years, and would continue housing them for two more months until they moved into the new Arts Center, was on Broadway. But the wrong end of Broadway, next to the Goodwill store and a vacant garage. Even during the shank of the evening, there was virtually no traffic there; and I was confident that at this hour the place would be deserted. I'd simply break in the back door, and there was no way anybody would see me. I'd have plenty of time to search the Arts Council—and even Penn's old apartment upstairs for good measure.

And if by some amazing freak I actually got caught, I figured on getting a break for sure. After all, not only was I more or less the executor of Penn's estate, but I'd been burglarized twice and I was just trying to catch whoever did it. So I got into my rusty old '85 Camry and drove off. The muffler needed fixing, which was highly noticeable in the silent night streets. One of these days I'd have to accept the fact that I really was rich now, and could afford a new vehicle.

The Arts Council was a mile and a half away, but I only spotted a single moving car, a nondescript mid-sized sedan which followed me down Franklin for a while, but then turned off onto Washington. There's not a lot of action in Saratoga Springs on a late Thursday night in mid-May.

I parked on a narrow backstreet one and a half blocks away from what would soon become the scene of my crime. Hammer and gloves in hand, I stepped out into the eerie three a.m. darkness, then eased along an old nineteenth-century alley toward the rear of the Arts Council building.

The alley was pitch black. The streetlights didn't make it back there, and the moon and stars were smothered by clouds. The rain that had drizzled off and on for two days had stopped for now, leaving behind a strong wind that whooshed down the alley, rattled a fence, and whistled through a couple of half-open garbage cans. The only other noise I could hear above the wind was a solitary streetlight buzzing way off in the distance.

But then I heard a scream.

I stood still. Then came another scream, from the direction of the Arts Council, even more bloodcurdling than the first.

I gripped my hammer tight. Somewhere in the darkness ahead of me was a damsel in major distress. My duty was clear: charge forward, attack the villain, save the girl, and maybe get on *Oprah*.

On the other hand, I could always just sneak back into my car and hightail it the hell out of there. Maybe dial 911 after I made it safely home and locked the doors behind me. As Groucho Marx used to say, "Are you a man or a mouse? Squeak up!"

Unfortunately (or maybe fortunately), I didn't get the chance to find out which I was, because life intervened. There was a scrambling noise in the alley. Then something slammed hard into my ankle.

I jumped several feet high, and screamed myself. And then the cat—that's what it was—screamed, too.

The same scream I'd heard earlier. My damsel in distress. As the cat tore off for parts unknown, I felt my heart come back down to its usual spot. I even managed a laugh, but stopped quickly because it sounded so hollow. I gripped my hammer more tightly than ever as I headed up the alley toward the Arts Council.

Just as I had remembered, the building's back door was well hidden. On one side of it the wall jutted outward, and on the other side were some large yew bushes that hadn't been trimmed in years. I'd been inside the building several times before, while judging children's poetry for the annual Saratoga County Apple 'n' Arts Festival, and I didn't recall seeing any alarm systems. I was about to find out for sure.

The back door had a large glass panel that glinted invitingly in the darkness. This whole Donald Penn business is a real boon for local glaziers, I reflected, as I took a deep breath, brought back my hammer . . .

And walloped the windowpane. *Smash*—the whole pane jumped right to the floor. I waited breathlessly for an alarm. But nothing happened. I couldn't believe how easy this was. I put on my gloves and reached in, felt around for the lock, and opened the door.

Broken glass crunching under my feet, I stepped inside the dark forbidden hallway. Every nerve in my body was tinglingly alive. People who say burglary is as exciting as sex are full of shit; burglary is *much* more exciting. To heck with writing, this was my new career right here.

I edged upstairs, holding on to the rails. Next time I'd bring a flashlight. So far as I knew, the first floor was unoccupied; the Arts Council office was on the second floor, and Penn had lived on the third.

On the second-floor landing, my gloved hand felt a doorknob. I tapped above it hoping to find a windowpane, and did. *Yes.* I bashed the pane, unlocked the door and stepped inside the Arts Council. Piece of cake.

I closed the two windowshades that faced onto Broadway and turned on Gretchen's desk lamp.

And then, feeling like an old pro, I got down to business.

The Arts Council office had the kind of haphazard look you find in a place where everything is donated. Classy oak chairs were sitting alongside cheap blue plastic ones. A state-of-the-art color laser printer was hooked up to a hopelessly outdated late-80s Mac. Beneath the side window was an antique rolltop desk that looked pretty nifty—except for a broken leg that was propped up by *World Book Encyclopedia* volumes from 1958. A variety of desks, file cabinets, and bookcases covered every available square inch, and they were bursting with hundreds or maybe even thousands of files. Where in the middle of this whole mess would Gretchen keep this year's NYFA grant applications?

I started with the biggest file cabinet in the room, but all six feet of it were devoted to the new Arts Center. A quick gander at the files showed that getting the Arts Center up and running had taken up a major portion of Gretchen's life for more than a decade. And other people's lives, too; the files were full of memos and letters from such familiar figures as Bonnie Engels, Antoinette Carlson, and even Mike Pardou, the King of Spoons. They had all served on the Arts Center Advisory Board and put in a lot of grassroots grunt work promoting the project.

It was fun snooping on people I knew. In another cabinet I found a drawer marked *"National Bookings of Local Artists."* Gretchen had files on a lot of local artists, but the biggest one belonged to George Hosey, the ersatz Uncle Sam. How could Gretchen possibly take this guy seriously? But evidently she did, because the file contained correspondence from Gretchen to arts councils, city halls, and business conventions all over the world promoting Hosey's dubious services. And sometimes she succeeded. I found a letter from a marching band in Auckland, New Zealand, offering Hosey *five thousand dollars* for a one-day gig.

Five grand? For a guy whose major talent was wearing a long white goatee? Wasn't that just a trifle excessive?

I mean, New Zealand is basically full of kiwis and sheep. Couldn't they just make a goatee out of wool and tape it to someone's chin? Or if that failed, maybe they could make a goatee out of glued kiwi fuzz.

I was curious to read up more on Hosey, but it was closing in on 4:00 already. Where were those damn applications?

I ran around the room like a chicken with its head cut off, throwing open drawers and files, until finally, in the very bottom shelf of the very last bookcase in the room, I struck gold. Underneath a batch of files about local community theaters there was a plain cardboard box, about as high as a shoe box and twice as wide, with NYFA, 98 written on the cover.

I tore the box open. Sure enough, it was full of applications, each one five pages long, stapled together. I lifted them all out.

I quickly skimmed the top one, from "Albanese, Albert." "*. . . Requesting one thousand dollars . . . support me while I write poetry . . . need money.*" Jesus, artists are so desperate. At the top of his application were two boxes, "*Accepted*" and "*Rejected*", and Gretchen, or someone else on the grant panel, had put a check mark in the "*Rejected*" box. Another dream dead. I briefly pictured poor Albert Albanese coming home from his lousy day job and discovering the rejection letter from the Arts Council in his mailbox. I'll bet his girlfriend had to listen to him bitch for weeks.

I tossed Albanese aside and zipped through the pile, searching for Penn. Applebaum, Atwater . . . Alphabetical order. I jumped ahead. Engels, French . . . I jumped again. Orsulak, Pardou, Preller . . .

Wait a minute. Where the hell was Penn?

Molly had said his application would be here, hadn't she? I checked again. Orsulak, Pardou, Preller . . .

Shit.

Maybe it had been misplaced. I went through the entire pile of applications carefully, one by one.

But Donald Penn's application wasn't there.

Someone had taken it away.

Great. This was just perfect. *Now what?*

I checked my watch: 4:15. A wave of exhaustion poured through me. The top of my head was radiating dull throbs and my eyes ached. Outside the wind was picking up again, rattling the windowpanes. There was some kind of unpleasant smell in the air, probably dust from all those old files.

I looked down at the applications in front of me, and on a whim checked out the one from Mike Pardou. He had applied for $1500 to support him while he composed a "one-man, folk-music opera about lost love, with harmonica and spoons." Just what the world needed. Bad enough people had to listen to him cry and warble "Midnight at the Oasis" whenever he got high; now he wanted to be paid for it.

But the panel had actually *accepted* his application. And not only that, they'd awarded him the entire $1500. Come on, this guy hadn't done anything of artistic note since the Jim Kweskin Jug Band broke up, and that was so long ago, people still said "groovy."

Intrigued, I decided to check the grant applications from the other artists who were also members of the panel. Bonnie Engels had applied for $2000 to produce her boxing video; and her application had been accepted in full, too. Now Bonnie was a legit artist—I'd seen a couple of plays she directed, and they were pretty good—but two grand seemed like a lot, given how little money the Arts Council had to spread around.

I kept on going. Antoinette Carlson: $1800, accepted in full. George Hosey: also $1800, also accepted in full.

What a joke.

And to top things off, Steve Simpkins, the Novella Man, had applied for $1200 "to support me while I complete my novella. Several publishers have already expressed interest." Give me a break, the Novella Man didn't need any grants to support him; he had a trust fund. And besides, I would bet my wife and at least one of my children that no publisher anywhere on this planet had ever "expressed interest" in anything this chump had ever written.

But his application was accepted in full. *Every single application* from members of the grant panel was accepted in full.

Talk about conflict of interest.

Weird. With such small sums of money involved, you'd think people wouldn't bother to be dishonest. They'd just figure it wasn't worth the trouble. But I guess that's not how it works. What the heck, Spiro Agnew, one Watergate heartbeat away from the presidency, gave it all up for a $25,000 bribe.

Of course, with these NYFA grants it wasn't just money at stake, it was prestige. But still, it seemed so petty.

And what about Gretchen? Why did she go along with it? Because she needed these folks' help to do the grunt work for her Arts Center?

Disgusted with people in general, and artists in particular, I threw the box of applications back in the bookcase. And that's when I noticed, sitting right there on the bottom shelf, two more cardboard boxes. They were labeled NYFA, 97 and NYFA, 96. I quickly opened the '97 box, tore through the pile, and there it was: *Donald Penn's application.* With his cramped meticulous handwriting covering the page. A year old, but still, maybe it would have that magic hidden clue. I started reading.

I got so engrossed in the application, I didn't notice the unpleasant smell in the room getting stronger.

And I didn't notice the fire until I looked up and black smoke was already racing through the broken windowpane.

15

I was so lost in Penn's words, the smoke didn't register at first. I just stared at it blankly.

But then that old chestnut flashed into my brain: "Where there's smoke, there's fire." No shit; the whole stairway was lit up in bright orange, and burning wet wood was crackling loudly. How the hell had the fire gotten so big, so fast? Snatching up Penn's application, I ran for the door and opened it.

Big mistake. Smoke poured through the now open door, choking me. I gasped, coughed, and jumped backward.

Then, insane with fear, I charged forward into the hallway, covering my nose and mouth with my sleeve. Another big mistake. I was so blinded by smoke, I couldn't even find the steps at first, and when I did, I only made it down three of them before the smoke and flames drove me back. My lungs were burning up.

I dashed back into the office, tripped on a chair and fell down. I leaped up again and ran through the smoke to the nearest window. I ripped down the windowshade and, since my hammer was lost in the smoke, kicked at the window. Nothing happened. The windowpane, though old, was made of stern stuff—either that or I was weakening fast.

I reared back my foot for another, stronger kick, but lost my balance and fell down again. Smoke enveloped me. I tried to scream, but all that came out were desperate coughs.

Served me right, of course. If I died of asphyxiation, it was only fitting punishment for having written *The Gas that Ate San Francisco.*

Actually though, I probably owe my life to B flicks. Because just then an image of Bruce Lee somehow popped into my brain. I jumped up and delivered a classic kung-fu B-movie kick at the window, and it crashed open. As the glass splintered onto the ground way down below, I stuck my head out and gulped the fresh air. I coughed and sputtered, then gulped some more of that delicious stuff.

Feeling revived, I held my breath and looked behind me. Suddenly I felt my right arm getting hot. I glanced down and realized I was still holding Penn's application, and it was in flames—it must have caught on fire in the hallway. I dropped the application and was about to stamp out the flames when I saw my jacket sleeve was on fire, too.

Terrified, I wriggled out of the jacket and threw it to the floor. But my arm was still burning hot; there were angry red sparks parading from my wrist up to my elbow, and even higher. I frantically rubbed the fiery spots with my other arm, trying to get them to go out.

Only now I couldn't breathe. The smoke was getting thicker and thicker, blurring the room. I leaned out the window again, but smoke was billowing out of it like crazy now, right next to my head, so even when I stuck my head way out, I still could barely breathe. Meanwhile, the wet wood was crackling so loud it sounded to my frightened ears like explosions. From across Broadway, I heard a siren wail. I didn't know if they were cops or firemen, but either way, they were too late. I had to jump.

I looked down. Two stories, with nothing but grass

to ease my fall. I'd break something for sure—hopefully not my head. Two concussions in two nights would probably not do wonders for my neurological future. I started coughing and it turned into an uncontrollable spasm, racking my body. A sudden flame shot out at me from the wooden desk. No time to think; I better just pray I had some kangaroo in my blood. I got up on the windowsill and bent my knees.

But wait—what about that goddamn application? Holding my nose, I turned and looked back. A couple of feet away, through the smoke, I saw a small pile of yellow and orange fire. Perfect. The '98 application had been stolen, and now the '97 application was turning into ash.

First I just felt disappointed, but then, out of the blue, a burst of fury seized hold of me so hard I actually started shaking and almost fell off the windowsill. This was so unfair. Here I commit a felony offense, my ass is burning off, I'm about to jump sixty feet and risk turning into a paraplegic—and all for nothing? Screw that!

I got down on all fours. The smoke wasn't quite as harsh down there, and I actually managed to get something resembling oxygen into my lungs. As tears fell from my stinging, half-closed eyes, I felt my way around the desk to the bookcase where I'd left the box labeled NYFA, 96. My hands found the box before my eyes did. I grabbed it and crawled back to the window, then climbed up on the sill.

Beneath me a cop car, siren blasting, roared up Broadway and screeched into the Arts Council driveway to my right. When the cop leaped out I thought about shouting down to him, then thought better of it. A quiet little burglary was one thing; a four-alarm fire was something else. If I got caught now, I was in for some serious grief. So I watched silently as he raced around the back of the building.

The cop car's headlights lit up the grass beneath me, and I looked down dubiously at the sparse-looking stuff. Hopefully no one had mowed it for a while, because I needed every extra eighth-inch of cushioning I could get.

What's more, I had better hit that tiny little patch of grass, and not the concrete sidewalk right next to it.

And I better not land on any jagged shards of windowpane.

And I better not hit my head again, or I'd spend the rest of my life doing the Muhammed Ali shuffle.

I was so scared, I didn't even remember to pray.

I just closed my eyes and jumped.

I opened my eyes just in time to see the grass hurtling toward me at warp speed. My feet hit first. My knees buckled and hit the grass a nanosecond later, then my whole body buckled. The hard sidewalk came rushing at my head.

I still think that box of grant applications saved my life. Certainly it saved me from another concussion. Because by some primitive survival instinct, I thrust the box at the sidewalk just before my head got there. And instead of banging right into the concrete, my head landed on fifty grant applications loosely filling a soft cardboard box. Painful but not deadly, and not bad enough to mash my brains into overripe broccoli.

At first I didn't realize how lucky I was. I lifted my head and was somewhat surprised to find it was still attached to my body. Then I moved my knees—or tried to. But they wouldn't budge. I tried again. Still nothing. *Oh Jesus, this is it, I'm paralyzed.* I was already imagining life in a wheelchair, wondering if I'd ever learn to enjoy wheelchair basketball, when I tried a third time and at last my knees lifted up.

Mud. That's all it was. The ground was so soggy from the rain, my knees had gotten stuck in six inches of mud. I wobbled to my feet, and took a tentative step. My God, I could actually walk! I hobbled around in a small circle to prove to myself that my walking was no fluke. I was so thrilled and relieved I started laughing hysterically.

"Hey, you!" someone shouted. I looked up—oh no, the cop! I had forgotten all about him. Now he was moving swiftly toward me from the driveway.

It was still dark out and I thought about running, but I wasn't exactly operating at full speed. More like quarter speed. In the light from his headlights I could see the cop was fat and balding, but unless he'd had knee replacement surgery in the last week or so, he would catch me, no problem. And sirens were coming from everywhere now. I better just give up and beg for mercy. Trying to escape would definitely not be a smart idea.

But it's funny how clichés can come into your head at the strangest times. This time it was my agent's favorite standby, which had also become my favorite ever since I struck it rich with that hack movie: "It's better to be lucky than smart."

So I trusted in luck and ran. The cop ran after me.

I ducked into the back alley. The cop ducked after me shouting "Halt! Police!" just like in the movies. Amazing, I thought—the movies actually got it right.

He was gaining on me. I heard his footsteps, and I felt myself running out of gas. This was the end. Fuck luck; I put my hands up and started to turn around.

And then the guy fired his gun at me.

BOOM! A piece of wall chipped off right above my head. Maybe he was aiming above me and not at me, but I didn't wait to find out. Talk about incentive. I found new gas. I found gas in places I didn't even know I had gas. I became Michael Johnson and the Roadrunner combined, on fast forward. That fat, balding, trigger-happy cop didn't stand a chance. I raced up one alley and down another one, zipped across a side street and through some back yards, and left him in the dust like Wyle E. Coyote.

I hid behind a rotting picket fence for twenty minutes or so until I was pretty sure he'd given up. Then I crouched down low, scurried alongside some hedges, and darted warily across driveways until I made it back to my car. I had to hurry; dawn was coming, and I didn't want the cops catching me with no jacket on and little burn marks all over my arm. They might wonder. So I opened the car door as quietly as I could, checked to make sure no cops were around, and started the engine. *CHUGGA VUGGA!* Oh God, I thought, that's it; no more burglaries until I buy a new car.

I backed into someone's driveway and took off down Washington Street. My car felt like the loudest thing in all of Saratoga at that hour. I might as well have had a bumper sticker that said, HERE I AM! ARREST ME! But I guess the cops were hanging out watching the firemen or something, because I made it home without incident.

No question: It's better to be lucky than smart.

I picked up the box of '96 grant applications from the seat beside me and went inside. Then I tiptoed upstairs and peeked in our bedroom. Andrea was still sound asleep, her long black hair flowing off the pillow to her bare shoulder.

And that's when it hit me: I had almost died. Not only that, I had almost lost Andrea forever.

I took off my smoky clothes, lay down in bed, and

snuggled up close to her. But then she shifted in her sleep and her nose twitched, and I thought: What if she smells the smoke on my body? I'd never be able to explain that away. Andrea had gotten pretty pissed off about my little safety-deposit box episode. How would she react to my breaking and entering, jumping out of a burning building, and getting into a foot chase with a wild and crazy gun-toting cop?

Probably not too well. In fact, if Andrea found out I did something so stupid I almost got myself killed, she might kill me herself.

So I eased carefully away from her and slipped out of bed. I wasn't ready for sleep anyway. Even though I felt totally burned out, pun intended (why do people always say "pun not intended" when it really is?), my mind was still running a marathon inside my head. I went downstairs and opened up the box of '96 applications. My hunch was right: The Penn had applied that year, same as '97 and '98.

I glanced at the top of The Penn's application, where the grant panel had recorded their verdict: *Rejected.* Same as '97. No doubt his '98 application would have been rejected too, if he'd still been alive. But he wasn't. He died just two days before the grant panel met.

Someone killed him.

In my bones, I was sure of that now. Just like I was sure in my bones that someone had just tried to kill *me.*

Or at the very least, someone knew I was in that building when they set it on fire. The fire had spread too fast for it to be anything but arson.

So what was the deal here? That nondescript mid-sized sedan that followed me briefly on my way to the Arts Council, then disappeared; maybe it kept right on following me and my kamikaze muffler from a distance. And then whoever it was saw me breaking into the building, figured out I was searching either Penn's digs or the Arts Council for evidence about the murder, and panicked. So they got hold of some gasoline and . . .

But wait, who had that screaming cat been running away from? Maybe the arsonist was already there outside the building, preparing to set the fire, when I happened along and drove him off temporarily—or should I say *her*, given those high heels. Then, when I went inside, she decided to go ahead and torch the place anyway. Probably figured torching me was just an added bonus.

I shivered. How many people was I dealing with here? Burglaries, intimidation, arson, someone possibly following me . . . could this all be the work of just one person? Maybe Penn's murder was a conspiracy.

Or maybe there were two or more unrelated people running around and committing desperate crimes in order to keep Penn's writings from ever seeing the light of day. How many people had Penn blackmailed? His words, *"No one is a saint, and no one is immune,"* rang through my head. I got up to make sure all the doors were locked, then realized it didn't matter, because the windowpane was broken.

The sky outside was slowly brightening, but it still felt ominously quiet. I wished I had a gun, but all I had was The Penn's grant application. I better hope that old cliché was true, the one about The Penn being mightier than the sword. I smiled to myself. The more tired I got, the worse my jokes were getting. I poured myself a much-needed cup of coffee, sat down at the kitchen table, and started to read.

Name: Donald Penn.

Category: Writer.

Amount Requested: $172.32.

$172.32. The exact same amount he requested a year

later. I'd read that far in the '97 application before the fire hit.

Statement of Purpose: I am requesting these funds to assist me in writing my three-volume work The History of Western Civilization Careening, as Seen through the Eyes of One of Its Primary Practitioners. *After working on this book for three decades, I am now nearing completion.*

I shook my head with amusement at that bald-faced lie—"*nearing completion.*" But was it really a lie, or had he somehow managed to delude himself into believing it? Having spent so many years as an unproduced screenwriter, deceiving myself about one project after another, I knew how amazingly powerful self-delusion could be. I had a swig of my coffee and continued.

This book will have a major impact on the way Americans perceive themselves as the millennium draws to a close. My thesis is that the merest act of love can bring almost unbearable responsibility, and this is why we, all of us, live our deepest lives isolated in clear sky, in Ethiopian, in newspapers . . .

Oh, terrific, his Statement of Purpose was just another version of that goddamn preface. And it was three pages long. I couldn't bear the thought of reading the whole thing, so I just skimmed it quickly for hints about blackmail, then moved on to the next section: Budget of Project. (*Please be as specific as possible.*)

Having filled out my share of grant applications over the years, I knew what you were supposed to do when you hit the budget section: Come up with some random numbers, inflate them as much as you think you can get away with, then double them for good luck and write them down. It's a con game. You'll find more truthfulness in a Republican campaign document than in your average arts grant application.

But I guess no one ever told this to Donald Penn, because he was painfully honest. And talk about specific—his Budget went like this:

EXPENSES, MONTHLY	
Rent including utilities	$350
Coffee—3 cups daily, at various restaurants (*necessary* for creativity)	87.00 (includes tips)
Food—daily consumption of 1 can chunk tuna, 8 oz. milk, 2 cups Tastee-O's breakfast cereal, 8 oz. frozen orange juice, 4 slices day-old bread, and 2 tbs butter	62.40
Notebooks, pens of various colors, pencils, erasers, and other writing material	14.36
Entertainment—1 movie matinee	4.75
Toothpaste, miscellaneous	4.75
Safety-deposit box	1.25
Transportation—bus to and from mall for movie	1.20
Telephone, clothing, shoes	0
TOTAL EXPENSES, MONTHLY:	$525.71

INCOME, MONTHLY	
Social Security disability	$504.36
NYFA grant (projected)	14.36 ($172.32 annual)
Can and bottle returns	7.75
TOTAL INCOME, MONTHLY:	$526.47

Boy, talk about living on the edge. This guy's life was a regular Flying Wallenda Brothers routine.

I suppose, though, that he wasn't really so different from all the other millions of "emerging artists" in the world, subsisting in tiny bug-infested apartments, stealing salt and sugar packets from their local fast-food outlets, working their asses off for years for zilch money while dreaming of fame and fortune. No wonder so many artists are crazy. The surprise is that more of them aren't. Like most people—including artists themselves—I have mixed feelings about "emerging artists"; I vacillate between pity, scorn, and admiration.

I turned the page. Under Additional Comments, Penn wrote: *A grant of $172.32 will enable me to write for the entire year, free of financial worries. I will not have to dip into my savings, which total $18.57 (recent bank statement enclosed). I hope you will be able to assist me in this very important project.*

"Very important project." I couldn't read anymore. I sighed and rubbed my tired eyes, then gazed out the window. Dawn was bursting forth at last, in spectacular fashion. Three broad red streaks laced the soft blue morning horizon. I wondered, where was The Penn now?

Hopefully, he was busy applying to some great arts panel in the sky.

And hopefully, some divine panelist would check the box marked *Accepted.*

16

I showered, shampooed, put on new clothes, and stuffed my old smoky clothes in a plastic shopping bag in the basement. Then I made a phone call. It rang three times before Molly Otis answered. "Hello?" she said, her voice squeaking with fear.

I spoke fast, trying to get it all in before she had a chance to slam down the phone. "Look, the application. Any other copies?"

She didn't answer. *"Molly, are there any other damn copies?"*

Finally, a small, beaten voice: "In New York."

"New York City?"

Her voice got tight with hysteria. "We send one copy of every application to NYFA. Now please stop bothering me!" she yelled, and hung up.

I was still sitting there holding the phone when Andrea came in wearing her birthday suit, though I was almost too distracted to notice. "Hi, honey, you sleep okay?" she asked.

"Like a log," I answered.

She pointed at the phone in my hand. "You calling Dave?"

I stared at her in confusion. "Are you kidding?" No way was I telling any cop about my little B and E job, even if he did snow-blow my driveway every winter.

"Why not?"

"Well, he is a cop, after all. I doubt he looks too favorably on burglaries."

Andrea frowned, puzzled. "Exactly. So let's call him."

It took me a moment, but then I got it. She was talking about Ms. Silver Heels's burglary of our house, not my own burglary of the Arts Council. She wasn't aware of that little escapade of mine yet.

And I better keep it that way.

She came closer, sniffing the air. "What's that smell? *Smoke?*"

Despite my shower, evidently my pores were still oozing smoke. I hid my right arm, with its blackened spots, incipient scabs, and singed-off hair, behind my back. "I don't smell anything," I said. "Hey, you're right about Dave. Why don't you call him?" I nervously held out the phone with my left arm, extending it as far as I could so Andrea wouldn't step too close and realize the smoke smell was coming from my body.

She eyed me like I was acting strange, but then took the phone from my hand with a small shrug. I guess she was used to my acting strange lately. As she got Dave's number out of the phone book (we finally remembered—Dave *Mackerel*), I went upstairs to take another shower.

Andrea opened the bathroom door and called in that Dave was already at work, having been called in early to help redirect traffic on Broadway because of some big fire, but he promised to drop by later that morning to see us. Oh God, now I had to worry about Dave sniffing out my secret. How long would it take me to get rid of that smoke smell? I scrubbed so vigorously even my arm that *wasn't* singed turned red, then put on a long-sleeved shirt.

When I came back downstairs, I told Andrea—without telling her about my illegal activities the previous night—that I needed to go to New York City immediately. I had to examine The Penn's 1998 NYFA application and find out if he really wrote that someone was threatening his life, and who it was.

Andrea stared at me, incredulous. "What are you saying? You think someone *killed* Penn?"

"Yes, I do," I said solemnly, and then showed her what The Penn had written about blackmailing people. But I couldn't tell her about the arson and my involvement in it, and I couldn't convince her that The Penn was killed. In addition to being an upbeat person, Andrea is also very no nonsense.

"For God's sake," she said almost angrily, "the guy wasn't murdered. We've got enough excitement around here already, we don't need to make up more. And besides," she continued, "if he actually *was* murdered, that's a job for the cops, not you!"

"I'm just trying to goose the cops into—"

But Andrea still wasn't done. "We just got burglarized two times in two nights," she reminded me, "and now you want to leave me alone with the kids? Forget it!"

I had to admit, she had a point. I promised to be back from The City (as we upstaters refer to it) by nightfall, but that didn't mollify her. "The kids and I will be off at school all day. What if someone breaks in while we're gone?"

The fact that she was right didn't make her any less annoying. Dagnab it, I'll bet old Sam Spade never had to deal with anything like this. No way. Nero Wolfe, Travis McGee, Kinky Friedman—all of those guys were single, and I was beginning to see why.

Luckily, Andrea and I have developed pretty solid communication skills during our nine years of marriage. Whenever we have a difference of opinion, we simply shout and scream at each other for a while, then talk it over semi-rationally (emphasis on *semi*), and finally compromise, after which I buy her flowers. The quantity and quality of flowers depends on how much of a jerk I was.

So that's what happened this time. After our requisite marital squabble (worth a $5.99 bouquet of red tulips, I estimated), we eventually came up with a plan we were both happy with. Then I went to Madeline's to carry it out.

But I must confess, I added a little wrinkle to the plan that I didn't exactly tell Andrea about. I had a feeling she wouldn't like it.

On the other hand, Sam Spade would have loved it.

When I hit Madeline's at 8:40, smack in the middle of the morning rush, the place was packed. Just like I wanted it.

There was an excited buzz in the air, with everyone talking about the fire at the Arts Council building. From snatches of conversation that I heard, like "I bet it was that asshole from New Jersey who owns the place," the main theory seemed to be landlord arson.

Madeline, Marcie, and Rob were all behind the counter, and as usual at that hour, a large assortment of local notables were standing in line. The Mayor's elderly secretary, who makes all the day-to-day decisions about running the city, was chatting with the wheelchair-bound assistant editor of the *Daily Saratogian*. He wasn't actually standing in line, of course, he was sitting. A couple of bureaucrats from the Office of City Planning were ordering iced lattés. The arts community was well represented too, with Bonnie Engels, Antoinette Carlson, and George Hosey sharing a table nearby.

Bonnie spotted me first. "Jacob!" she exclaimed,

crushing me with a welcoming hug that sent tingles of pain through my scorched right arm. Then she gripped my wrist, causing instant agony, and gazed into my eyes with deep concern. "So, they let you out of the hospital? Are you okay?"

Gritting my teeth, I looked down at Bonnie's feet, trying to picture them in size-eight silver high heels. Then I sneaked glances at every female foot within glance-sneaking distance—is this how foot fetishists spend their time? How odd!—but unfortunately I couldn't tell their shoe size just by looking. I wanted to ask all of the women in the espresso bar to remove their shoes, but I was afraid that might be considered a little déclassé.

"I'm fine," I told Bonnie loudly. "But we got burglarized again."

Announcing that you've just been burglarized is a great way to attract attention; try it at a party sometime if you're feeling wallflowerish. Instantly, everyone in Madeline's was staring at me. The asshole from New Jersey was forgotten.

"Burglarized *again?*" Antoinette called out dramatically, eager to place herself at the center of attention. I'd noticed this trait before; maybe it was why she got so many grants. "And on the *same night* the Arts Council burns down? Is this town going crazy or what?! How utterly, awesomely *bizarre!*"

"No, not so bizarre." I solemnly held aloft a brown grocery bag. "They were looking for *this.*"

Everyone strained their eyes for a closer look at the mysterious grocery bag. In the excitement someone dropped a coffee cup to the floor and it shattered, but even that didn't distract anyone. "What in the world is in the bag?" breathed the Mayor's secretary.

"Something that *somebody* is desperate to get hold of." I took out a notebook and showed it to the assembled throng. "This is *Donald Penn's book.* I'm taking it to my safety-deposit box right now, so no one tries to burglarize our house a third time."

Their eyes followed Penn's notebook as I waved it in the air and smiled to myself. Everything was going exactly according to the plan Andrea and I had cooked up. With Madeline's chock full of people from City Hall, the Arts Council, and the *Daily Saratogian,* and with small-town Saratoga being the most gossipy place in the universe, I figured that by tonight any potential burglars would know that searching our house for Penn's manuscript would only be an exercise in futility, similar to searching Billy Joel songs for interesting lyrics (at least, that's my opinion).

Yes, everything was going exactly according to plan. But now . . .

Now it was time to throw in my little Sam Spade wrinkle.

Madeline provided the opening when she asked me, as she filled a take-out cup with Ethiopian, "I don't get it. Why would anyone be desperate for Donald Penn's book?"

I could feel everyone's eyes glued to me. I let them stick there for a moment, then declared portentously, *"Because it's fucking dynamite."*

Nobody said a word. This is way cool, I thought to myself, I should take up acting. Then Marcie broke the silence with a nervous giggle. *"Dynamite?* You mean like, really good, or like, TNT?"

I gave my audience a grim Jack Palance nod. "Like, hydrogen bomb. This book will do to Saratoga what Monica Lewinsky did to Washington. Hell, it'll do what Rambo did to North Vietnam."

Another cup fell to the floor and shattered. Bonnie, Antoinette, and George stared up at me from their table, their jaws hanging comically open. The Mayor's secretary tried to insert a muffin in her mouth but missed, hitting her cheek instead. The assistant editor of the *Daily Saratogian* got a strange tic in his nostrils.

I plunked down a dollar for my java and walked out.

As soon as I was out the door and out of sight, I allowed myself a huge grin, feeling like Dashiell Hammett on one of his good days. *That ought to stir the pot a little,* I thought, and chuckled.

Maybe I should have felt guilty about trying to scare people, but I didn't. Not in the slightest. So far I'd been burglarized, beaned, burned, and shot at. It was high time to fight back.

Besides, the pot I was stirring had a murderer inside, which ought to give me some moral leeway.

And most important, I figured announcing to everyone publicly that The Penn's book was "dynamite" was a good way to ensure that nobody would try to kill me again . . . assuming that had indeed been the arsonist's intention last night. I had worked it all out very rationally, or so I thought. Donald Penn had picked the wrong person to blackmail. That person—or persons—killed him to shut him up. Then the killer or killers burglarized my house and burned down Penn's apartment and the Arts Council office in order to get rid of anything dangerous he might have written.

But now, as I had announced, Penn's manuscript was going into a safety-deposit box, out of the killer's grasp. So there was nothing any more that the killer could do. He, or she, or they, would have nothing to gain and everything to lose by killing me too. That would just prod the cops into doing a more serious investigation of Penn's death, two dead writers in one week being a little too hard to blow off. And after my performance at Madeline's, the cops would doubtless check into the very same "dynamite book" the murderer was so afraid of.

Maybe this was a little convoluted, but I was feeling pretty pleased with myself as I strutted down Broadway, swinging my brown grocery bag. But then a terrifying thought smacked me in the gut. I froze. *Now is the perfect time for someone to kill me.* While I still had Penn's manuscript on me. Just put on a mask, shoot me, grab the bag, and drive off down the Northway.

Oh, come on, that was paranoid. I even said it out loud: "You're getting paranoid. Totally fucking paranoid." A purple-haired teenager walking by started laughing. I smiled nervously at Purple Hair and hustled up the street, eager to make it into the safety of the bank already. But I had to wait for the light to change at the corner of Division Street, and suddenly someone hit me from behind.

I screamed, jumped, and whirled, gripping The Penn's manuscript tight against my body, prepared to fight to the death. Then I stood there staring at my assailant. A three-year-old girl. She must have run into me or something. She looked up at my terrified face and burst into tears.

Her mother grabbed her hand and pulled her away from me so hard I was afraid she'd wrench her daughter's arm off, then the two of them raced away at top speed. I guess with my panicky eyes, and the way I was wildly clutching a brown shopping bag to my chest, I looked like a particularly deranged homeless person.

As I watched them run off, I wondered if the woman's fear, the child's cries, and Purple Hair's laughter were the same ways that people had treated Donald Penn for most of his life, upon seeing his long unkempt hair, threadbare jacket, and off-kilter eyes. What would that sort of treatment do to your psyche if it continued for, say, a third of a century?

But I didn't wonder about it for long, because I needed to quit screwing around and unload Penn's manuscript pronto, before I died of a heart attack myself. For God's sake, who was I trying to fool? I was a neurotic Jewish artist, not a hard-boiled private dick. I wasn't cut out for this shit.

I hurried across the street, jumped the steps to the Saratoga Trust Bank two at a time, and was about to go inside when I was accosted by a young man with greasy hair and a cheap brown suit, smoking a cigarette. "Hey," he said. Then he put a hand in his jacket pocket.

I backed away. Holy Toledo, could this really be happening? The guy was straight out of *The Godfather.* He wouldn't shoot me in broad daylight in the middle of Broadway, would he? Of course he would, if he wanted to. I tried to scream, but all that came out was a gulp.

"So how'd it go with Spielberg?" the Mafioso asked.

Spielberg? How did *what* go with Spielberg? That concussion must have been worse than I thought. Maybe I should check back into the hospital immediately. If not sooner.

"Did he like your mutant beetle idea?" the Mafioso continued.

My battered mental gears clicked back into place. Aha! It was Young Gray Suit! That's why I hadn't recognized him at first—he was wearing brown today. A bad choice, I thought, and told him so. "You look better in gray."

He pursed his lips, chagrined. "I know. I screwed up." He glanced around to make sure no one was listening, then whispered confidentially, "But it was cheap, and I needed another suit for this lousy job." He raised his voice again. "So what's the word?"

"It's a go," I told him. "Look for mutant beetles soon, at a theater near you."

"Hey, that's *excellent.* Congratulations, man," he

said enthusiastically. I nodded and started past him, but he stopped me. "So, you putting your disk back in the safe-deposit?"

"Yes." I opened the door to the bank, impatient to be rid of this guy.

"Well, don't worry, it'll be safe, all right. They just ran a special security check last night."

A what? I thought. "A what?" I asked.

"Special security check. You know, the lock system, timing mechanism, all that stuff."

I nodded calmly, but my mind was racing. *A special security check? Why?* Did they somehow find out that someone had broken into The Penn's safety-deposit box? Was Young Brown Suit just playing with me, knowing I was about to get busted?

I looked at his innocent face, and realized I had indeed turned paranoid. It was absurd to think that this guy had it in for me, or that the bank's security check had anything to do with me or Donald Penn. My head was spinning again, and I wondered how much of what I remembered from the past five days had actually happened, and how much I had just imagined. Probably Penn wasn't even really killed in the first place; it was just a heart attack, like everyone said.

But even though I knew I was being ridiculous, I couldn't help asking, "So why'd they do a special security check?"

"You got me. I thought I'd have to stay late and help out, but they said I could go home."

A dim light bulb came on in some cobwebby recess of my brain. "Who is this 'they' you're talking about?"

Young Brown Suit shrugged. "You know, the big honchos. The guys that own this crummy joint."

The dim light bulb turned into bright red neon flashing through my cerebrum. "Like the mayor? Was he here?"

Young Brown Suit nodded. "Yeah, he set up the whole thing. Why?"

Why, indeed. "Do they run a lot of these security checks?"

"No, this is the first one since I've been here. Eight months and counting."

I got the feeling I had just uncovered further proof of that ancient proverb: Just because you're paranoid, doesn't mean they're not out to get you.

Sure, maybe there was an innocent explanation. But City Hall had given Penn free Ethiopian, which, if I had it figured right, meant *someone* there was being blackmailed. And the mayor certainly got upset when he heard me trying to confront Gretchen about Penn. And I remembered how oddly intense he'd been on the post office steps when he asked me about Penn's writing. Was he afraid that his blackmailer would return from the dead, via the written word, to haunt him?

The more I thought about it, the more I wondered if the mayor had thought up this bogus "special security check" as a means of breaking into Donald Penn's safety-deposit box himself and stealing whatever was in there. And for all I knew, maybe breaking into *my* box, too.

Which meant my box might not be the safest place to deposit Penn's manuscript. I let go of the bank's front door and headed back down the steps, still carrying my damn grocery bag. My ball and chain.

"Hey, aren't you going in the bank?" Young Brown Suit called after me, puzzled.

"I changed my mind," I said, as I got myself the heck out of there and walked back down Broadway.

17

Okay, so I couldn't trust the Saratoga Trust. But then whom *could* I trust?

I thought about depositing Penn's magnum opus in another bank in Saratoga, but after this experience, I was spooked. Besides, I had no time to do all the paperwork for opening a new safety-deposit box. Andrea was at home frantically finishing up her students' semester grades, which were overdue as usual. So I needed to pick up the kids from Judy Demarest's house, drop off the Sultan of Swat at school and the Great One at the babysitter's, and then hit the Albany Amtrak station in time for the Friday 11:25 to New York City. I needed to be on that train; otherwise, I wouldn't make it in to the NYFA office until Monday. No way was I driving into the city today, with my head the way it was.

So I decided to lock up The Penn's stuff in an Amtrak locker in Albany. Until then, I'd have to lock it in the trunk of my car.

I'd parked on Broadway right in front of Madeline's, so when I opened my rusty trunk to put the grocery bag in, I felt like all eyes were upon me. I stared aggressively at Madeline's plate glass window, trying to scare off any potential murderers who might be watching. Then I slammed the trunk door down and drove off, my muffler chugging out a noisy good-bye.

I turned onto Phila Street, then went right on Henry, doubled back on Circular, and went up Henry again, checking my rearview mirror to see if any cars were following me. Unfortunately, my surveillance efforts were hampered by the fact that as a teenager, I was too busy getting high and grooving on the Grateful Dead to learn about cars. To this day, all cars look alike to me.

Besides, with my muffler from hell, a car would be able to follow me from a mile away. But I did the best I could, putting on fake turn signals and speeding through red lights, and made it to Judy Demarest's house in record time. Record *slow* time, that is.

It was already past nine-thirty, but Judy had graciously agreed last night to keep the kids until whenever we showed up and go in to the *Saratogian* late. My five year old would be late to school again himself; I guess that's the price you pay when your Daddy is a high-powered private eye.

Judy did favors like this for us from time to time, and seemed to enjoy it. She didn't have a spouse or kids of her own, and our children were the closest thing to nephews or nieces she had.

It was odd that my wife and Judy had grown so close, because these days it seemed like Andrea only got close to other women if they were mothers of young children who understood the traumas of peepee and preschool. But Andrea met Judy four years ago, when she had a major identity crisis, decided there must be more to life than work and family, and insisted on getting out of the house by herself at least one night a week. She wound up doing volunteer work for the Literacy Volunteers of Saratoga, Judy's special project. They soon discovered that not only did they share a passion for teaching children to read in this barren television age, they also shared an even deeper passion: bowling.

When I walked up Judy's front steps, Gretzky and Babe Ruth bounded outside to greet me. "Daddy! Daddy!" they shouted gleefully, then immediately started telling me some complicated tale about a dog named Doughnut, or a doughnut named Dog, or a dog that ate a doughnut, or vice versa. I couldn't figure it out for the life of me, but whenever they stopped for my reaction, I said "Wow!" or "Way cool!" and that seemed to do the job.

Judy came outside dressed for work, air kissed me hello, and asked how my head was. I started to tell her about the latest burglary of our house, but decided to wait until the kids were safely out of earshot. They'd already had to deal with more than enough scary stuff this week. I hoped all the craziness wouldn't make the Babe's sleepwalking episodes, or the Great One's peepee boycotts, even more frequent.

When the kids ran off suddenly in search of anthills to attack, I thanked Judy profusely for her babysitting and was about to whisper to her about the burglary when she threw me a curve. "Hope you don't mind," she said, "kids were up late last night. Took 'em to Madeline's."

I looked at her, feeling confused. Something was bothering me, but I wasn't sure what. Judy got nervous. "That's okay, isn't it?" she asked.

"Sure," I answered, but meanwhile I'd figured out what was bothering me. "Did you mention to people at Madeline's why you were babysitting? Because Andrea was visiting me at the hospital?"

"I guess so, yeah. Why?"

Why? Because this meant whoever was at Madeline's last night knew our house was empty—and ripe for burglary. "So who was at Madeline's?"

"Totally packed. Hey, your kiddos were the life of the party. Got all the grownups playing with the barrel of monkeys."

"When were you there?"

Judy stiffened, getting annoyed at my interrogation. "I don't know. Maybe eight-thirty to ten."

Eight-thirty to ten. We'd been burglarized around nine-thirty.

Of course, maybe the burglar had been nowhere near Madeline's last night. But that silver high heel did make the burglary look like a spur of the moment thing. Which fit my scenario: Judy pops into Madeline's with my kids, shoots her mouth off, and Ms. Silver Heels, inspired by our first burglary the night before (hell, maybe even the *perpetrator* of our first burglary), slips out of Madeline's and drives over to our house.

Judy misinterpreted my frown as criticism for keeping the kids out late. "Hey, sorry I took 'em to Madeline's, but the Literacy Volunteers special events committee was meeting there last night, and I had to bring them some info about last year's silent auction—"

"Who's on the committee?" I interrupted.

She threw me a look. "Why?"

"Just curious."

She gave one of her characteristic world-weary shrugs. "Usual gang of suspects. Diane Gee, Annette Dobrow, the mayor . . ."

The mayor again. To use the Novella Man's favorite word, he was ubiquitous. Harder to escape than the theme song from *Scooby Doo*.

I nodded thoughtfully to myself. It fit, all right—it fit perfectly. The mayor devises a sneaky scheme to get his hands on The Penn's safety-deposit box, but it's empty. He figures out I've already made off with The Penn's stuff, and he's furious. Desperate, even.

But later that same night he's at Madeline's, and finds out there's no one at my house. So he immediately carpes the diem and drives over there so he can break in and nab that elusive manuscript at last.

Only one problem with this theory. The high-heeled shoes. Did the mayor dress as a woman to disguise himself?

If this were a movie, yes. Since it wasn't, no. Besides, his feet were too big.

Did he get some woman at Madeline's to do the burglary for him? That seemed more likely. But who? And why?

"Judy, were there any women at Madeline's last night wearing silver high-heeled shoes?"

Judy raised an eyebrow at me. In fact, she raised both of them. "What the hell is this all about?"

I didn't answer her. And it wasn't just because both kids were pulling at my shirt sleeves and insisting that I join them in their ant demolition project. At this point I was so paranoid, I even suspected Judy.

I mean, hey, she'd been awfully eager to publish Penn's opus. So eager that she pushed me real hard to get her own paws on it and do the editing all by herself, before I even had a chance to read it. Was she just being a conscientious newspaperwoman? Or was there something more sinister at play?

For all I knew, she went to Madeline's last night expressly to tip somebody off that my house was empty. Maybe she even left the kids in someone else's care for a while and slipped out to my house herself. It would have taken her three minutes max to drive there, five to break in and do a quick search, and three more to drive back. And if she got caught, she could always say she was looking for an outfit for Gretzky or something.

So I didn't give Judy a straight answer. Instead I dropped my car keys, bent down, and took a close look at her feet.

And wondered if they were size eight.

18

As we drove away from Judy's house, I questioned the kids about whether Judy had left them alone at Madeline's for a while last night. Gretzky said yes, the Babe said no, and further attempts at cross-examination were unsuccessful, because the witnesses kept interrupting with loud burps and giggles.

I was desperate to hit the 11:25 train and ditch that grocery bag in an Amtrak locker. But even after I dropped off the kids, I still had to have a talk with Dave the Fish before I left town. He was in our kitchen when I got there, doing his dusting-for-fingerprints routine on the silver high heel. Unfortunately, the mud and rain had eliminated all fingerprints but my own.

I put my arm around him. "Listen, old pal, old snowblowing buddy—"

"Yeah, yeah, what do you want?"

I cut the clowning. "Dave, so far there have been one arson and two burglaries that are all connected to Donald Penn. Also, I have reason to believe that Penn was blackmailing people."

Dave looked up from his dusting. "Who?"

"I'm not sure yet. But the point is, the police should reopen their investigation of his death. Exhume his body, find out if someone put poison in his coffee or whatever."

Dave rolled his eyes. "Poison in his coffee?"

"Did anyone check his blood for some kind of poison?" Dave simply rolled his eyes again. Just as I thought, no one had checked. "Look, the guy had three cups every morning—at City Hall, the Arts Council, and Madeline's. Any one of those coffees could have killed him."

"Three coffees, huh? Well, that explains it. Probably got a heart attack from all that caffeine." I started to reply, but Dave held up his hand and stopped me with a patronizing, wise-cop-to-naive-civilian smile. "You've spent too much time in Hollywood, my man. We still don't even know for sure that any of these crimes are really connected to Penn."

"Oh, come on—"

"We're not even sure it was arson."

"Give me a fucking break!"

Dave narrowed his eyes. Our relationship was entering uncharted territory. I'd never cussed at him before, we were just friendly acquaintances. "Look, I'm sorry, but—"

Dave waved off my apology. "Hey, even if it *is* arson, you still gotta suspect the landlord first. From what I hear the guy's a sleazebag, and he's got a vacant first floor, a second-floor tenant that's leaving, and a third-floor tenant that's dead. What's a poor absentee landlord to do?"

If I told Dave about the brick that flew through Molly Otis's window, maybe I could convince him. But I'd promised Molly to keep that little golden nugget to myself.

So I gave Dave my fiercest look, which I got from watching Roger Clemens's face when he's about to fire his high hard fastball, and declared intensely, "Dave. *Trust me.* That fire was about Donald Penn."

Dave didn't answer. I gave the Clemens face some extra juice and he looked away, but he still didn't give in, just sat there shaking his head at the floor. So I changed tacks. "Man, if you don't help me out on this, you can forget about me trimming your hedges this summer."

Dave laughed, the tension broken. "Kind of trimming job *you* do, is that supposed to be a threat?" Then he clapped me on the shoulder. "Jacob, I tell you what. I'll take it up with the chief."

I nodded, but I had a feeling Dave wouldn't push this too hard for me. He was a nice-enough guy, but no Mel Gibson. Then again, who is? Probably even Mel Gibson isn't Mel Gibson, if you know what I mean.

Having concluded my unsatisfactory conversation with Dave, I proceeded to have an equally unsatisfactory conversation with Andrea while I hurriedly packed a peanut butter sandwich for the train. I was pumping her for any possible links between Judy and The Penn, or Judy and the mayor, but she wasn't very helpful. In fact, she was practically homicidal. "What?! You think *Judy* had something to do with this?" she sputtered.

"I'm just—"

"Jacob, don't be an idiot!"

"But—"

"Judy is my best friend!"

I steeled myself against her sisterly wrath. "How much money does the mayor contribute to the Literacy Volunteers?"

"I don't know, maybe ten thousand last year, but who gives a shit? What are you trying to say? The mayor gives to all kinds of charities. He's rich!"

True, but still . . . Ten grand was pretty darn grand, especially by Saratoga Springs standards. It was probably a third of the entire Literacy Volunteers budget, maybe more. Why had the mayor been so generous?

Judy was an absolute fanatic about the Literacy Volunteers, giving it the same kind of love other women give their children. Was the mayor himself also enamored of the Literacy Volunteers, or was he just trying to curry favor with the editor of the town's only newspaper?

Of course, currying favor with people isn't exactly illegal. Usually it's not even immoral.

I waved good-bye to my still-angry wife and roared off, finally, to the Albany train station. Looking around to make sure no one was watching, I stashed the fateful grocery bag in a locker and pocketed the key.

Then I raced to the 11:25 train, and made it with one and two-thirds seconds to spare. I opened my peanut butter sandwich, and was so beat I fell asleep before I even got around to eating it.

I didn't wake up until we rode into Penn Station. Which was fortunate, because if I'd been awake, I'd have gone berserk. The train was an express, scheduled to get in at 2:10, but because of "undiagnosed engine troubles"—the Amtrak version of delayed concussion syndrome, I suppose—we did the last leg of the trip at groundhog speed and didn't arrive in New York City until 4:44. I had approximately 16 minutes to get to NYFA before they closed for the weekend.

To make matters worse, when I came up from the bowels of Penn Station onto Eighth Avenue, I discovered that seven years of living outside The City had dulled my street savvy. Other, more ruthless pedestrians kept beating me out for taxis. I was reduced to racing the many blocks to the NYFA office on foot, hoping against hope I could make it by 5:00.

When I finally got there, at 5:02, the secretary had her jacket on and was halfway out the door. She was a cute fake blonde—or as they say in the New York *Daily News*, "bottle blonde"—who would have been cuter, in my opinion, without the two purple lip rings. Though I did like the Groucho Marx tattoo right above her left breast.

I played on Groucho Girl's sympathy by huffing and puffing for breath after my long run. I played on the rest of her emotions by putting my left hand in my pocket so she wouldn't see my wedding ring. Unmarried men who are into the arts and don't "look gay" are at a premium in New York, and I was hoping that would help me out.

It did. After I did the requisite fawning and flirting, Groucho Girl took off her jacket—revealing tattoos of *all* the Marx Brothers, *including Zeppo and Gummo,* which was so classy I almost forgave the purple lip rings—and found me the 1998 Saratoga Springs file. Since NYFA is publicly funded and their grants are a matter of public record, their files are open to anyone, especially cute guys who might be single.

I reached out for the file with trembling hands—actually, just one trembling hand, because I kept my left one hidden in case I needed any more favors from Groucho Girl. Then I opened up the file. *At last: the moment of truth.* Now I'd find out who threatened The Penn's life. Maybe I'd even find out who The Penn was blackmailing . . . and who had the motive to kill him.

I zoomed through the applications. Albanese, Atwater . . . alphabetical order again. Hosey, Introcaso . . . almost there. Orsulak, Pardou, Preller . . .

What? Orsulak, Pardou, Preller.

Shit! It wasn't there!

I groaned, miserable, but Groucho Girl didn't notice. "It's funny, you asking for the Saratoga stuff," she said cheerfully, making conversation. "There was someone in here a couple days ago, asking for the same thing."

I stared. "Who was it?"

She shrugged her shoulders and gave her head a pretty shake. Unfortunately her lip rings shook too, destroying the effect. "I don't know. Some lady."

Some lady? "What'd she look like?"

She wrinkled her eyebrows in thought. "Um, pretty old, like in her fifties? Short hair, big earrings . . ."

"And big teeth?"

She nodded and smiled brightly. So did Groucho, Harpo, Chico, Zeppo, and Gummo. "You know her?"

Yeah, I knew her, all right.

Gretchen Lang.

I took my left hand out of my pocket and rubbed my chin with it, so Groucho Girl would see my wedding ring and wouldn't ask me out to dinner or whatever. Though for all I knew, I was greatly overestimating my appeal. Before I met Andrea, I used to always get mixed up about which women were interested in me and which weren't. I wondered briefly how you kiss someone who's wearing a lip ring, but decided I'd wait until another lifetime to find out.

I waved good-bye to her and all her Marx Brothers, especially Zeppo and Gummo, and hustled back outside. This time I managed to catch the very first cab that came along, showing some true New York spirit by beating out an elderly man with a cane, and made it back to Penn Station in time for the 5:28 train home.

Sorry about the elderly guy, but I was in a hurry.

I needed to go back to Saratoga and kick some ass.

The return train was miraculously free of engine troubles, diagnosed or otherwise, so I made it back to Saratoga just after nine o'clock. I called Andrea from the Mobil station south of town to make sure all was quiet on the home front, and it turned out Dave was over at the house watching TV with the kids. My family was in good hands. Maybe Dave wasn't Mel Gibson, but at least he was a good solid Jimmy Stewart.

Andrea commiserated with me about not being able to get hold of Penn's application, then asked, "So where are you calling from?"

"Um," I began, and then, "I'm on the pay phone in the train. We're still south of Hudson. Be back in about an hour and a half, okay?"

"Okay, honey. Love you."

"Love you too, honey," I replied, and hung up, feeling guilty. Oh well, it wasn't like I was having an affair or anything. I just didn't want to get into an argument with her about what I was about to do. If I was going to try out my Philip Marlowe imitation, I needed some freedom to maneuver.

I borrowed a phone book from the Mobil cashier, found Gretchen Lang's address, and chugged over there. Gretchen lived in an old Victorian on North Broadway, which was emphatically the *right* end of Broadway, where heirs, heiresses, CEOs, and others of their ilk reside during the racing season. I knew Gretchen was well off, but I had no idea she was *this* well off. The front facade of her mansion was a wild melange of Corinthian columns, captain's walks, French doors, and intricate flourishes painted in "traditional Saratoga colors"—purple, white, and green. It looked kind of like a giant gingerbread house, and would have been cutesy if it weren't so grand.

Gretchen's salary at the Arts Council must be pretty minimal, so I speculated, as I walked up the long tulip-fringed path to her front door, that her husband must be a robber baron businessman type. Moneymaker husband, artistic wife—a classic combo dating back 50,000 years to when some cavewoman in southern France figured out how to draw woolly mammoths on the wall with berry juice while her man went off hunting the real thing.

The wind shook the leaves of Gretchen's stately oak trees. It was a cold spring night, the kind that gets people talking about that big May blizzard of '78. I missed my jacket, the one I'd left behind in the burning Arts Council. Hopefully, it had been reduced to ashes before any cops got hold of it.

The outdoor light came on before I made it to the door, which made me think someone was home. But then I realized it was just one of those motion-sensitive anti-crime gizmos. In this part of Saratoga, homeowners don't forget to lock their doors. Some of them have bathroom fixtures that cost more than my entire house.

I rang the doorbell and waited. There was an exquisite antique stained-glass window next to the door depicting Noah's ark, and I tried looking through it, but I couldn't see inside. It wasn't even 9:30 yet, so Gretchen couldn't be asleep. Actually, it was hard to picture Gretchen *ever* being asleep; she seemed like way too much of a fireball to lie still long enough.

I rang the bell again and waited some more, blowing on my hands to keep warm, then headed back down the path. Gretchen's husband was probably away on a business trip—I recalled her mentioning that he was gone more often than not—and Gretchen must be out at a gallery opening or something. I'd have to try again in the morning. I stopped briefly to admire Gretchen's black tulips . . .

And that's when I noticed, from a corner of my eye, the curtains in a darkened window upstairs part ever so slightly. I lifted my hand and waved. But the curtains closed right back up.

So I marched to the front door and rang the doorbell a third time, then a fourth, but still no one answered. The wind was swirling and rain started coming again, and I was hopping up and down to keep from freezing. This was incredibly aggravating. How was I ever going to solve Donald Penn's murder if I couldn't even get Gretchen to open her front door? I stared up at those window curtains on the second floor and, without looking, pounded at the door angrily.

Only I missed the door. I was so riled up, I pounded the antique stained-glass window.

And broke it.

Instantly an alarm bell shrieked and kept on shrieking. The Noah's ark had sprung a leak right in the middle, and two giraffes and two elephants had fallen out. Yet more work for the glazier, and expensive work, at that. I was tempted to make a run for it, but just then Gretchen came racing toward me up the front hall, barefoot and wearing a white terrycloth bathrobe.

She stabbed some buttons on the wall to shut off the alarm, then turned on me, furious. "Do you know how much that window costs?" she screamed.

No, and I didn't want to know. I started to apologize, but some imp must have grabbed hold of my tongue, because what I actually said in a blustery John Wayne voice was, "You know, we never did get a chance to talk about Donald Penn." I guess I was following the principle that the best defense is a good offense.

Gretchen stared at me, speechless, then managed to stutter, "I should have you arrested!"

"We'll go to jail together, Gretchen. Obstruction of justice. You stole Donald Penn's application from NYFA."

Gretchen's mandible fell. Then it came back up again. "Where did you get that ludicrous idea?"

"From the Marx Brothers who gave you the file," I answered coolly.

The mandible fell again, but not as far this time, and

it came back up a lot quicker. A complacent sneer formed on Gretchen's sweet, pleasant face. I'd never seen her sneer like this before. What else had I missed?
"You're saying someone *saw* me steal something?" Gretchen asked, sarcasm dripping from her long teeth. "Someone *actually observed me,* what, putting something in my purse? And so now I'm going to jail? Is that what you're saying?"

I rocked back on my heels. No, Groucho Girl hadn't observed Gretchen stealing that file, and Gretchen knew it. As I tortured my brain for a clever comeback, a cop car roared up the driveway. In this part of town the cops responded quickly.

I looked back at Gretchen. She smiled grimly, enjoying watching me squirm. I was about to get busted for malicious vandalism or whatever the hell they call it. God, how much of my hard-won nest egg would this stupid stained glass window cost me? For all I knew about antiques, we were talking fifty grand. To say nothing of lawyers' fees and court costs.

What a fool. I had completely misplayed my hand. I thought I was holding the ace of trumps, and it turned out to be just a lousy joker.

The cop came out of his car. Oh, no. Just my luck, it was the same fat, bald, trigger-happy cop who'd taken a pot shot at me outside the Arts Council that night. He'd better not recognize me.

Accurately reading the tension between Gretchen and me, Mr. Fat, Bald, and Trigger-Happy kept his hand close to his gun as he headed up the path toward us. "You all right, Mrs. Lang?"

Gretchen bared her teeth in a leonine grin. She was about to throw me to the cops, and she was loving every minute. I tried a desperate shot in the dark. I hissed at her sharply from the side of my mouth, "I know all about the conflict of interest. You want me to spread the word?"

Like I say, it was just a desperate shot. It was just a wild half-court heave as the final buzzer sounded.

It was just fucking inspired.

Gretchen's mandible fell, and this time it stayed down.

Fat, Bald, and Trigger-Happy came cautiously closer. "Mrs. Lang, you okay?"

Gretchen quickly stepped outside and stood right in front of the broken window so the cop wouldn't see it. "I'm fine," she said, flashing him one of her patented warm smiles. "Just a false alarm, that's all."

Fat, Bald, and Trigger-Happy eyed us uneasily. "You sure?"

"Absolutely. I'm so sorry I made you come all the way out here for nothing."

The cop knew something was wrong, but didn't know what to do about it. He peered at me, and I could see a confused glimmer of almost-recognition on his face as he tried to remember where he'd seen me before. Finally he gave up, going back to his car and driving off while Gretchen invited me inside.

Not too graciously, I might add. In fact, she was downright rude about it.

But hey, you can't please everybody. At least I was making the glaziers happy.

19

Gretchen led me into her living room. I was intrigued to find the walls covered by bizarre postmodern art, a hodgepodge of odd geometric shapes and skewed perspectives. Despite Gretchen's professed admiration for pointillist fat people, I would have expected her personal tastes to be utterly middlebrow, with an emphasis on still lifes of peaches. The lady was full of surprises.

Speaking of surprises, why did she get so spooked when I threw up that half-court shot about "conflict of interest"? I mean, sure, if people found out her panelists had cheated and given themselves grants without following the legal guidelines, it would look bad. But how much of a threat would that be to Gretchen herself?

Actually, maybe a big one, I realized. It could discredit Gretchen sufficiently that NYFA would stop giving her any grant money to disburse. That would take away a major source of her power.

And then it suddenly dawned on me: If Gretchen got into a controversy over misuse of NYFA funds, she might very well have *other* grant money withdrawn from her. The NEA and the New York State Council of the Arts were both helping Gretchen build her beloved Cultural Arts Center. What if they decided they'd better steer clear of her and turn off the public money hose? And then how would Gretchen's private donors react, once she got the smell of corruption on her?

Were we talking about a serious domino effect here? Might those piddling eighteen-hundred-dollar grants that the panelists awarded themselves spell the death of Gretchen's lifelong dream to be in charge of her very own highly glamorous Cultural Arts Center?

And most important of all, was I the first person who'd confronted Gretchen about this—or the second? Was this what The Penn had blackmailed her about?

And how would Gretchen react if she saw her grand and glorious lifelong dream in danger of being destroyed by some pathetic sniveling bum, some caffeine-addled frustrated writer with one moth-eaten pair of pants to his name, blackmailing her about a two-bit, no-account "conflict of interest"? Would she have killed him?

I sank into an antique leather easy chair and eyed Gretchen, wondering who this middle-aged woman really was. She scowled back at me. "How dare you break my stained glass like that?"

The thing was, I really admired Gretchen. Like The Penn, she had devoted her life to art. But now was no time to be a sensitive guy, so I stuck to my Philip Marlowe routine and shrugged. "I'm sure you're insured."

Gretchen set off on an angry tirade. "All you people, you artists, you think I'm so rich. *I am not rich!*"

Sure, and Nixon was not a crook. I lifted an eyebrow or two at her, possibly even three. This fancy mansion, these paintings on the wall by artists with unpronounceable French and German names . . .

Gretchen read my mind, and gave a frustrated growl. "Damn it, that's my *husband's* money on the wall, not *mine.* He won't let me use *his* money for the Arts Council. He won't even let me buy any paintings from Saratoga artists. Hell, I have to pay my lousy twenty-five-dollar membership fee for the Arts Council out of my own pocket!"

I didn't know where this was going, but I had a feeling it was going *somewhere,* so I kept quiet and listened as Gretchen ranted on. "People act like I could just pay for the new Arts Center *myself* if I wanted. Hah! If you knew how much spending money I get, you'd laugh! I bet your wife gets more cash than I do. I bet she got more even *before* you wrote that stupid screenplay of yours."

On the other hand, maybe this *wasn't* going somewhere. As I'd discovered earlier, Gretchen was a master of distraction. "Why don't we talk about that conflict of interest," I told her. *And about whether you killed Penn,* I thought to myself, but didn't say it. I figured I'd ease into it later, try to catch her off-guard somehow. Hey, it worked for Perry Mason.

Gretchen banged her fist on the coffee table. "I can't believe you'd turn against me like this. I've spent fifteen years trying to help people like you! I'm the best friend Saratoga artists ever had!"

It was true, and I felt like a heel. Speaking of heels, I looked down at Gretchen's feet. They looked about size eight to me, but as I've said before, I'm not a foot man. Meanwhile, Gretchen kept right on. "Do you know how important that Arts Center is going to be for the artists of this—"

"Spare me the speech, Gretchen," I interrupted.

"Look, why do you even *care* about some little—"

"Just tell me the truth, and I won't do anything to hurt you."

She slammed the table again. Pretty hard, too; maybe she was taking boxing lessons from Bonnie. "Christ, you are such a typical *artist.*" For someone who supposedly loved artists so much, she sure made it sound like an insult. "You have *no idea* how the world works, you are totally clueless! I had no choice! I had to make that deal with the mayor!"

Come again? *Deal with the mayor?*

Gretchen read the puzzlement on my face, but misunderstood the reason for it. "Get real," she snarled. "You think those jerks at City Hall would have given me that building for a dollar a year if I didn't grease their palms a little? Forget about it!"

Grease their palms?

Gretchen was really rolling now, nostrils flaring and lips curling in disgust. "Those philistines don't care about *art*. They go to *The Nutcracker* once a year and that's it! This is a bunch of Chamber of Commerce know-nothings we're talking about! And they run this town! So what do you expect me to do? If you want to play ball with the big boys, you gotta get up there and swing the bat!"

She poked a finger at my face and raved on. "How much money are we talking anyway?" This question threw me—did Gretchen think *I* was blackmailing her for money now?—but then she kept going and I realized she was just being rhetorical. "Even if we did the whole competitive bidding thing like we were supposed to, the renovation still would've cost *at least* two hundred grand, for those stupid handicapped ramps, elevators, a million other things. So when I gave the contract to the mayor's buddy from Hudson Falls for two fifty, all we're talking is a measly fifty grand at the max. Big deal. So the mayor and his buddy get forty, a couple of councilmen split the rest, and the city of Saratoga gets a terrific state-of-the-art Arts Center right on Broadway that'll benefit everyone in this entire town! So what's the harm in that? Why don't you quit being so goddamn self-righteous and tell me: Who's getting hurt?"

She eyed me challengingly, waiting. But I was still trying to get my bearings.

This was too weird. So I'd been right about Gretchen getting caught up in a conflict of interest, but I'd been wrong about *which* conflict of interest. No, cut the euphemisms, this was much worse than that—it was downright bribery.

"Why don't you tell me exactly how this deal worked?" I said.

"What, are *you* gonna blackmail me now?" Gretchen snapped.

Aha! "So this is what Penn was blackmailing you about?" Gretchen didn't answer. "How did he find out about this 'deal'?"

Gretchen snorted disgustedly, but then something seemed to fall apart inside her. She leaned back heavily in her chair and rubbed her forehead. All of a sudden she looked tired and vulnerable, sitting there in her white terrycloth bathrobe. "The little turd listened through the floorboards. Heard me talking to the mayor."

"And that's when he started blackmailing you for free coffee?"

Gretchen nodded. "Yeah, about six months ago. Knocked on the Arts Council door one day while I was eating lunch." She gave a loud, rueful sigh, then looked up at me pleadingly. "Honestly, Jacob, I didn't feel like I was doing anything wrong. Legally maybe, but not morally."

I kept my sympathy valve clamped down tight. "So what did he say to you?"

She shook her head unhappily. "Not much. It was bizarre. He kind of shuffled in and stared down at the floor. Then he mumbled the whole thing in this strange, real quiet monotone. How he knew about my deal with the mayor. But if I gave him a hot cup of coffee every morning, he'd keep his mouth shut." Gretchen laughed bitterly. "He said it had to be Ethiopian, in an eight-ounce cup. And it had to be ready at nine o'clock sharp every morning." Her eyes appealed to me. "Can you believe it? Every day I had to come in at eight forty-five to make coffee for that awful creep. Thank God we finally got an intern to make it for him. Otherwise I would have killed him, I swear."

Now or never, I thought. I hit Gretchen with my toughest Marcia Clark look and said slowly, "You would have killed him?"

Gretchen stared at me.

"*Did* you kill him?" I asked.

Her face was a study in disbelief. "Is that what this is all about? You think I killed him?"

"Yes, I do." And I was only half lying.

"The man had a heart attack."

"You poisoned his coffee."

"You're crazy."

"I don't think so. You killed him to shut him up, and then you burglarized my house to get rid of his manuscript." Gretchen's mouth opened and then closed again, like a goldfish. "And you're the one who threw that brick in Molly Otis's window, aren't you? And *you* burned down the Arts Council office."

Gretchen gave me an incredulous look. "Why would I burn down my own office?"

"Because you were afraid I might find something in Penn's apartment upstairs."

Gretchen stood up and wrapped her terrycloth robe tightly around her. Her voice was cold and dignified. "I would like you to leave my house."

"No." Time for another shot in the dark. "Not until you give me Donald Penn's grant application."

She scowled at me. "*I don't have it.*"

Maybe she was telling the truth, maybe not. I pushed harder. "Then I'm going to the police."

Gretchen hesitated for a quick moment—just long enough so I knew she was lying. "I told you, I don't have it."

I shoved myself out of the easy chair and stood toe to toe with her. "Gretchen, I don't give a shit about your deal with the mayor. It's not my fucking problem. But Donald Penn *is* my problem. Frankly I don't know if you killed him, but I intend to find out who did. And if you don't help me, you're going down. You better believe that, lady. You're going down so far you'll forget what up looked like."

I turned on my heels and strode toward the front door. I had a quick mental image of Gretchen pulling a gun from the pocket of her bathrobe and shooting me in the back. When I had my hand on the doorknob, she stopped me. "Wait."

I waited.

"I'll get you the damn application," Gretchen said.

"Thank you," I answered.

20

About a minute later, I left Gretchen's house with The Penn's NYFA application in my hot little hands. Gretchen and I were pretty sick of each other's company by now, so I told her I'd read it at home and call her if I had any questions. "I'll certainly look forward to hearing from you," she said dryly.

As I set the application down next to me in the Camry, I realized I'd forgotten to ask for one of Gretchen's shoes, to check the size. I thought about going back, but decided I'd already harassed the poor woman enough for one night. I could always go back later.

So I drove off. The street was dangerously slick, but it wasn't raining anymore; we were having one of those quick weather changes you get sometimes in the Adirondack foothills. The wind had chased the clouds away, and a thin crescent moon shone through the windshield.

I started feeling melancholy. The adrenaline rush of interrogating someone just like a real Humphrey Bogart–type private eye was wearing off. The truth was, Gretchen was good people. Okay, I wasn't wild about her bribing the mayor, but it wasn't like she'd done something really horrible, like rooting for the Yankees. In a way, the fact Gretchen cared so much about the Arts Center that she committed a crime in order to get it built made me like her even more.

My liking her, however, didn't make her innocent of murder, as I well knew. When I taught a screenwriting course in prison a couple of years back, I took a particular liking to an affable fellow named Marvin Melrose who, I later learned, had murdered three young women in cold blood while robbing a bridal gown shop.

Well, what the hell, maybe I'd get lucky and Gretchen's criminal activities had stopped short of murder. Maybe Penn's killer had actually been . . .

. . . the mayor?

That idea flustered me so much I didn't see the red light until I was practically underneath it. A purple minivan whizzed past less than a foot in front of me while I screeched to a halt. The driver blared his horn at me and I backed up, feeling like an idiot. So now I was suspecting the *mayor* of killing Penn? Absurd. I shook my head, annoyed at myself. The heck with this Columbo nonsense, I'd never in a million years be able to solve The Penn's murder—if that's what it was. I should just throw that NYFA application out the car window and forget the whole thing, go back to being a hack movie writer. Mutant beetles, here I come.

But high above me, through the windshield, I could see what looked like thousands of tiny stars. Maybe The Penn was somewhere up there with them. The light changed and I drove on, so spaced out that when a long white Cadillac drove past me with a long white goatee hovering above the steering wheel, I didn't recognize it at first. But then it hit me. *Ersatz Uncle Sam.* With another screech of my brakes, I pulled over to the side and craned my neck.

Ersatz's Caddie stopped at the red light. Nice car, I reflected—and paid for largely by that New Zealand cash Gretchen hustled for him. Then the light turned green, and Ersatz took the left fork up North Broadway . . . toward Gretchen's house.

Hmm. So was this how Gretchen amused herself during her husband's long business trips? I grinned. I had to admit it—this private-eye stuff could be a lot of fun.

The clock above the Saratoga Trust Bank said 10:20 when I got out of the car and headed for Madeline's, carrying The Penn's grant application. I wasn't ready to go back home and do the whole husband-and-father routine; I wanted to read this application already. Andrea had said that Dave would stay at the house until I got back, and they weren't expecting me until around 10:45, and I figured I could stretch that to 11:00. So I was footloose and fancy free . . . for forty minutes, anyway. Married life.

Madeline's was jammed, as it always was on weekend nights. Madeline and Rob were nowhere in evidence, but Marcie was working behind the counter along with three college kids. She was wearing a low-cut red dress, held up—barely—by two skinny little shoulder straps. Spaghetti straps, I think they're called. As usual, I forced my eyes modestly away from her. Or tried to.

While I waited to buy coffee I looked into the back room, which was packed with teenagers and twenty-somethings listening to a long-haired guitar plucker singing about how the answer was blowing in the wind. I always found it reassuring to go in there at night and find that the 60s still ruled. Or at least, they still ruled in the back room of Madeline's on a Friday night.

The front room was full of folks of various ages discussing whatever movie they'd just come back from, *The Postman* or *Scream* 2 or some other junk. Sometimes it gave me a thrill that only eight months from now people would be sitting in this very room, and rooms much like it across the world, discussing *my* movie, *The Gas that Ate San Francisco;* but sometimes I didn't really give a hoot. I mean, I'll take the dough, thank you very much, but *Gas* is not exactly going to be a modern screen classic.

Jonas, a Skidmore sophomore whose passion was collecting memorabilia from local minor league sports teams, took my order. They hadn't made Ethiopian that night—I guess no one expected me to show up—and I was relieved. I was getting sick of the stuff. Give me good old-fashioned Colombian any time.

I looked around for an empty table but couldn't find any until someone got up from the corner table in the back room, by the basement stairs. Donald Penn's old spot again. Must be fate. I sat down just as the guitar plucker went on break and everyone applauded, chanting "Yo! Yo! Yo!" That chant is one of the few entertainment innovations of the past twenty years that I approve of.

I put The Penn's application on the table in front of me, took a deep breath, and eagerly started to read. "Spill it, Donny baby," I whispered. "Who did you think would kill you?"

Name: Donald Penn.

Category: Writer.

Amount Requested: $5000. Whoa, *five grand?* A far cry from the $172.38 he'd asked for the last two years. Why so much all of a sudden?

"Hi, Jacob," breathed a silky voice right next to my ear.

I turned. I gulped. Lord, those teensy spaghetti straps would be so easy to lift off. "Hi, Marcie," I managed.

She was carrying a huge coffee sack, one of the 50-

pound jobs. "Could you help me?" she asked. "I'm supposed to carry this downstairs, and it's *so heavy.*"

"Sure," I stuttered. Forget about cooking; the best way to a man's heart is asking him to carry something heavy for you. (Asking him to open a jar also works well.)

I put Penn's application in my back pocket and watched Marcie's chest muscles tense up as she handed me the sack. "You sure it's not too heavy for you?" she asked.

"No problem," I answered, trying not to groan audibly beneath the weight. Mr. Macho Man. She opened the gate to the stairs and stepped aside. I bumped into her right hip as I went by, and shock waves trembled through me.

I headed downstairs with Marcie and her smoky scent following. As we descended into the darkness, with the noises from the espresso bar fading away, her smell was almost overpowering. What was it about this girl that seemed to activate all my illicit fantasies at once? I tried to stop the growing tightness in my jeans by focusing on the task at hand. "So where do you want this bag?" I said gruffly.

"In the back. I'll show you." She pointed ahead of me to the end of a long dark aisle filled with coffee sacks and old coffee machines. I walked up the narrow aisle, with Marcie again right behind me, close enough to touch. If I stopped short, she would rub up against me. My body tingled with the thought.

"Don't you love the smell?" she said. I looked back at her, startled. Then I figured it out. She was talking about the smell of coffee, not the smell cascading from her body. I could barely even smell the first thing, I was so overwhelmed by the second.

I felt hot blood rushing to my face, and other parts

of me too. "Yeah, it smells good," I said lamely, and turned away.

The 50-pound sack, and Marcie's body, were leaving me breathless, but I made it to the end of the aisle without fainting and found an empty shelf at around chest level. "Up here?" I asked.

She nodded. "I'll help you."

"No, that's okay."

But she came up next to me anyway, and took hold of part of the sack. Our hands touched. As we strained to lift it, our arms brushed against each other, and then our legs. I gasped, and not just from the physical effort.

As we hoisted the sack up onto the shelf, a corner of it brushed against one of her shoulder straps. The strap came right off, just like I'd pictured, leaving her shoulder bare and her dress barely hanging on. She wasn't wearing anything underneath it that I could see. And God knows I looked.

With one last push, we got the sack all the way onto the shelf. That push did something else too. It brought her left thigh into contact with a part of my anatomy that I had tried to keep politely pointed away from her. My face turned flaming red. Marcie gave me a look, her eyes shining. Her lips parted. I gasped again.

She took hold of my hand and brushed the other shoulder strap with it. The strap came down, she did a little snakelike move with her arms, and her dress fell completely off.

I was right. She was totally naked under it. *Oh, my God.*

Then she slid her hand under my shirt and felt my chest. My heart felt like it would jump right out of my body. Her nipples rubbed my arm as she came closer. My goose bumps were about ten inches long. Or maybe that was something else.

No one will ever know. You'll never get another chance like this again in your life.

Marcie's fingers were circling my belly button.

This is something you'll smile about in your old age. You'll be sitting in a rocking chair with Andrea . . .

She knelt down.

Oh God oh God . . . Three more seconds and it'll be too late . . .

Her hand reached down to undo my belt buckle. I moaned, anguish and ecstasy combined.

Two seconds . . .

She unzipped my fly.

One second . . .

I bit my lip so hard I drew blood.

And jumped backward.

She looked up at me in surprise, her blue eyes glittering in the darkness. I took one last longing look at her gorgeous perfect breasts, mumbled "I'm sorry," and escaped down the aisle, up the stairs, and out the front door.

Out on the sidewalk, I gasped for breath yet again. The crisp night air helped to evict Marcie's smoke from my nostrils, and I started to wake up from this whole wild dream. My hard-on began subsiding, and I shifted it around under my jeans to get more comfortable. But then a woman's voice behind me called out, "Jacob!"

I almost fell down, my legs got so weak. Great Scott, was Marcie going to follow me through the streets? I instantly started bursting out of my jeans again. I wanted to run away but I was glued to the sidewalk. Lord have mercy, how much more of this could I take without giving in?

Not much.

My heart pounding out some fast primitive melody,

I turned around. But it wasn't Marcie; it was Bonnie Engels. She must have come out of Madeline's right behind me, and now she was heading straight for me, arms wide, preparing one of her patented boa constrictor hugs. I cringed. I didn't want Bonnie hugging me close and getting the idea that the little guy between my legs was meant for her. That was one complication I didn't need.

I put my arms up to stop her. But she was coming at me so fast, my hands banged up against her breasts. As it turned out, Bonnie wasn't wearing a bra either, which made her the second woman I'd felt up in the past two minutes. My lucky night.

I pulled my hands back, and Bonnie stepped back too, her eyes shooting darts at me from out of her angular face. I reddened. "Sorry, didn't want you to catch my cold." I sniffed my nose to try and make it sound legit.

Bonnie didn't buy it for a second. "Jacob," she said, "I've noticed a certain tension between us lately."

I couldn't think of what to say, so I focused on a blue vein that was sticking out on Bonnie's right temple. This boxing regimen of hers was something else; unless it was my imagination, even her *face* was growing more muscular. And her neck was filled with more of those thick, pulsing blue veins; they stuck out of the ungainly looking muscles that poured out of her T-shirt. How was she getting so big so fast? Every time I saw her, she looked more and more like Mike Tyson. Was this really healthy, or would she soon start going around biting people's ears off and giving away large cars to total strangers?

"Jacob?"

I snapped back to attention. This ability of mine to remove myself mentally from whatever is going on in my life is why I became a writer in the first place.

Looking back, maybe I should have gone into therapy instead. "Yes?"

"Am I right?"

About what? Oh yeah, tension between us. I attempted a nonchalant shrug. "I haven't noticed any. I'm just a little sick, that's all."

Bonnie's jaw thrust forward, and hard green light flashed from her irises. "Look, we need to talk. Get everything on the table."

I recognized that look, all right. It meant she was about to push me to invest in her video again. "Hey, I'd love to talk, but I really need to get home—"

"I don't mean right now." She paused. "We'll get the whole grant panel together."

If she was examining my face for a reaction, she got one. *The whole grant panel.* What was Bonnie saying to me? Was this something about The Penn?

I didn't want her to realize how ignorant I was, so I just said, "Good idea," and nodded my head knowingly. From watching Hollywood executives at work, I've learned that nodding your head knowingly usually works just as well as actually knowing something.

"How about tomorrow morning at ten?" Bonnie suggested.

Great. After being away from home all day today, tomorrow I'd have to leave again first thing in the morning. On a weekend, no less. Andrea would read me the riot act. No way could I say okay.

"Okay," I said.

"How about we meet at Madeline's?"

Between Penn's death, Marcie's near-seduction, and that lousy Ethiopian, Madeline's was starting to fill up with bad vibes. But I was too tired to argue, so we agreed on Madeline's and said good-bye without a farewell hug, though it would have been okay by now since Little Big Man had gone south.

I headed south too, to Uncommon Grounds, Saratoga's other upscale coffee shop right down the street. It's not as nice as Madeline's—it's narrow and too well lit, and feels a little like an airport runway—but it's passable. So I went in, got myself some Colombian, and sat down at one of the two empty tables in the back. I heaved a sigh of relief. *Finally,* I would get to read the application. I reached into my back pocket.

But the pocket was empty. The application was gone.

Bonnie must have ripped it off, was my first thought. But that was just a lame attempt to ward off my second thought: *I must have dropped it in the basement of Madeline's.*

I'd have to go back to the devil's lair. Not that Marcie was the devil, but you know what I mean. I hurried out of Uncommon Grounds, regretfully leaving my undrunk java behind. I was leaving behind undrunk java at every coffee joint in town. People would start thinking I was eccentric.

If anyone wanted even more evidence of my eccentricity, they got it if they were watching me a minute later. I was hiding behind a wall outside Madeline's, sneaking occasional peeks through the window. I know I was being cowardly, but Marcie was clearing tables in the front room and I wanted to make it down to the basement without her seeing me. I wasn't ready to face her again; it would be too embarrassing. And besides, I'd barely succeeded in retaining my virtue the first time around; pushing my luck would be foolish. Especially since I could already feel my blood rise when she bent down to clear a table and her dress fell slightly, revealing her breasts.

If I were British, maybe I'd have tried thinking about the queen; being American, I tried thinking about

Karen Carpenter singing "Close to You." But even that didn't work. Sneaking peeks through the window was making the whole damn thing even more erotic.

Marcie looked up from her wiping, and I ducked quickly behind the wall. It took me a whole minute before I got up the nerve to look back inside. I sang "Close to You" to pass the time. Four middle-aged couples walked up the sidewalk, throwing me questioning looks as they passed by. Maybe they thought I was singing for quarters.

Then they stopped and went into Madeline's. Screwing up my courage, I slowly eased my head around the wall and eyed the front room. Just as I'd hoped, Marcie wasn't cleaning tables anymore; she was behind the counter now, taking orders from the four couples, hemmed in. *Go.* I opened the door and slipped past the counter to the back room, pretty sure I hadn't been noticed, and hurried straight for the basement stairs.

But Jonas, the sports memorabilia collector, was cleaning tables in the back room, and he looked up at me and nodded. If I tried going down to the basement, he might hassle me. So I stopped short at the big green bookcase lining one wall and pretended to studiously examine the books, an eclectic mix of Leo Tolstoy and Danielle Steele. As slow as Sports Memorabilia was working, it looked like I'd have time to read *War and Peace* before he finished. I just hoped I could make it downstairs before Marcie spotted me, or we might end up giving Danielle some fresh material.

Sports Memorabilia finished wiping a table and headed for the front room, so I sidled toward the back stairs. But then he did a nifty 90-degree turn and walked up to me. "Hey, did you hear the Albany-Colonie Diamond Dogs signed Bam Bam Mueller to a two-year contract?" he asked.

I contemplated braining him with a Tolstoy tome. But instead I just smiled slightly—*very* slightly, so as not to encourage him.

Unfortunately, the guy didn't need any encouragement. He spent the next ten minutes telling me in painful detail about every single one of the Diamond Dogs' offseason roster moves, as well as the moves made by the Catskill Cougars, the Elmira Pioneers, the New Jersey Jackals, and all the other teams in the Northeast Independent Baseball League. *War and Peace* wasn't nearly heavy enough, I realized; true justice would require that I drop the entire seven-foot-tall bookcase on his head.

Finally, after one last parting comment about the Allentown Ambassadors, Sports Memorabilia moved off. I glanced around quickly, unlocked the gate, and dashed down the back stairs.

My eyes took a few moments to adjust to the darkness, but then I found the aisle where I had almost sampled Marcie's forbidden fruit. I was in such a hurry to find the application and get the hell out of there, I tripped on a coffee sack and sprawled headlong. Marcie's scent was still lingering in the air, impairing my ability to think straight. As I stood back up, I wondered if my concussion had somehow improved my sense of smell. I couldn't believe Marcie's odor was still so powerful, even though she hadn't been down here for fifteen minutes, maybe more—

"Hi," Marcie said.

I jumped, tripped on another coffee sack, and landed back on the floor. Marcie came and stood over me. "Are you all right?" she asked in her husky voice.

From where I lay, I couldn't help but look up her dress. And her smell was stronger than ever—so that's where it comes from, I thought . . .

And then my brain just plain gave out. My synapses exploded.

Helpless with lust, I reached up to pull Marcie down on top of me. My hands stretched toward hers, my fingertips shivering as they rose through the air.

21

"Looking for something?" Marcie asked, her eyes on my outstretched fingers.

"Yes," I breathed.

"Here." She brought her hand close to mine.

I started to grab her. But then I saw she was holding out some sheets of paper in her hand. *Huh?* I stared blankly at them for a few moments before the lust fog finally lifted enough for me to recognize The Penn's application.

I blinked up at Marcie, then took the application from her fingers and stood up. The act of standing finally got my brain synapses working again, and I started coming back to myself. *I am Jacob Burns,* I thought, *I'm married with two young children.* My mind repeated it like a mantra. *I'm married—*

"Jacob, there's something I have to say to you."

—with two young children. "Sure, yeah," I said, smiling with false cheer that fooled neither of us. "Let's go upstairs, we can talk there."

I started past her, but she put a hand on my chest. "I'd rather talk down here."

My lips flopped around for a while, then I found my voice. "Marcie, I know how you feel. But—" *But I'm married with two young children,* I was about to say, until she interrupted.

"Yeah, I figured you knew," she said bitterly. "It's in that dumb book he was writing, isn't it?"

Now my synapses all began firing simultaneously. *What* is in that dumb book?

When in doubt, nod knowingly, I reminded myself, *just nod knowingly.* So I did. I was glad my body was more or less following my brain's instructions again. Though to be honest, my head wasn't the only part of me that was nodding knowingly.

"It was just a one-time thing," Marcie complained, her baby blues looking pained. Still at sea, I nodded knowingly again. Marcie shook her head, exasperated. "I can't believe he made such a big deal out of it. It didn't *mean* anything. It would be like if we did it—I mean, you and me. Just a fun thing, you know?"

Holy cannoli, what was Marcie telling me here? Had she made love to *Donald Penn?* I was so baffled, I forgot to nod. This seeming lack of sympathy got Marcie even more riled up, and she started whining. "It's just so unfair. I mean, Madeline is my cousin. She's like my *sister.* I'd never do anything to hurt her."

Come again? How would Marcie's one-nighter with The Penn hurt Madeline? But then, finally, I started to get a glimmer of understanding.

Marcie put her hand on my shoulder, and I was surprised that for some reason it didn't turn me on. Strange. "Hey, Jacob, you and I almost made love, right? But that wouldn't have made us *bad people.* It wasn't something we should be *punished* for."

She threw me a desperate look, then started up again. "So did he write down the whole thing? How he heard me and Rob in the basement?"

Me and Rob in the basement. So my glimmer had been right. I nodded to myself. But Marcie thought I was nodding yes to her question, and she let out a petulant growl. "That pathetic little *shit*," she spit out, "did he write down about how he was *blackmailing* me?"

Whew, this Penn guy was some piece of work. Marcie kept on going, driven by fury. "Every single morning I had to give him *ninety-seven fucking cents* for a cup of coffee. I had to sneak it in a goddamn envelope and then hide it under the magazines so he could get it when he came in. And it had to be exact change, or the bastard wouldn't *accept* it!" She swatted a coffee bag angrily. "If anyone ever deserved to *die*, it was *Donald fucking Penn.*"

I stared at Marcie, wondering something, and I guess you know what it was. But Marcie was wondering something else. "So what are you gonna do?" she asked, with a hard stare.

I didn't know, so I nodded knowingly. I figured that would provoke her into talking some more, like it had before. But it didn't. She just stood there, her hard stare icing over. So I sighed thoughtfully, then nodded noncommittally, then tried raising my eyebrows questioningly, but nothing seemed to work. Marcie's glare was so fierce it definitely made me think she was capable of murder, but she still wasn't saying anything. Finally I gave in and broke the silence first. "What do *you* think I should do?"

"Just shut the fuck up!" Then she pulled herself together, and softened. "Look, I know you're a serious writer and everything, and I respect that, and you probably don't want to interfere with that asshole's *artistic integrity* or whatever the hell you call it when you get his book published"—she paused for breath, and to bat her big blue eyes at me—"but would it be so hard to just, you know, *leave out* the part of the book that's about me and Rob?"

I took a moment to try to frame an answer, and Marcie started to cry. Her tears would have been more effective if I hadn't suspected that she knew the same actor's trick for making yourself cry that I did. "Jacob, you gotta understand, if Madeline finds out he slept with me while he was engaged to her, it'll just *kill* her. She's so *old-fashioned,* white wedding dress and all that stuff, I mean Rob is only, like, the second guy she ever slept with." Marcie wiped away a tear. "Please, Jacob, Madeline doesn't deserve this. You can do anything you want to me, but not to poor Madeline," she ended melodramatically.

You can do anything you want to me. My chest sagged.

So that's why Marcie had been so eager to wiggle out of her clothes. It wasn't because I was so incredibly desirable and sexy, it was because she wanted to buy my silence.

Or maybe *blackmail* my silence. Maybe she was tearing a page out of Donald Penn's book, as it were. Man, what a comedown. Here I'd been burning with insane ballbusting desire, and the whole time the woman was just playing me like a kazoo.

I would have felt worse, except for one thing: as I looked at Marcie's mute pleading face, I realized that my crush on her had dissipated somehow. Maybe because in the last few minutes Marcie had transformed from a gorgeous fantasy queen with perfect smile, perfect breasts, and even perfect coffee, to a regular person who pleaded, sighed, and got self-centered and furious just like everyone else in the world. Now that I'd seen the reality of her, it only took a short mental jump for me to picture Marcie as a harassed thirty-something married woman with young children, nagging her husband to change a damn diaper every once in a while.

In other words, I belatedly understood, Marcie was not all that different from my wife. Except, of course, that I love my wife.

I allowed myself a small smile. I felt like I had dodged a bullet tonight.

"What are you smiling about?" Marcie broke into my thoughts.

"Nothing," I answered, and quickly shifted gears from 90s sensitive guy back to 30s private dick. What was the score now: one murder, two burglaries, assault, arson, following me around town, throwing bricks through windows . . . It seemed like too much for Marcie to pull off alone. But what if she'd conspired with Rob? "So was The Penn blackmailing Rob too?" I asked.

"No, I made him promise not to tell Rob. That was part of our deal." She sighed. "See, it wasn't really Rob's fault we slept together. I seduced him."

Suddenly she surprised me with a girlish giggle. "I couldn't help it. I mean, I worked right next to him for ten whole months, just *dying* to sleep with him, and I couldn't stand it anymore." She gazed up at me, her eyes getting that familiar lewd twinkle. Her nostrils flared a little, and she moistened her lips. "Just like I've been watching you every morning for two years. And getting hotter and hotter for you every single day."

Our eyes locked. My head pounded. Maybe she meant it. Maybe not.

But one thing I was sure of: I wanted coffee right now more than I had ever wanted coffee before in my life. Maybe more than I had ever wanted sex. "Marcie," I said, "let's go upstairs."

She didn't miss a beat. "What about Penn's book? Will you take out the part about me and Rob?"

I would have reassured her, but I guess I was still pissed off about being a kazoo. So I just said, "I don't know what to say," and led the way upstairs.

After we got there, it occurred to me that for all of

my lustful ogling, I had never once thought to look at Marcie's feet. Must be a shortcoming in my erotic makeup. So I turned and looked.

Like the rest of her, Marcie's feet were gorgeous. And two other interesting things about them:

They were medium sized . . . and they were clad in high-heeled shoes.

They weren't silver, but they were definitely high heels. This gave me yet another thing to think about as I headed back to Uncommon Grounds with The Penn's application folded up small and stashed carefully in my front pocket. It was 10:50 already and I really should be going home, but I figured Dave wouldn't mind staying a little late. And I didn't feel like going home to my wife right after Marcie.

Not that I had anything to feel guilty about, I reassured myself. Hell, I'd been a veritable pillar of virtue. Okay, so maybe I did sway a bit, but I didn't fall. The devil thought he had a slam dunk, but I blocked his shot. I had been tested, true, but I'd passed with a C minus.

I was still thinking up metaphors as I ordered Colombian, headed for an empty table . . . and practically ran into Madeline and Rob. I was so taken aback, I spilled my drink. Shoot, another java wasted. Fortunately Uncommon Grounds offered free refills, so I was able to get myself another hit of caffeine without forking over my fourth dollar bill of the night. Also, the whole episode gave me time to rearrange my face so I could act nonchalantly cheerful when I passed Madeline and Rob's table again. "Hey guys," I said, "how come you're giving money to your competition?"

Madeline grinned. "They have better coffee here."

"No way, Jose."

"Yo, what about you?" Rob asked. "How come you're not at Madeline's?"

Because Marcie was playing my kazoo, just like she did yours, I thought. Out loud I said, "Hey, nobody goes to Madeline's anymore, they're too crowded."

Madeline thought about that one, then laughed. "Hey, good line. No wonder you're a writer."

Actually I stole that line from Yogi Berra, but I didn't correct her, just shrugged modestly and changed the subject. "So what's that, an invitation list?" I asked, pointing to a long handwritten list of names on a yellow legal pad in front of them.

Madeline nodded. "How many people did you have at *your* wedding?" she asked me, glancing sideways at Rob.

"Including all my great-aunts and my long-lost relatives from Philadelphia, about a hundred and fifty."

She turned to Rob triumphantly. "You see? A hundred and twenty really isn't all that much."

Rob looked pained. "At sixty dollars a person?"

"Don't worry. We can afford it."

"I just don't feel right. I mean, it's your money."

"Honey, it's *our* money. Please, you gotta start thinking like that." She stroked his cheek. "Besides, once you sell your sofa and the rest of your stuff, that'll take care of twenty people right there."

Rob looked to me for support. "*Women,*" he said.

"*Women,*" I agreed.

"What about women?" Madeline asked.

Rob kissed her on the lips. "Did anyone ever tell you, you look just like Andie MacDowell in *Groundhog Day*. Except with more freckles."

I watched as they started cooing and rubbing noses. It did my heart good. Sure, Rob had his moment of weakness with Marcie, but God knows the temptation had been strong, and besides, he hadn't been married yet. One last little premarital fling didn't by any stretch of the imagination mean their marriage was doomed. Far from it. Madeline and Rob truly loved each other, and they were perfect together.

I just hoped neither of them were murderers.

Madeline, at least, was in the clear, so far as I knew. She'd told me the truth when she said Penn paid for his coffee; she didn't realize he was blackmailing Marcie for the ninety-seven cents.

But Rob, on the other hand . . . He'd been after me pretty hard for The Penn's manuscript. Had The Penn been blackmailing him, too, without Marcie knowing? It didn't make sense, though, because The Penn didn't need Rob for free coffee; Marcie was already supplying it. And besides, Rob started talking about holding a memorial service for The Penn before he even knew that manuscript existed. Why would you kill someone and then want to hold a memorial service for him? Rob might be a frustrated filmmaker, but he wasn't psychotic.

While I was thinking all these things I beamed at the happy couple, my face on automatic pilot. Madeline took my hand and held it. "Jacob, keep Columbus Day weekend free. You made the list."

"I'm truly honored," I said, and I was. "Well, you guys are getting a little too sickeningly sweet, so I guess I'll leave you alone now."

I took my Colombian to the empty table and had a sip. No, not a sip, a guzzle; it was the best coffee I ever tasted. Of course, at this point even moldy Sanka would have tasted good. As the caffeine kicked in, I took The Penn's application out of my pocket. If Marilyn Monroe herself came back from the dead and wrapped her legs around me, it wouldn't have mattered; I was going to finally read this damn application, right now.

But then a shadow hovered over me; Madeline, on her way to the bathroom. Was it my imagination or was she reading over my shoulder as she passed by? I gave her a friendly nod, but pulled the application closer to me.

Statement of Purpose: I am requesting $5000 to assist me in writing my three-volume work, The History of Western Civilization Careening, as Seen through the Eyes of One of its Primary Practitioners. *After working on this book for many years, I am now nearing completion.*

The book's thesis is that love can bring almost unbearable responsibility . . .

I was so disgusted I threw the application to the floor. *Another* version of the *preface?!* The Penn had made a fool out of me yet again! For *this* I had committed burglary, almost fried to death, and come within a pubic hair of losing my extramarital virginity? I stood up to go. Then, with an exasperated sigh, I reached down for the application and read on. *Dark and snowy night . . . live our deepest lives isolated . . .* I impatiently skimmed the key words, not even bothering anymore to hide the application from Madeline's eyes when she returned from the bathroom. *Clear sky . . . clister . . . computer . . .*

Wait a minute. *"Computer?"* I backed up.

I have been somewhat blocked in my writing for the past couple of years. No kidding, pal. *You see, I learned when very young the fearsome power of words. Even seemingly innocuous ones like "Have you seen my clister?" can kill. Therefore I rewrite assiduously, which has become both my joy and my bane. I have concluded that the solution to the problem of rewrites is purchasing a computer. Only a computer, I believe, now lies between me and greatness.*

Not the first time I'd heard this sentiment. The screenwriting class I taught in prison was full of guys who were sure that if they only had a computer, they'd become the next Spike Lee.

Sure, and if I had a tutu, I'd be the next Rudolf Nureyev.

An artist, like every man, or every woman as one must add in this pseudo-egalitarian age, will grasp for greatness by any means necessary. Six months ago a heartless, malicious bureaucracy decreased my Social Security disability income (or, as I prefer to think of it, my federal writing stipend) by $89.60 per month. Ever since then, I have taken extraordinary measures to insure that poverty will not abate my intake of Ethiopian—believing, as I do, that a steady flow of Ethiopian is imperative to my creative flow. Members of the grant panel are only too aware of some of the extraordinary measures I have taken.

I read that one twice. *Members of the grant panel are only too aware of some of the extraordinary measures I have taken.* Like blackmail? Did Penn somehow manage to blackmail the panel members, too?

So Penn had dirt on Gretchen, the mayor, Marcie, Rob, and now maybe the grant panel. Man, this guy got around. Maybe he was a failure as a writer, but as a blackmailer he was aces.

At this point in time, mere Ethiopian is no longer sufficient. To fulfill my destiny as official chronicler of the final years of our wobbling millennium, it is necessary that I receive funding for a PowerBook 1400 computer; an Apple LaserWriter 12/640, with accompanying toner cartridges and printer paper; and eight ballpoint pens and other items.

Panel members should know that if my extremely reasonable request is denied, I am prepared to take even more extraordinary measures. Be forewarned.

Penn's "Statement of Purpose" ended right there. "*Be forewarned.*" Pretty impressive; Penn had gone from blackmailing people for cups of coffee to blackmailing people for expensive computers. A step up.

What was he blackmailing the grant panel about? Obviously he felt he had something juicy. But even if he did, how could they possibly award him $5000? True, in theory they were permitted to fund requests of up to five grand; but in practice they rarely gave more than twelve or fifteen hundred. The two grand that Bonnie Engels got, and the almost two grand that George Hosey and Antoinette Carlson both got, were probably the biggest grants the panel had awarded this year.

Which put the panel members in a dangerous bind. Ever since the NEA awarded money for some guy to exhibit a crucifix in a jar of piss, oversight on arts grants has gotten more rigorous. Maybe not rigorous enough to stop every little conflict of interest, but definitely enough to uncover a preposterous $5000 award to a derelict with no résumé. If the panel said yes to The Penn, they'd have to face fierce questioning from both NYFA in New York and the Arts Council Executive Board in Saratoga. At best they'd come off looking like total idiots; at worst, someone would smell something shady.

On the other hand, if they said no, they'd risk having Penn expose whatever nefarious deeds he'd been blackmailing them about. They were lucky that The Penn died just in the nick of time, only two days before their big meeting, so they never had to decide what to do about him.

But maybe it wasn't luck at all. Maybe someone on the grant panel had solved the problem by killing The Penn.

Suddenly The Penn's application started shaking in my hands; then I realized it was my hands that were shaking. He had dropped dead at 9:50, less than an hour after guzzling his daily Arts Council Ethiopian. Maybe that was the Ethiopian that killed him.

One or more of the panel members could have dropped in at the Arts Council that morning between 8:45 and 9:00, after Molly Otis made the coffee but before The Penn picked it up, and slipped a hit of poison into his drink. It would have been as easy as making fun of Ross Perot's ears. That early in the morning the Arts Council was probably deserted, so the killer could sneak in and out the back door with no one ever seeing him.

Except, of course, for Molly.

Oh, my God. Why hadn't I seen this before? I sipped the last dregs of my java, trying to steady myself.

Was this the real reason why someone was so desperate to shut that girl up?

If Molly Otis saw somebody in the Arts Council office between eight forty-five and nine a.m. that morning, then she might know, without realizing it, who killed Donald Penn.

22

I checked my watch. Eleven-twenty already; Andrea would be seriously pissed. I better haul my ass back home immediately.

But first, it was high time to give Molly Otis another call. After all, Dave was at my house holding down the fort, and I could always blame my lateness on Amtrak. So I pocketed the application and headed to the pay phone outside Uncommon Grounds.

Unfortunately, the pay phone was booked. Some Skidmore pib (person in black) was having a conversation with either her boyfriend or her worst enemy. The way she was cussing at him, it was hard to tell which. I withdrew a few yards to give her fury some room and took out the application again, looking for further clues. I turned the page and found The Penn's *"Budget of Project,"* which started out looking like the exact same pathetic budget he'd submitted two years before.

EXPENSES, MONTHLY

Rent including utilities	$350
Food—daily consumption of 1 can chunk tuna, 8 oz. milk, 2 cups Tastee-O's breakfast cereal, 8 oz. frozen orange juice, 4 slices day-old bread, and 2 TBS butter	62.40

Notebooks, pens of various colors, pencils, erasers, and other writing material	14.36
Entertainment—1 movie matinee	4.75
Toothpaste, miscellaneous	4.75
Safety-deposit box	1.25
Transportation—bus to and from mall for movie	1.20
Telephone, clothing, shoes	0
Coffee, 3 or more cups daily, at various establishments (necessary for creativity)	0 (donations)

I stopped and reread the last entry. That *"0 (donations)"* business was new. I guess "donations" was The Penn's cute way of saying "blackmail money." And I was pretty sure *"3 or more cups"* was new too; it used to be just *"3 cups."* Was an increased caffeine intake responsible for The Penn's increasingly grandiose schemes?

Those schemes were very much in evidence in the next budget item:

Computer (PC portable PowerBook 1400, with RAM expanded to 64MB, 1.0GB hard disk, and added CD-Rom drive)	$2458 (includes shipping charges)

A damn nice computer. The same type of machine I used to use at Madeline's, back when I was writing, but about three levels fancier. The Penn may have been thinking portable, but he definitely wasn't thinking small.

Printer and supplies (Apple LaserWriter 12/640; one year's supply of toner cartridges—i.e., four cartridges; and printer paper)	$2207. 96 (includes shipping charges)

Once again, the same type of machine I used to use; but once again, a lot fancier. I put the application down for a moment, intrigued that The Penn was both mimicking me and one-upping me at the same time. Just coincidence? Or was he jealous of my sudden success? I had gone from fellow unsuccessful writer to millionaire in one stroke of a Hollywood producer's pen. Maybe The Penn thought if he got himself a computer that was more expensive than mine, it would sort of even the score.

Also, I was willing to bet the guy convinced himself the only reason I broke through and he didn't was because I had a computer. It scared me how well I understood this guy. I guess that was one dubious benefit of my many unsuccessful years as a screenwriter: I understood failure.

And I felt like I understood his blackmailing, too. It wasn't just about the money or the free java. No, it was about all the bitterness, rage, and despair that had built up inside him during his three decades as an unsuccessful artist, until he finally exploded.

I wondered, since I never brought my printer to Madeline's, how did The Penn know what kind I had? He must have eavesdropped on me talking about it. Or maybe he was even *spying* on me, looking for stuff to blackmail me about. What a creepy thought. This guy Penn was a sick fuck. Of course, if I hadn't gotten lucky with *Gas,* and if I'd kept writing unproduced screenplays for another fifteen years, no doubt I would have turned into a pretty sick fuck myself. I turned the page.

Software, disks	330
Eight ballpoint pens (for revising hard copy of manuscript)	4.04

I had to smile about those eight ballpoint pens. The old Donald Penn poking through. He poked through later too, in the "*Income*" section, where he still listed $7.75/month from bottle and can returns.

But when I turned the page again, my smile froze. Under "*Additional Comments,*" The Penn had written: *Thank you, but I've said all I need to say. The threats that have been made against my life do not frighten me. I may be killed, but I will not be silenced.*

After those ominous words, there was nothing but extremely aggravating blank white space.

Goddamn it, *who? Who* had threatened The Penn's life?

I stood there staring at the whiteness, perhaps hoping that the answer would mysteriously reveal itself there, but my thoughts were interrupted by a loud shout of "You prick!" It was the Skidmore girl, slamming down the phone. She glared at me and snapped, "You, too!" and then stormed off. Oh well, at least now the phone was free. Hopefully I'd get a friendlier response from the Skidmore girl I was about to call. I dialed the operator and asked for Molly Otis's number.

"Unlisted at the customer's request," some woman with a lisp informed me.

"No, that's not possible. I got her number from the operator just two days ago."

"The number has been changed since then, sir."

"Let me talk to your supervisor," I began, but she hung up. Terrific.

What were my chances of getting Molly's new number from her overprotective father? Probably about as good as the Mets' chances of winning the pennant.

I'd have to leave Molly for the morning. Right now I figured I better not push my luck with Andrea, so I got in the Camry and drove home. Oh no, *11:45.* I'd tell

Andrea and Dave the train got stuck for an extra hour near Albany. Unless they had called Amtrak for info, in which case I'd have to come up with something else. But what? I had a feeling that "I'm sorry, honey, it's just that I was busy almost getting seduced" wouldn't play too well in Peoria.

I opened the door and called out, "Hi, guys."

No one answered. "Hi, guys!" I called again, louder.

Still no answer. I went in the living room. Dave wasn't there.

My heart raced, and I did too, frantically dashing upstairs and opening my bedroom door. There was Andrea, sprawled on the bed, not moving.

I gasped, sure she was dead. But then she gave out a loud snore.

I sat down and listened. Funny, I'd never noticed before how truly beautiful Andrea's snore was.

I took off my clothes and snuggled into her, with my nose next to her right armpit. Her post-workout odor was still clinging to her, and I lay there inhaling her, letting her smells flow into my muddled brain, cleansing it of Marcie's smoke and all the other events of the night.

I did have one last mental image of Marcie, a momentary flash of red from her skimpy dress. But the red quickly faded into darkness and slipped away into the night.

Then I relaxed and fell asleep.

Andrea and I were in the west of Ireland on our honeymoon. We slipped into an abandoned medieval fort, threw off our clothes, and were about to make passionate love when I happened to notice that Donald Penn was dead on the ground next to us. A pair of cross-country skis lay on his body, forming an X. I woke up.

Donald fucking Penn.

So far as I could figure it out, something had happened to him "one dark and snowy night" when he was young. Something involving his father, clister, and cross-country skiing. This event was so traumatic that he spent every single day of his entire adult life trying to put it into words. And failing.

I got out of bed, went to the study, and turned on my trusty, if slightly outdated, Powerbook. Maybe the miracles of modern technology would help me get to the bottom of this strange, obsessed man who had somehow taken over my life.

Through her work at the community college, my wife had access to a database called Nexis that I vaguely knew how to use. Unfortunately I didn't know the first names of Penn's parents. I didn't even know if Penn was his real name, or just a "pen" name. But in any case, I searched for "Donald Penn" and got a grand total of zero hits. Then I widened my search to "Penn" and got more than five hundred hits. I settled into my chair. There were probably ways to speed up this search, but I didn't know them, and I doubted Andrea would appreciate it if I woke her up to ask her.

The first hit was from the *Seattle Post-Intelligencer,* about a Doris Penn from Spokane who won first prize for a coffee cake recipe. Hardly the sort of traumatic event a son would spend his whole life obsessed about. Though come to think of it, my grandmother used to make an incredible chocolate cake that none of her six children was ever able to replicate after she died, and it's haunted them for decades.

I got umpteen hits for William Penn, the seventeenth-century Quaker. There were three more hits for Doris's coffee cake, from as far away as Birmingham, Alabama; maybe I should print out that recipe. Up in Minnesota, a man named Joe Penn ran for Congress as a Republican, and lost. Served him right. A Buffalo man named Elmer Penn died in 1992, survived by his wife and three daughters, none of whom was named Donald.

I started to recognize a pattern; none of these hits came from before 1970, and most of them were from no earlier than 1988 or so. Evidently Nexis hadn't gotten around to incorporating older newspapers and magazines into their database.

Which probably made my whole search useless. Since Penn was fifty-three when he died, and a child when the traumatic thing happened, that meant my search needed to cover the period from about 1948 to 1958.

I looked up a few William Penn hits for further evidence that Nexis didn't go back that far . . . and was surprised to find a *New York Times* hit from 1949. Hmm. Apparently the nation's "newspaper of record" was considered sufficiently important that Nexis had gone to the trouble of incorporating their older issues.

Personally I'd always found this "newspaper of record" business ridiculous. Or I'd felt that way ever since they began reporting on the making of *The Gas that Ate San Francisco,* and I noticed there were at least three factual inaccuracies in every article they wrote. But what the heck. Right now the newspaper of record was my last hope. I figured out how to search the *Times* for other articles about the Penns of the world . . . and on my very first hit I got lucky.

John Penn. A headline from 1953: *"Tragedy in New Hampshire."*

My fingers trembled as I hit the computer keys to bring up the article. My Powerbook, which felt incredibly fast when I first bought it, now felt like something out of the Old Stone Age. Finally the article appeared.

> "Berlin, New Hampshire, January 23. In one of the worst tragedies in this state in recent history, a Berlin man killed his wife and then himself early this morning with his shotgun, as their eight-year-old son hid in a bedroom closet.
>
> Policemen and neighbors at the scene were unable to offer any explanation as to why John Penn, a factory worker at International Shoes in nearby Gorham, might have committed this horrific deed. Louise Wentworth, the next-door neighbor who was awakened by the shots and found the bodies, says that John and Marian Penn were a quiet, unremarkable couple—"a typical family," she says. "Marian went to church every Sunday, and John loved his cross-country skiing. We always thought the skiing business was a little odd, but we sure never thought he'd kill someone."
>
> Another neighbor, Dennis Olson, was similarly baffled by the horrible crime. "Maybe it was just the weather," he said. "It's been blasted cold around here."
>
> The young son, Donald, is temporarily under the care of a neighboring family.

During the next few days the *Times* ran two follow-ups. I guess horrific crimes were more rare in those days; if this happened now, the *Times* probably wouldn't bother. In the first follow-up, there were background interviews with coworkers and friends. In the second one they talked to the cops, who had gotten a statement from the distraught young Donald.

Apparently, all week long Donald's father had been looking forward to going cross-country skiing. According to Al Wenningham, who called himself "the closest buddy John had, even though we weren't all that close," John Penn lived to go skiing, "the same way everybody else up here lives to go hunting."

Reading between the lines, working at the shoe factory offered little in the way of job satisfaction, and there was no way out except on Sundays, when John Penn strapped on his skis and glided off alone into the snowy yonder and found peace.

Unfortunately, that Sunday, when his long-awaited day off came, there had been a freezing rain and the top layer of snow was so icy and crunchy that none of the usual ski waxes worked. So John went down to the basement searching for a special clister that he had carefully stashed away, which might possibly allow him to ski in this god-awful snow.

But he couldn't find it. His wife had rearranged the basement to store her canning supplies. As Donald lay in bed half-asleep, he heard his father storm upstairs and ask his mother furiously, "Where did you put my clister?"

In response, Marian said, "Shut up, I'm sleeping."

So John repeated himself, louder and even angrier. Marian snapped back at him. They began shouting. John yelled at her for ruining his life, along with his bosses at International Shoes. Marian yelled back. Donald, listening, huddled in his bed.

Then he heard crashing noises from the other room—they were throwing things at each other. Marian must have picked up a ski, because Donald heard his father yell, "Put that ski down!"

But she didn't. She swung the ski at a wall or something, and it broke in two.

The next thing Donald remembered was a shotgun blast. His father killed his mother with one point-blank shot in the face.

Donald ran to his closet and hid, just before John came in the room looking for him. John sobbed out his apologies for killing Marian, and promised to make everything all right again by killing Donald and then himself.

Then the closet door opened. John called his son's

name. The son lay still, not daring to breathe, beneath his old gray Army blanket.

Finally the door closed again. Donald wasn't sure if his father had seen him or not. For a while there was silence. Then a shot blasted out. Then more silence. Eventually Donald snuck out of his closet and went in his parents' bedroom, where he found John and Marian lying in bed together. As one of the cops quoted in the article put it, "neither of them had faces left."

I turned off the computer and sat there for a while in the dark. Then I went into the boys' room and hugged and kissed them as they slept. They both had warm blankets curled around them, just like Donald Penn, many years ago, on that deathly cold winter morning.

It was five a.m. and I was finally slipping into a troubled semi-oblivion when Gretzky came into our bedroom crying. I found out soon enough what the problem was: His pants were soaking wet.

For several months now Gretzky had been wearing "big boy pullups" to bed, sort of a cross between diapers and regular underwear. Usually they absorbed any bedwetting easily. But tonight he had so much peepee from holding it in all day that when he finally let loose he got flooded. "Honey, let me change your pants," I said.

"No!" Gretzky shouted, irate.

"But they're all wet—"

"No, they're not!"

"Sweetheart, they're full of peepee—"

"Hockey players don't make peepee!"

From the other side of the bed, Andrea broke in. "I can't stand this anymore. If he doesn't stop this hockey-players-don't-make-peepee business, I'll put him in diapers again!"

This horrible threat sent Gretzky bawling. "No! Nooooooo!" he howled desperately.

While Andrea covered her ears with a pillow, I finally talked the Great One out of his wet pants and back to bed. But then Babe Ruth came in carrying yesterday's sports page and demanding to know why the Mets were starting John Olerud at first base instead of Butch Huskey. Before we could get that issue resolved, Gretzky woke up again and ordered me to get up *this very minute* so I could go to the store to buy him a goalie helmet. When I told him it was only 5:30 and the stores were all closed, that didn't faze him in the slightest. "You can open the store yourself, Daddy, with a key," he explained impatiently.

Then Babe Ruth announced that if the stores were still closed, we should just go outside and play baseball. So Gretzky angrily declared that we had to play hockey first, because he was younger. Rationally, I knew the kids were just acting out their frustration that I'd been so busy with my murder investigation, I hadn't been paying them enough attention. But I was too exhausted to listen to my rational mind, and I could feel a primal scream rising in my gut when I happened to look over at Andrea. Our eyes met, and for some reason we both burst out laughing.

Instantly the mood in the bed changed. Gretzky and Ruth dropped all their demands and decided to beat us up with pillows instead. Andrea and I would have gotten seriously clobbered except we had a secret weapon: Magic Tickle Fingers.

The Fingers were so successful that the children retreated to their bedroom to plot out a secret weapon of their own. Andrea took advantage of the battle lull to ask me, "So when did you get home last night?"

I hemmed, then hawed, then said, "Uh, I'm not sure. When did you go to bed?"

"Ten-thirty or so. I was beat. I told Dave he could just go home, since I figured you'd be getting back any minute. Hope you didn't mind my not waiting up."

"No, that's okay. I got in a little after 10:30." Which wasn't really a lie, strictly speaking; I mean, 11:45 *is* a little after 10:30.

"There's about a hundred messages for you on the machine," Andrea said.

I jumped up. "From who?" Molly? Gretchen? The mayor?

"They're all from your agent. I got sick of talking to him, so I turned the machine on."

I slapped my forehead. Talk about engine trouble—I had completely forgotten about my $750,000 deal. "What did he want?"

"He said to hurry up and express mail that contract back to him. The producer wants you to start immediately."

Immediately. Well, hey, for three-quarters of a mil I could deal with that. Today was Saturday; I'd express the contract today, then receive a copy of the mutant beetles screenplay on Monday morning. At which point my month of Hollywood hack work would commence with instant fury.

Monday morning. That left me forty-eight hours to solve The Penn's murder.

"Sorry the New York trip didn't go well," Andrea said, and massaged my back. I wanted to tell her about my confrontation with Gretchen, and how I'd gotten a copy of the application after all, but I couldn't figure out how to do it without admitting I'd lied about the train being late. Frankly, I was getting sick of all the little lies I was telling Andrea lately. I thought about telling my wife what I'd really been doing the last two nights, even though I knew she'd be livid at all the risks I'd taken, when we were suddenly interrupted by loud shouts of "Batman!" and our two superheroes raced in flailing their pillows fiercely.

This time not even Magic Tickle Fingers were enough to fight off the savage onslaught. The grown-ups were soundly and utterly trounced, and only the promise of homemade waffles allowed us to escape with our lives.

We had a nice couple of hours together, and I wish I could have brought my little warriors with me for moral support later that morning when I met with the grant panel at Madeline's. They were all waiting for me when I got there, and they all looked about as cheerful as Bosnian war refugees.

Even worse, Marcie was working the counter. I didn't want to deal with her, but I sure needed some java to pull me through this. So I went up there and pushed my dollar bill across the counter, and she pushed the Ethiopian back at me. Our hands never touched; in fact, we did the entire transaction without even looking at each other.

I surveyed the Grim People as I headed for their table. George Hosey rubbed his eyes somberly, resembling Uncle Sam on a particularly bad day. Like, say, Pearl Harbor. Mike Pardou, the King of Spoons, was absentmindedly beating spoons against his cheek, but it didn't interfere with his hangdog expression. The man was definitely not an advertisement for recreational drugs.

Steve the Novella Man sat next to Antoinette the Grant Queen, as usual. But he didn't look as shrunken as he usually did next to her, mainly because she looked pretty shrunken herself this morning. Her lanky six-foot frame slouched over the table, and her dreadlocks came dangerously close to falling into her coffee. I would have said something, but I was afraid she'd get insulted.

The only member of the Grim People who was sitting tall and proud, looking in prime fighting mood, was Bonnie Engels.

"Hey, guys," I greeted them.

"Sit down," Bonnie said peremptorily. The other Grim People grunted.

"Thank you." As I sat down, Bonnie gave me the evil eye. Mike Pardou, meanwhile, began beating his spoons faster and louder—*clickety click clack clack*—as Ersatz Uncle Sam cleared his throat and said, "Listen, Jacob, we've been hearing a lot of, uh, strange rumors."

"Uh huh." Hmm, pillow talk from Gretchen?

"It's like this, Jacob," Antoinette broke in, lifting her dreadlocks and shining her earnest chocolate-colored eyes on me. "We know you've made it big and everything, and we're happy for you, but see—*Jesus fucking Christ, Mike, would you shut up?!*" she shouted.

The *clickety clack* suddenly stopped as Pardou dropped his spoons, stunned. The rest of us were stunned too, not just by Antoinette's outburst but by seeing Pardou without spoons in his hands. It was like seeing him stark naked.

Antoinette collected herself and continued. "See, Jacob, for the rest of us, we really *need* these NYFA grants. If they get taken away from us, word gets around. I can kiss good-bye to the NYSCA grant I applied for, and that means no Pollock-Krasner grant. Which means I get shut out by the National Endowment for the Humanities, which means my teaching jobs dry up. Basically, my career goes down the toilet."

"Getting a NYFA grant from the state of New York enhances my credibility worldwide," seconded Ersatz Sam. "Even as far away as New Zealand."

"The thing is, I already called my mother and told

her I got the grant," Novella Man chimed in. "She'll be really upset if it gets taken away."

"I don't get it. Why would your grants get taken away?" I asked, genuinely puzzled.

Bang! Bonnie Engels slammed her fist on the table. My coffee cup jumped and tipped over, spilling steaming hot Ethiopian all over my jeans. I leapt up, cursing, and tried to pull the scalding pants away from my leg.

Bonnie leapt up too, but not so she could help me. She just wanted to do a better job of getting in my face. "You slimeball," she snarled, "don't you play any of your asinine games with us. We know you're trying to close down the Arts Council."

I stared at her, incredulous. *"Close down the Arts Council?"* Jesus, talk about rumors. "Next thing, you'll be accusing me of burning down that building." I examined their faces carefully to see if any of them gave a sudden guilty look, or eyed each other nervously, but no one rose to the bait.

Bonnie just ignored what I said and kept on snarling. "And all because of some stupid little formality. Not leaving the room when our grant proposals were being discussed." She waved her arms, disgusted. "Everyone at this table would have received those grants anyway. We're all serious artists."

Unfortunately for Bonnie, the credibility of her last statement was damaged when Pardou picked this moment to beat his spoons again. We all turned and looked at him, and I'm sure everyone else was thinking roughly the same thing I was: If this guy was a serious artist, then I was a dill pickle.

As if reading our thoughts, Pardou said, "Hey, man, my one-man folk opera is gonna be hot."

Bonnie jutted her sharp chin back in my direction. "Forget about him," she said, jerking a disdainful thumb at Pardou. "My women's boxing video is for real, and a two-thousand-dollar grant from the Arts Council is entirely appropriate. Put that together with the six thousand I just got from Virgil Otis, and—"

"*Virgil Otis?*" I asked, astonished. Whoa, there was a connection between Bonnie and Virgil, the fat funeral home director?! That would mean a connection of sorts between Bonnie and Virgil's daughter Molly, who—

Bonnie stamped her feet impatiently. "I *told* you the project was attracting private investment. What, did you think I was making it up?"

Virgil, Bonnie, Molly. . . . Something stirred in my brainpan, but before I could scoop it out Antoinette interrupted with a noisy, flamboyant, "It's *outrageous.*" Bonnie's combativeness had put the fire back in Antoinette, and she gave her dreads an angry toss. "First this dirty, smelly, little man tries to *blackmail* us, and now even after he's dead we *still* have to deal with his sniveling schemes. Jacob Burns," she said, and then shifted her voice to a subtly menacing whisper, "I have always respected you, even after you sold out. But if you publish this man's lies, then as they say in Zimbabwe"—and here she gave a low hiss—"*I will spit on your toenails.*"

The coffee had soaked through my pants, my legs were damp and clammy, and now someone was threatening to spit on my toenails. Enough already. "Let's see if I got this straight," I said, taking them all in with my eyes. "Donald Penn eavesdropped on you people through his floorboards, right? And what he found out was, you all sit around the Arts Council every year giving each other grants. You did it this year, and I bet you did it last year too, and the year before that."

"We have an ongoing body of work—" Novella Man began.

I interrupted. "Yeah, and an ongoing body of bullshit, too. So finally The Penn called you on it. He said, give me five grand or I blow the whistle on your little grant panel scam."

"The bastard had us on tape—" Mike Pardou sputtered, before Bonnie shut him up with a look.

I threw them all a shiteating grin. "How interesting. So are you afraid you'll get busted for spending public money *fraudulently?*"

No one answered. No one even moved.

"Well, good news, folks," I told them, "no need to worry about the tape. It must have fried in the fire." Novella Man gave out an audible sigh of relief, but I wasn't finished. "However, the bad news is, Penn transcribed the entire panel meeting from last year—and I have it. Makes very entertaining reading. Would be a crime not to publish it. Maybe I should send complimentary copies to NYFA and a few other people too."

If looks could kill, their combined gazes would have put me twenty feet under. "Give me a fucking break!" Bonnie exploded. "We did nothing wrong, and you know it. You can't expect artists like us to follow every little rule like regular people. When the whole world is against you, you have to be willing to sell your own grandmother to succeed!" She threw every word at me like a dagger. "Admit it, you *hypocrite.* Until six months ago, if you were on this panel, you'd have done the exact same thing we did!"

She was right, of course. Being an unsuccessful artist had corrupted my spirit, just as it had corrupted everyone else at this table. Bonnie shoved her finger an inch from my nose. "So don't you dare sit there acting all high and mighty. You don't have any more talent than we do, you just got lucky, that's all! And you know it!"

I was getting real sick of people yelling at me. I yelled right back at Bonnie, "You jealous *fool,* I don't care about your stupid little grants. I just want to find out *who killed Donald Penn!*"

That stopped them, all right. They stared at me. So did Marcie and everyone else in the joint. I leaned over the table at the Grim People and fixed them with my Roger Clemens glare. "So tell me, which one of you people visited the Arts Council office on Monday morning—the morning Penn was poisoned?"

I caught Bonnie's eyes darting around, scared, looking guilty as sin. But when I glanced over at Ersatz, he looked guilty too. And so did the Grant Queen, and the King of Spoons, and Novella Man. But they couldn't *all* be guilty, could they? What was this, *Murder on the Orient Express*?

Ersatz was the first to speak. "You're crazy," he said.

Think F. Lee Bailey, I told myself, and fastened my eyes on Ersatz's, trying not to get distracted by his impressive goatee. "Answer the question. Were you at the Arts Council office on Monday morning shortly before nine o'clock?"

"No."

"Do you have an alibi?"

"No, I don't," Ersatz replied, but he didn't act nervous, and his eyes continued to hold mine.

"I have an alibi," Novella Man volunteered—and there was a sudden blur of motion. It was Bonnie, slapping him hard across the face with a vicious backhand.

It happened so fast, I don't know if Bonnie even meant to do it. Maybe it was just an unconscious reflex. We all sat and watched dumbly as blood spilled from Novella Man's cut lower lip. He looked like he was in shock, and I was afraid he'd pass out.

"Sorry, I didn't mean to do it," Bonnie said. She didn't look too broken up about it, though. She was always babbling about how boxing was good for a person's soul, but Bonnie's soul seemed to have taken on a few extra twists lately.

Novella Man just stared at her, eyes wide, blood dripping down onto the table. Antoinette stood up. "I'll get you a napkin, Steve."

As Antoinette went up to the front counter, Bonnie turned to me. "You should be ashamed of yourself, trying to pull this crap. Donald Penn wasn't killed, and even if he was, it had nothing to do with us. Get serious."

"I'm dead serious."

"If you are, you're an idiot."

"Jacob, we had no reason to hurt him," Antoinette cut in, as she returned with the napkin. "The whole affair between us and that man was over and done with."

"How do you figure that?"

She opened her eyes wide and gave me another one of her earnest looks. This must be the look she used when hitting up potential funders for cash. "It's like this, Jacob. Me and Bonnie met with him last week, three days before he died. We called his bluff. We told him we planned to reject his application, no matter what the consequences."

"What did he say?"

Bonnie answered for Antoinette, with a derisive sneer. "What *could* he say? He wasn't happy about it, but it was all just a joke anyway. The little shrimp didn't even have the balls to look us in the face. And he *definitely* didn't have the balls to actually carry out his ridiculous threats."

"You're right. Especially if he was dead."

"For God's sake—" Bonnie began, but I stopped her. "What about you, Bonnie? Where were you that morning?"

Big angry purple veins stuck out on Bonnie's hand as she balled it into a fist, and I was sure she'd punch me. I had to force myself not to back away from her as she said, "I will not put up with this insane harassment."

"Sure, you will. Either from me or from the cops."

Bonnie's veins got even bigger and purpler. "Burns, you're sticking your nose in places it doesn't belong." Her eyes turned into thin green slivers. "That could be dangerous. *Very* dangerous."

My throat dried up. With as much toughness as I could muster, I asked, "Are you threatening me?" I probably would have sounded tougher if I hadn't been squeaking.

Then, as if a faucet inside her had been suddenly shut off, Bonnie's fists relaxed and she burst into an amused smile. "Of course not," she laughed lightly, and stood up. "You're still one of us, Jacob. I just don't want anything bad happening to you, that's all."

And before I could stop her, she stepped up and hugged me. I heard several sharp cracks. Either I'd just received some inexpensive chiropractic, or she'd broken a few disks in my spine.

While I was still assessing the damage, Bonnie took my hand and gently put a couple of tickets in it. "I'm doing a performance piece with my students tonight. A new piece called *The Devil Comes to Town* that we wrote ourselves." She squeezed my fingers so hard they ached. "I do hope you can come, Jacob. You need to take a break from Hollywood and get back in touch with what grassroots art is all about. It'll renew you spiritually."

And darned if she didn't hug me again. The woman's arms should have been registered as lethal weapons. Then she gave us all a wave and walked out of Madeline's.

I sighed with relief, glad that my spinal column was finally out of danger. Then I looked back at the other Grim People, who were still sitting there at the table. Lost in the Sixties was beating his spoons again, eyes half closed, while Ersatz Uncle Sam stroked his goatee, and the Grant Queen applied a wet napkin to Novella Man's lips. He was gazing up at her adoringly.

Could any of these people have committed murder?

I had no idea.

23

Sam Spade, Jr., needed a break. He needed one bad.

And he got one, at Virgil Otis's house.

That's where I headed after Madeline's, to see if I could somehow hustle the man into giving up his daughter's phone number. Luckily, just as I was driving up I spotted the girl herself coming out of her dad's house with a laundry basket full of clothes. It was nice to see that although web sites and megabytes have changed a lot of things, the grand old tradition of doing laundry at your parents' house lives on into the new millennium.

I almost confronted Molly right then and there, while she dumped the clothes in her car. But Virgil appeared at the front door waving good-bye, and I decided to wait until we were out of his sight. As Molly pulled out of the driveway and took off, I followed her discreetly—or as discreetly as you can with a muffler that sounds like an Ozzy Osbourne CD. When would I get time to fix that thing?

Molly led me onto the hallowed grounds of Skidmore College. Not wanting to spook her, I stayed a respectful distance behind. *Too* respectful as it turned out, because she found a parking spot right in front of her dorm and went inside while I was still stuck at the corner playing stop and go with a thirty-yard-long food service delivery truck.

Molly's dorm was seven floors high, the biggest and most modern building on campus. I went in the foyer, but the inner door was locked and I didn't know which of the hundred or so doorbells to ring, since the students' names weren't listed. For security reasons, no doubt.

Back outside, I went behind the dorm and found a broken window on the far corner of the first floor. So Molly had been telling the truth about that brick. Evidently the town's glaziers hadn't gotten around to fixing it yet, though in fairness to them, they'd been kept plenty busy lately.

I returned to the foyer, rang a bunch of doorbells, and in no time at all four or five people buzzed me in. Great security. No match for a veteran B and E man like myself. I walked up the first floor hallway, found the room at the far corner, and knocked.

"Who is it?" Molly called out. I could hear her voice quavering through the door.

"Jacob Burns."

A gasp. "Go away!"

"We need to talk—"

"I said, go away! I'm calling security!"

"That won't do any good," I began, then heard a noise which sounded like someone taking a phone off its cradle. "Molly, stop—" I tried, but she said, "Hello, security?"

"You've got to listen to me—"

"I'm calling from Merrill Dorm! There's a man trying to break into my room!" Molly screamed into the phone.

"Look, you were right about Donald Penn!"

"I'm in Room one-eighteen!"

"Penn was murdered!"

I waited. Molly was silent. "He was murdered," I repeated, more softly this time.

Finally Molly spoke into her phone again. "Uh, I'm sorry, sir, it's okay, it's just my, uh, father. Yeah, I'm sure. 'Bye."

Meanwhile two doors opened down the hall and two fearful young women peered out at me. I gave them my friendliest smile but they recoiled like I was Hannibal Lecter, or Marv Albert. "Molly, are you okay?" one of them stammered when Molly opened her door.

"I'm fine," Molly said, nodding for me to come into her room. I stepped inside, gazing around at the Alanis Morissette posters on the walls and the feminist literature on the floor. It was a long time since I'd been in a college girl's boudoir, and it felt like a foreign country. Molly had instinctively referred to me as her father. Ouch, was I really that old?

With boards covering the broken window, it was dark in there. Molly pointed a reading light in my direction, folded her arms, and waited silently for me to speak. I felt like I was being interrogated, but since it was me who wanted something from her, I put up with it.

I sat down on her desk chair and told my story. It reminded me of all the Hollywood movie pitches I used to do, but with one difference: This time, my story was real.

Molly frowned as she listened, looking a lot older than the first time I'd seen her, only two days ago. Though even then, despite her sweet freckled face, she'd looked more mature than her age. I guess growing up in a funeral home will do that to you.

I was afraid Molly would find my suspicions of the panel members absurd, but she surprised me. After I finished, she shook her head and said, "Yeah, they could've done it, all right. They are the most neurotic people I have ever met."

"Which of them in particular?"

"All of them. *Artists.*" She waved her arms expansively to include every artist in the universe in her condemnation. "I've only been at the Arts Council three months, and I'm already thinking of switching my major from arts administration. I just can't deal with these people. Every time they come in the office, it's instant crisis. They're always totally freaking out about this grant, that exhibition, this production, whatever." She rolled her eyes, exasperated. "Everything people say about artists is true. *They're all crazy.*"

After my recent encounter with the grant panel at Madeline's, I was inclined to agree. But I felt obligated to defend the artists of the universe, especially since I was one of them, or at least had been until recently, and hopefully would be again. "Artists aren't crazy. They're just poor."

Molly gave me a dismissive shrug. "That's just crap, and you know it." Man, this was a no-nonsense kind of girl; her boyfriends better watch their asses. "Look, I still don't get it. I don't mean to be rude, and I do hope you find out who killed the guy, but how exactly can I help you? I'm really nervous about you being here," she went on, flicking a glance at her boarded-up window. "What if someone followed you?"

She was right. I was putting her in danger.

Whoever tossed that brick through her window might not stop there.

"Molly," I said, "think back to early Monday morning at the Arts Council. Was there anyone who had the opportunity to poison The Penn's coffee?"

She frowned, thinking. The seconds ticked away. Then she answered, "Yes."

My heart jumped. At last, I would learn who killed Donald Penn. "Who?"

"Anyone," she shrugged. "First I made the coffee,

then I went out to the Xerox store to pick up some stuff for the panel. Donald came in and got his coffee before I came back."

I groaned. "And you didn't lock the door when you went out?"

"No. Anyone could have snuck in and poisoned the coffee while I was gone, no problem."

I found a straw to grasp at. "It had to be somebody who knew it was Penn's coffee."

"Sure, but everybody knew. They all made jokes about it." Suddenly Molly shuddered.

"What is it?"

"I thought Gretchen and I were just being nice to the guy. She never told me I was making him coffee because he was *blackmailing* her. That's so creepy."

I nodded sympathetically, then got back to business. "Were you expecting someone that morning? Any appointments?"

"No, but people came in and out all the time."

"Like who?"

She thought about it, and a network of worry wrinkles formed on her forehead. "All kinds of people—panelists, artists, building contractors—it was like Grand Central Station in there sometimes." She slapped her hand angrily on the bed, but I had a feeling she was really more hurt than angry. "Damn it, I'm gonna call Gretchen and tell her I'm quitting. She should have told me the truth. I trusted her."

"I don't think you should call Gretchen right now," I said.

"Why not? I'm quitting that dumb job. It's just an internship anyway."

"Well, be careful what you say to her." Molly stared at me. "Gretchen might be the one who threw that brick in your window. She might even be the murderer."

Molly tried to laugh, but it came out sounding hysterical. "Come on. Gretchen? A murderer?"

"Why not? She's the one who warned you to shut up about the application, right?"

"Yeah, but it wasn't just her."

"Who else?"

"Well, like my dad . . ." Suddenly Molly faltered. Her eyes avoided mine.

I prodded her. "Your dad?"

She nodded slowly. "Yeah. He's going out with Bonnie."

"Really?" *Virgil and Bonnie?*

My mind flashed on muscle-bound Bonnie and fat Virgil humping each other. Not a pretty picture. Well, I guess that was one way to get someone to invest in your video.

Molly's eyes opened wide, full of pain. "I thought my dad was trying to keep me out of trouble. But maybe he was really trying to keep *Bonnie* out of trouble."

Suddenly Molly's whole body gave a start. "You don't think *my dad* threw that brick at me, do you?"

I didn't know, so I didn't say anything. There was no question, Bonnie was *desperate* not to lose that grant. So yeah, the brick thrower could have been her, or Molly's dad, or both of them together.

And it was possible Bonnie killed The Penn without Virgil knowing it, and now she was manipulating Virgil.

Molly drew up her knees, put her head on them, and rocked back and forth. All this fear and betrayal was turning her catatonic.

"Molly, it's going to be okay," I finally said, realizing even as I said it how lame it sounded.

She scowled at me, disgusted. "How the hell do *you* know?"

She was right. I didn't. I awkwardly stood up to leave . . . and banged my toe against something hard on the floor. Which was odd, because there was nothing down there except a copy of *The Feminine Mystique.* A heavy book, it's true, but not something you'd expect to stub your toe on. Out of curiosity I stooped down and lifted the book out of the way. Underneath it was a mottled red and white brick.

I picked the brick up. "This is the one?"

Molly nodded. "If anybody tries to break in, I'm gonna hit 'em with it. Listen, Mr. Burns—"

"Call me Jacob," I said, but she went right on, not acknowledging my interruption. "When you leave, could you go out the back door? I don't want anyone to see you."

Finally, something to smile about. This was like my younger days, when I'd have to sneak out of girls' dorms at Mount Holyoke in the early morning before the dorm mothers woke up.

Molly frowned, upset. "What's so funny? You think I'm silly for being scared?"

I looked away from her, embarrassed, and set the brick back down on the floor. "I'm sorry. There's nothing silly about it. I'll go out the back door."

So I did.

And ran straight into the mayor.

24

"What are *you* doing here?" the mayor asked.

"What are *you* doing here?" I countered.

The mayor gave me a toothy Tom Cruise grin. "Same thing as you, I guess, you old sly dog. At least *I'm* not married."

I didn't buy his routine for a second. "Are you here to see Molly Otis?"

"Gentlemen don't tell," the mayor said with a wink.

I wasn't sure what he was here for, but I seriously doubted he was up to any good. Feeling a guilty need to protect little five-foot-two Molly, especially since I seemed to be exposing her to danger every time I talked to her, I stepped up so close to the mayor I could see where his teeth had been capped. "Mr. Mayor, if you threaten Molly in any way whatsoever—"

He stepped back with a surprised look. "*Threaten* her? I have no intention of threatening anybody. I'm here to offer her a summer job."

Now it was my turn to look surprised. "A what?"

"A summer job. Gretchen says she's terrific. And a local girl, too—good politics." The Cruise grin came back.

But I still didn't buy it. While he was busy grinning, I was busy thinking, and now I felt pretty sure I had the mayor figured out. "What's the matter, Harry? You scared she heard something she wasn't supposed to hear? So you and Gretchen figured it might get her to keep quiet, if you handed her a cushy job?"

The mayor's face hardened. "Burns, you got something you're trying to say?"

"I guess you figured throwing a brick at her might not be enough to shut her up. Right, Harry?"

The perfect eyebrows shot up. "What's this about throwing a brick?"

I eyed him closely. I read an article in the *National Enquirer* once: "Seven Sure Ways to Tell if He's Lying." Unfortunately, I can never remember any of them.

"Harry, don't play games with me," I said sneeringly. "I know all about your fifty-grand sweetheart deal with Gretchen. I imagine the cops would want to know about it, too."

The mayor didn't bat an eye. "And you've got some evidence, I suppose? The cops won't think you're just some half-baked Hollywood screenwriter?"

He was right, of course, but I didn't bat an eye either; damn it, I was going to nail this yuppie politician scum. Since the best defense is a good offense, I decided to be as offensive as possible. "Where were you on Monday morning of this week?"

The mayor shook his perfectly coifed head, amused. "What are you accusing me of now?"

"Poisoning Donald Penn."

He exploded into guffaws. "I can't wait to see your movie. What a great imagination!"

I had to admit, it sounded pretty preposterous to me, too. But you never get anywhere in this world by admitting self-doubt. "It had to be you. The Arts Council people are all a bunch of crackpot artists, not killers. And no one at Madeline's had enough motive. So that leaves you. You're the only other person who was giving him free coffee."

"Oh, is that so? What about your wife's little friend?"

What? "Who?"

Tom Cruise came back again, but with a sarcastic edge this time. "Judy Demarest. At the *Daily Saratogian*. What, your wife didn't share that little detail?"

I found my voice. "Why was Judy giving him coffee?"

His eyes twinkled meanly. "Why don't you ask *her?*"

Yeah, sure. If I interrogated Judy, my wife would kill me . . . and the mayor knew it. Typical politician: not too bright maybe, but clever as hell.

I fought back against his Tom Cruise teeth with my most evil Jack Nicholson leer. "Listen, pal, evidence or not, all I have to do is go public with this and I wreck your political career. And if you don't answer my questions, that's exactly what I intend to do."

"I hear Andrea's up for tenure next year," the mayor said, in a seemingly total non sequitur.

"So what?"

"So I happen to be a very close friend of her college president," the mayor said, his leer out-Nicholsoning mine.

He didn't say anything more. He didn't have to.

If the mayor pulled some strings and got my wife's tenure denied, her career was up the creek. She'd go back to teaching adjunct courses for chicken feed. To get a decent job teaching college English these days, you have to have at least two or three Ph.D.'s, publish at least nine or ten books, and most difficult of all, take literary deconstruction seriously.

No question, the mayor had found my weakness. I was screwed. I wondered, was he about to pull some similar sort of scam on Molly?

"Out of the way," the mayor said triumphantly, as he stepped around me toward Molly's dorm.

What I did next was stupid, I guess.

I mean, logically speaking, I had no right to jeopardize my wife's career.

And I had no right to punch the mayor smack in the middle of his perfect nose.

And I definitely had no right whatsoever to kick him in the balls and leave him writhing on the doorstep.

But I did it anyway.

And, God, did it feel great. Not bad for a sensitive artist type, I thought proudly.

As I walked cheerfully away, it occurred to me that I had just added assault and battery to the growing list of major felonies I'd committed in the past six days.

Well, hell, you only live once.

William Goldman, the screenwriter of *Butch Cassidy and the Sundance Kid, All the President's Men,* and about a million other hits, as well as a million flops, has a famous saying about Hollywood: "No one knows anything."

Which, I suppose, is why everyone out there is always nodding knowingly.

As I drove back down Broadway, I reflected that this saying was turning out to be true of Saratoga Springs as well. No one in town, from the mayor on down, knew how much dirt Molly or I really had on them. In some ways that had been working to our advantage: Molly was being bribed with a cushy summer job, I had been propositioned by Saratoga's answer to Pamela Anderson, and neither one of us had been killed.

Yet.

When I got home, I found Andrea and the kids in the back yard playing a complex game of their own invention called "baseball-hockey." I've never managed to understand the rules, but if it keeps both Gretzky and Babe Ruth happy, then I'm happy. I decided now was not the ideal time to confront my wife about Judy. Of course, the ideal time would be never.

The phone rang as soon as I came inside. I grabbed it, but before I could even say hello, my agent shouted into my ear, "Did you send me the contract yet?"

Oh phooey, I'd totally forgotten. I'd brought it with me in the car, planning to hit the P.O. after Madeline's, but then I got sidetracked.

Andrew interpreted my telephone silence correctly. "Goddamn it, you fishmeal-for-brains," he roared, "these people are in a fucking hurry to get moving already and they're not like most producers, they won't do anything without a signed contract *in hand*, they've been burned on verbal agreements before—"

"Don't worry, big guy," I lied, "I sent it this morning."

"You did?"

"Of course." I figured I wasn't *really* lying, since I'd be hitting the P.O. as soon as I got off the phone. Unfortunately, by the time Andrew finished haranguing me about various details it was already past noon and the P.O. was closed. I called Federal Express in Saratoga, but they were closed, too. Ah, the joys of small-town life.

I could have driven fifty-five minutes to the P.O. or the FedEx office in Albany, but Gretzky was in the kitchen with me now, tugging at my shirt to make me stand up. "Daddy, time to go! Daddy, come on!" I had promised to take him, Babe Ruth, and Andrea to the Big Game today. Our team, the Adirondack Red Wings, was playing the Syracuse Crunch in the final and deciding game of the American Hockey League playoffs. Now was no time for worrying about minor matters like murders or $750,000 movie deals. There was a hockey championship at stake here.

Besides, FedEx in Saratoga would be open from nine

to twelve tomorrow, and I'd send the contract then. That was soon enough. No need to spend my entire Saturday afternoon driving all over upstate like a crazed chicken. Hollywood agents and producers are always trying to bum rush you into a loony, panicked state, because it makes them feel powerful. You can't fall for their shit, I told myself.

Of course, it doesn't take a degree in psychology to know I was really acting out my ambivalence about mutant beetles.

So Andrea, the kids, and I piled into the Camry and drove north to Glens Falls, the blue-collar town where Andrea teaches. Glens Falls was rocking with Red Wing fans, and parking took a good twenty minutes—which may not sound like much if you're from the big city, but in our part of the world it's practically unheard of. By the time we got to our seats the game was already two minutes old, the crowd noise was deafening, and the joint was so packed they weren't even selling standing room anymore.

It was an exciting first period, with the Red Wing goalie, a burly guy named Wenders, foiling the Crunch attack time after time. Meanwhile the Red Wings made good on a rare breakaway opportunity to take the lead, 1–0. Gretzky was so excited he spent the entire period bouncing up and down, while Babe Ruth and Andrea chattered away happily and chanted, "Munch the Crunch for lunch!"

But I had trouble relaxing. I had spotted Judy up in the press box, covering the game for the *Daily Saratogian*. She could have sent someone else, but she loved hockey almost as much as bowling. I kept glancing up at her and wondering how the hell I was going to deal with her and Andrea. When the buzzer sounded, I was relieved that Andrea and the kids left to buy provisions, so I could have time to myself to think.

My thinking time didn't last long, though. Someone broke in with a "Hi, Jacob," and when I looked up, it was Judy. "Great game, huh? Where's Andrea?"

I stared at her, my mouth open, wondering where to begin. "What's the matter?" Judy frowned.

My favorite writing teacher back in college always used to say, "When in doubt, tell the truth." So I did. "I understand Donald Penn was blackmailing you," I told her.

Judy's eyes darted back and forth as she thought about denying it. But then her shoulders fell and she sank into an empty seat. "Damn, damn, damn," she said. "How'd you find out?"

"The mayor."

"Bastard."

"Judy, I don't want to make this any harder than it is, but I need to know."

"Why?"

"Because I do."

She looked at me curiously. "I figured the whole thing was in Penn's book."

I didn't answer directly. "I'd like to hear it from you."

Judy glowered at me, then shook her head and turned away. "Stupid. This whole thing is so stupid." She sat and stared silently out at the ice. The Zamboni machine was going around and around in its slow circuitous path, and Judy seemed mesmerized. Just when I thought she had forgotten all about me, or had decided to stonewall me, she began to speak.

"I didn't mean for it to happen. It just did. I got sucked in." She turned to me with an imploring look. "It wasn't *extortion.* I don't even know if it was really *bribery.*" Her hands were squeezed tightly together. "It started so innocently. I was up in Hudson Falls one day, and I happened to notice the new City Hall there was being built by Kane Construction Company—you know, the mayor's company. And I happened to mention it to the person I was with, and it turns out the mayor's company had been awarded two other municipal building contracts in Hudson Falls recently. So I was kind of wondering, as I was driving home, why the Hudson Falls contracts went to a Saratoga Springs company, I mean, they're an hour north of here. There must be companies more close by that'll do it cheaper."

As she told this part of the story, Judy's hands flew apart and her eyes brightened with excitement. "And then, when I got to my desk that day, there's a press release announcing that the construction contract for the new Saratoga Arts Center has been awarded to the Hudson Falls Building and Renovation Company. So I get this funny feeling, and I call up my friend in Hudson Falls, and lo and behold, he tells me that Hudson Falls B and R is owned by the *brother* of the *mayor* of Hudson Falls. So I put two and two together, and it looks to me like the two mayors are trading kickbacks back and forth, with a little help from their friends. So I call up the three other construction companies that bid on the Arts Center job, and one of them tells me he was pretty suspicious himself of the way the bidding was handled, but never said anything because it's such a small town and he didn't want to make waves. So I promise him anonymity and he brings over the initial Request for Proposals on the job, along with some memos and statistics and so on, we go over them, and it looks to me like, yeah, we got something here. So I call up the mayor. Of Saratoga."

Here Judy's shoulders slumped, and once again she gazed out at the Zamboni. "So what happened?" I pushed her.

With effort, and haltingly, she continued. "He said

he was busy. But we made an appointment for the following Tuesday. Then, on Monday, the Literacy Volunteers receives a check in the mail. Unsolicited. From the mayor. A donation—for fifteen thousand dollars. Next day, I go to meet him, like we'd planned. Only he doesn't show up."

The Zamboni was almost done. "Then what?"

Judy closed her eyes. "Nothing. I just forgot about the whole thing." She opened them again and looked at me, begging for understanding. "I couldn't help myself. You know how I feel about the Literacy Volunteers. That's my baby. And we're always *broke.* I figured the mayor's money would keep us from going bankrupt until we can stay alive on our own. Is that so horrible? I mean, what's more important—uncovering yet another sleazy political deal, or teaching kids how to read?" She waited for an answer, and when she didn't get one, threw up her hands as if surrendering. "That's it, Jacob. That's the whole story."

Not quite. "How did Penn find out?"

Judy's eyes suddenly flamed with anger. "The little shit. Always pretending he was writing, but half the time he was just eavesdropping. One night after bowling me and Andrea are at Madeline's, and there's no one else in the back room except for Penn, and I figure he's just a harmless nutcase. So like an idiot I start telling Andrea about this whole kickback and donation thing. Next day, Penn walks into my office at the *Saratogian.* Says if I don't make him coffee every morning, he'll tell everyone the mayor bribed me into shutting up." Judy sighed unhappily and shook her head. "Jesus, I can't believe I got into this mess. This is something they never taught in journalism school."

She eyed me, hoping for a smile. Out on the ice the Red Wing mascot was dancing around to the Village People song "YMCA," while the fans applauded. How did the gay anthem of the late 70s become so popular at 90s sporting events? It was interesting that my wife never told me any of this stuff about Judy. I was torn between admiring her loyalty to her friend and being pissed off that she hadn't told me. The buzzer sounded, announcing that the second period was about to start.

"Listen, Jacob, I have to go back to the press box," Judy said, with a tentative smile. "You guys can come on up, if you want."

"Just one more thing."

"What?"

"Please don't take this the wrong way, but where were you last Monday morning?"

"Last Monday morning?"

"The morning Penn died."

She stared at me, openmouthed, then said, "'Don't take this the wrong way'? What other way is there to take it?"

Good question. I was still trying to come up with an answer when Judy started walking away. Oh God, Andrea would throw a fit when she heard about this. "Judy, hey!" I called out after her. "Hey, Judy!"

But she kept right on going.

25

Just at that moment Andrea appeared from the other direction, loaded down with Gretzky, Ruth, pizza, hot dogs, popcorn, and various sodas. She saw her friend hurrying off through the crowd and called, "Judy!" But Judy didn't hear her, or didn't want to. Andrea eyed me curiously. "Is everything okay? Judy looked upset."

I shrugged nonchalantly. "No, she's fine," I lied. When in doubt, lie. "She invited us up to the press box."

"Cool, let's go. That sounds like fun."

Sure, great fun. A pleasant social evening with my wife's best friend, whom I had just basically accused of murder. "You go, honey. I'm happy here." To change the subject, I turned to Gretzky and Babe Ruth and asked, "How's the grub?"

"Mmf," Babe Ruth answered, his mouth full of hot dog. The original Babe once missed half a season because he ate too many hot dogs at one sitting. At the rate my Babe was going, it looked like the same thing might happen to him.

Meanwhile Gretzky was wiggling his butt and hopping up and down as he ate, doing what Andrea and I called "the peepee dance." Andrea bit her lip, frustrated, and told me, "Maybe you can get him to go to the bathroom. I couldn't."

"Hockey players don't make peepee!" Gretzky shouted between bites. I thought about picking him up and carrying him by force to the men's room, but it was four sections away and two floors down, and he'd be kicking and screaming the whole way. Ugh. Even if I didn't get arrested for child abuse, my lower back would spend the rest of the week complaining. Ah well, maybe when his bladder couldn't take it anymore, he'd finally come to his senses.

But then again, maybe not. Gretzky squiggled and squirmed like a crazed amoeba for the next hour and a half, but through it all he held tight to his dream: be just like a real hockey player and never make peepee again. You had to respect the little guy's determination.

Andrea went up to the press box with Babe Ruth for a while, and when she came back I scanned her face for a sign that Judy had told her about our conversation. But so far, I guess, Judy was staying mum.

Out on the ice, the second and third periods were even more rousing than the first, with Wenders continuing to work wonders in the Red Wing goal, and the Red Wing offense madly swarming the Crunch goal whenever there was even the remotest possibility of a score. Wenders was unable to shut the door entirely, but when the final buzzer sounded, the Red Wings had triumphed 3–2. We were now the official American Hockey League *champions.*

I was thrilled. Growing up in Boston and rooting for the Red Sox, I had reached middle age without my team ever winning a championship. But here my kids were only three and five years old, and they already had a championship under their belts. Maybe it was a sign their lives would be easier than mine.

My joy would have been complete if only Gretzky weren't so obviously uncomfortable, jumping up and down like a jack-in-the-box. And I was still feeling pretty jumpy myself, about the whole Judy thing. I wanted to go home, put the kids to bed, then sit down with Andrea and as gently as possible break the news that I suspected her bowling buddy of murder.

But first the kids insisted on going down to the ice and celebrating. The ecstatic Red Wings and their fans were filling the rink, cheering, clapping, and singing "We Are the Champions." Minor league sports at its best. On the ice Gretzky's jumping and wiggling fit right in; it looked like he was dancing to the song. He and Babe Ruth ran to the Red Wings goal and started playing baseball-hockey with each other.

I noticed Wenders signing autographs nearby. Minus his goalie mask he was odd-looking, scary even. With a pile of shaggy black hair hanging over thick eyebrows and a low sloping forehead, he resembled a Cro-Magnon Man. But he was signing autographs patiently even though he must have been exhausted, and there was a kind look in his eyes, and suddenly I got an idea. I left Andrea behind and squeezed my way to the front of the crowd that was surrounding him. "Uh, Mr. Wenders."

"Yeah," he said, without looking at me, as he signed a little girl's Red Wings cap.

"I have a rather strange request."

Now he looked up. "The last guy who said that wanted me to autograph his wife's breasts."

The other fans tittered.

"No, it's not that," I assured him. "This request is even stranger."

Wenders's caveman brows lifted all the way up his forehead when I explained what I wanted him to do.

"You're right," he said after I finished. "That *is* stranger."

"It would mean a lot to me."

"I can imagine." Wenders turned to the other fans and excused himself, then went with me to find Gretzky. Andrea watched us, wondering what the hell was going on.

Gretzky stopped his baseball-hockey game and gazed upward in awe as Wenders—*a real hockey player*—walked over to him. He was so starstruck, he even stopped wiggling.

"So you're Gretzky," Wenders greeted him. "I hear you're an awesome hockey player." He held out a huge, hairy hand, and after staring at it for a while, Gretzky solemnly lifted up his own little hand. They shook.

Then Wenders stooped down to get on Gretzky's level. "Gretzky, there's something I think you ought to know."

He paused, making sure he had the kid's full attention. Then he dropped his bombshell. "Hockey players actually *do* make peepee," Wenders said gravely.

Gretzky stared at him, astonished.

"It's true. We make peepee between periods, when the Zamboni is out there. I *always* make peepee, because then I play better. It's easier to concentrate."

The kid was wide-eyed. I only hoped Wenders's message was getting through.

"Now Gretzky, I have to go. So take care of yourself, buddy. And remember: If you want to be an even better hockey player than you already are, be sure to make peepee."

As he shook Gretzky's hand again and turned to leave, Babe Ruth called out to him excitedly, "Hey, Mr. Goalie, you know what? I make peepee, too!"

I watched Wenders fight back the urge to laugh. Amazingly, he succeeded. I wondered if the guy would be interested in doing babysitting during the offseason. Whatever he might charge, he was worth it.

As Wenders discussed peepee with Babe Ruth, I caught Andrea's eye. Then we both looked over at Gretzky.

The Great One's brow was furrowed in deep thought. He seemed to be trying to puzzle something out, like Einstein on the brink of relativity. Finally he turned to me. "Daddy," he said.

"Yes?"

"I have to make peepee."

Halle-fucking-lujah! I felt like whooping with glee, but I didn't want to scare him into reconsidering. "Okay," I said with studied casualness, "let's go."

So we went to the bathroom together, and Gretzky pulled down his pants. "I'm going to be a champion hockey player when I grow up," he told me as an ocean of peepee poured out of him.

"You sure are," I said, and hugged him.

We hit Manhattan-style traffic getting out of Glens Falls, but we were all feeling so terrific no one complained. Andrea started singing songs from *Oklahoma!* and the kids joined in. Between songs, she squeezed my arm and whispered, "I love you." The best way to a woman's heart: toilet train her children.

Andrea was feeling so good about me right now, maybe I could bring up Judy without us getting into a big argument. I tried to think of some opening lines. "Oh, honey, by the way, you won't be upset if I investigate your best friend for murder, will you?"

I waited for the kids to fall asleep. It was only 7:30, but they'd had such a full day, I figured they'd be down for the count pretty soon. And sure enough, right in the middle of the chorus about the bright golden haze in the meadow, they started snoring. We were back in Saratoga now, driving up Van Dam Street. Andrea put her hand on my thigh and gazed at me, full of love. Now or never, I thought. I cleared my throat. "Andrea?"

"Yes, beautiful sweetheart?" she cooed, her hand moving higher.

"There's something we need to talk about."

"Okay, baby, let's talk." But the way her hand was reaching into my pants made me think she wasn't exactly in the mood for talking.

"Listen, it's really important."

Andrea frowned and withdrew her hand. "What is it?"

"Well, uh . . ." I stuttered as I turned onto Pearl Street, and then stopped. Stopped talking and stopped the car too, with a sudden screech.

"What's wrong?" Andrea asked in alarm.

I didn't answer.

At the corner of Pearl and Van Dam was the Shoeshine and a Smile Theater School, with a sign out front: "THE DEVIL COMES TO TOWN—TONIGHT—8:00." Next to the sign several young girls were hanging out, all decked out in identical costumes for tonight's show. Standing behind them, talking on a portable phone, was Bonnie. Evidently she'd be performing tonight too, because she wore the same costume they did.

Very interesting costume.

Bonnie and the girls were dressed in silver from head to toe. From their silver horns and silver masks . . .

. . . right on down to their *silver high-heeled shoes.*

"Honey, are you okay?" Andrea asked fearfully. I

stared out at Bonnie and those shoes. It didn't make sense—or did it?

What if Bonnie wore her costume shoes to Madeline's one night, just for kicks, and then found out that my house was empty—

Andrea interrupted, touching my forehead. "What is it, the concussion? Does your head hurt?"

"No," I said, and started up the car again.

"Then what is it? What did you want to talk to me about?"

Good question. Not about Judy anymore. But I wasn't ready to share my suspicions about Bonnie either. I needed to get my head straight—if that was possible. Andrea got panicky. "Jacob, say something."

I forced a smile. "Sorry, honey, I was just thinking about how much I love you."

That line usually works, but this time Andrea eyed me skeptically. I tried again. "It's true. I was just so overwhelmed by sudden love for you, I had to pull over."

Andrea rolled her eyes. "You are so full of shit." But when I reached down and put her hand back on my thigh, things began happening that convinced her I really *was* thinking about her. In fact, thinking pretty hard.

As soon as we got home and carried the sleeping kids to bed, Andrea and I went to bed, too. We did some deep thinking for a while and came to some enjoyable conclusions, after which Andrea closed her eyes and instantly fell fast asleep.

I closed my eyes too, but I was far from sleeping. Those silver high-heeled shoes were dancing in my mind. It seemed clear to me that The Penn and his magnum opus had gotten Bonnie so scared and angry that she broke into my house.

Had she also been scared and angry enough to murder The Penn?

I lay there and theorized for as long as I could stand it before I slipped out of bed, grateful that Andrea had gotten so used to my nocturnal comings and goings that she slept right through them. Then I jumped in the car and drove off through the night to the Shoeshine and a Smile Theater School.

26

I don't know who or what I expected to find there. When I pulled up across the street from the school it was already past 10:30, and the place was deserted.

I sat in my Camry and surveyed the darkened building. Nice view, but I wouldn't get anywhere by just sitting there. I grabbed my flashlight from the glove compartment, planning to smash the window by the front door and break in. Hey, maybe I'd get lucky and find a bottle with a big XXX on the front along with Bonnie's fingerprints.

But when I sneaked through the shadows to the front door, I decided not to break in after all. Mainly because the door wasn't locked. In the excitement of opening night, someone had apparently forgotten to lock up. So I waltzed on inside with my flashlight and commenced operations.

First I checked out the desk in Bonnie's office, where I found a bunch of financial files. The school had failed to turn a profit last year for the first time in eight years; but based on my limited accounting expertise, everything seemed on the up and up.

I kept on searching. Tucked away at the back of a drawer I found a paperback book titled *In the Cockpit of the Plane: Women's Sexual Fantasies.* Hmm. I wished I had time to read it.

Behind the book were two other interesting items: a

packet of hypodermic needles, and a prescription. Was Bonnie diabetic? Unfortunately the prescription was in that standard handwriting they teach you in med school, so I couldn't understand a word.

Fascinating stuff. But I wasn't finding any files labeled "Donald Penn" or "Murder" or anything convenient like that.

I went in the storeroom and discovered Xerox paper and cleaning supplies. But no gasoline for committing arson with, no books describing how committing homicide could be a positive spiritual experience.

Heading through the double doors into the darkened auditorium, I shone my flashlight over the empty seats and then the stage itself. Bonnie had created a nifty set. Stage left, there were red and orange flames rising up out of a deep pit. This must be good old hell, home of the silver-tongued devil himself . . . or *her*self. Stage right, fluffy white clouds were hovering in the air above two tire swings, also painted white. That must be heaven. At center stage was the brick facade of a house—I guess this was where the regular mortals hung out.

It was all very sweet, but since I wasn't there to critique set designs, I left the auditorium and was already walking down the hallway when suddenly a bell went off in my head. I turned around and ran back inside the auditorium, tripping over a couple of dark steps and then vaulting onstage. I shone my light on the house facade and stared at the bricks.

They were mottled, red and white.

The *exact same type of brick* someone had thrown through Molly Otis's window.

My hand trembled with excitement as I felt the brick's surface. So now I had evidence linking Bonnie to the burglary *and* the death threat against Molly. Bonnie had always been intense as hell—but now she was turning destructive.

Why?

The answer came to me in a rush. *Because she was broke and desperate.* Her school was losing money, and she was going nuts trying to raise funds for that boxing video. But The Penn was blackmailing her, threatening to expose her unethical little grant, smear her name, and scare off any other investors.

And above all this, I realized, Bonnie was facing the overwhelming reality that she was getting older, like me, middle age looming like some horrible hulking Godzilla, but Bonnie's still fighting, she still has desperate dreams of fame and fortune, and it's even looking like maybe they'll finally come true, she's actually getting some money together for what she sees as her huge breakthrough project . . . but then, of all the bizarre, horrible things, some total worthless louse, some two-bit blackmailer, Donald Fucking Penn, threatens to rob her of her one last shot at the rainbow, forcing her to resign herself once and for all to a lifetime of endlessly hustling theater gigs on a shoeshine and a smile, struggling to make ends meet . . .

Was raging midlife crisis enough motive to kill someone?

From stage right came a sudden noise. Someone opening a door. I froze.

As if that would keep whoever it was from seeing me, standing there center stage with a lit flashlight in my hand.

"Who's there?" said a woman's edgy, fearful voice.

It was Bonnie.

"Oh hi, Bonnie," I replied, inanely cheerful, as if I'd just dropped in for tea.

"Jacob? Is that you?"

"Uh, yeah." I shone the flashlight on her, thinking in

some mixed up way that it might help her see me better. It didn't, of course, but I did get a good view of Bonnie squinting against the light . . . and holding a silver pitchfork in her hand.

She lifted the pitchfork to shield her eyes. "Oh, sorry," I apologized, and shone the flashlight on my own face, for what reason I'm not sure. Then I felt silly doing that and pointed the light down at the floor. I gave Bonnie a nervous smile, which made no sense because she couldn't even see my face anymore. This was too weird. Here I'd finally caught the murderer, or thought I had, and the main thing I was feeling was embarrassed.

No, not the main thing. Mainly I was hoping that Bonnie's pitchfork, which I couldn't see in the darkness now, was papier-mâché instead of the real deal.

"What are you doing here?" Bonnie asked. Since I couldn't see her face either, I couldn't tell if she was merely bewildered or filled with murderous rage.

"Great show, Bonnie," I said as I backed away from her, but trying to go slowly so she wouldn't notice. "Really enjoyed it."

"I didn't see you in the audience."

"I was in the back."

"Jacob, what the fuck is going on?"

I backed up some more, and Bonnie started toward me. Not that I saw her, but I heard her footsteps—and saw her pitchfork prongs gleaming in the shadows as she called out, *"Goddamn you, Jake, what the hell are you trying to do to me?!"*

Tapping some hitherto unknown reservoir of either panic, courage, or total stupidity, I stunned myself by shouting into the darkness, "That was your shoe in our backyard, wasn't it?!"

Bonnie's footsteps stopped. She was probably

equally stunned. Sensing I had the advantage, I pressed on. "And you threw that brick at Molly Otis!"

From the darkness, I heard a low growl. Then Bonnie snarled, "So what? She deserved it! The little bitch was gonna get us all in trouble!"

"And did I deserve to be burglarized?"

"I *had* to do that. I was just protecting myself from Penn's stupid book!"

Some silver-tongued devil inside me urged me on. By God, I would get the whole truth at last. *"And is that why you killed him?"*

My words hung there in the air. Would Bonnie try to deny it?

No. Instead she shouted, "You bastard! You *both* deserve to die!"

And then suddenly she leapt at me.

I sensed her more than saw her, and dodged wildly to my left. I saw the glint of the pitchfork as it went past me, then heard it hit the stage with a loud metallic clang. Shit—definitely not papier-mâché.

Strange guttural noises were coming from Bonnie's throat, like she was foaming at the mouth. As I dodged, the last piece of the Bonnie puzzle came to me: *steroids.* That's what the needles were for—and that's why Bonnie's natural aggressiveness was spinning crazily out of control.

Bonnie had been so sick of being a struggling artist, and so eager to make it big in boxing, that she pumped herself full of toxic levels of weird shit until she had turned herself into Frankenstein's monster.

And now this lunatic was trying to kill me. "What did I ever do to you?!" she was screaming. "Why are you assholes *crucifying* me?! It was just *two thousand dollars*!" I would have pointed out that awarding herself two thousand bucks was the least of her crimes, except it didn't seem like she'd be interested in my input. Besides, I was too busy running like mad away from her.

But unfortunately, I'd forgotten all about the hell at stage left. I fell right in. The pit was about five feet deep and I killed my right ankle when I landed, then my head smashed into the side wall. I got an instant wave of nausea, and felt myself starting to pass out. I sank to the bottom of the pit, down for the count.

The sound of Bonnie's pitchfork shocked me back into full consciousness. Hearing three sharp metal prongs jab into the floor right next to your face will do that to you. I rolled to the other side of the pit. But my flashlight was down there in hell with me, still turned on, and pointing right at the spot I had just rolled to. Now Bonnie could see exactly where I was, even though I still couldn't see her. She charged around the pit and thrust the pitchfork straight at me.

I saw a silver prong glittering in a stray beam from the flashlight and rolled away at the last moment. The prongs landed inches from my left shoulder, where my heart had been moments before. I quickly grabbed for the flashlight and turned it off.

Bereft of light, Bonnie made random vicious stabs into the pit. Another struggling artist gone berserk; even worse than disgruntled post office employees. Bonnie was so frenzied, I'll bet she barely knew who I was anymore. I wasn't Jacob Burns; I was all of the stupid jerks who for twenty years had failed to recognize her greatness as an artist.

And judging by the number of stabs, there had been a lot of stupid jerks.

I stilled my breathing and kept as quiet as I could, as I crouched down low and dodged from side to side, keeping my eyes on those shadowy silver glints, wishing I'd eaten my carrots like my mother always told me to.

But maybe I could somehow get this female Mike Tyson to listen to reason. "Bonnie, stop!" I called out between dodges. "You're only making it worse!"

In one way, my plea was effective: It told Bonnie exactly where I was. With a throaty yell she swung the pitchfork at my head. I jumped backward, but the side of the prongs hit me flush in the forehead. I screamed. Sparks of agony flew through my entire body at what seemed like the speed of light.

I staggered to the far side of hell, away from Bonnie, put my hands against the edge, and tried to hoist myself out. But she heard what I was doing and ran around the pit toward me. She swung her pitchfork with another low yell and this time my arms got hit. I toppled back into the pit, landing on my twisted ankle.

I lay on the floor moaning. Bonnie's shadow loomed over me. I was just about finished and we both knew it. I saw the pitchfork glitter as she lifted it up, then saw it streak downward as she plunged it at my face.

Desperately, I rolled away. The pitchfork clanged against the floor. Without thinking, I kicked out wildly at the silver glints with my damaged leg.

Somehow I connected, and Bonnie wasn't ready for it. The pitchfork slipped out of her hand and clattered to the floor of the pit. I dove and grabbed it.

"Give me that!" Bonnie screamed. "Give it back!"

Yeah, right. I struggled up, waving the weapon around in her general direction. "Back off, Bonnie! Back off!"

But she didn't. She went on screaming and feinting for the pitchfork. I started to lose it again, feeling tidal waves of nausea coming on.

So I stabbed her.

In the arm, just as she was taking a swing at me. I felt the pitchfork entering her flesh. I didn't know how far it went in, but it was far enough that she howled in pain and finally backed off.

I seized the moment and hoisted myself out of hell. Because I couldn't put pressure on my messed-up ankle, I needed to use both hands to get myself out of there. That meant I had to leave the pitchfork behind. If Bonnie just jumped in the pit and grabbed the pitchfork, then came after me, I'd be dead for sure.

But luckily, Bonnie was too busy howling. I dashed offstage, dragging my leg behind me, and found the side door. Somehow I made it into my car and back home.

I looked in on Andrea, who was still snoring away happily, then called 911 and left an anonymous tip about a woman at the Shoeshine and a Smile Theater School who might need medical assistance. I figured she probably did need assistance; and more important, if a cop or EMT showed up at her door, she'd be less likely to come over to my house and start pitchforking me all over again.

Then I attempted to call my cop friend Dave to tell him about Bonnie, but in my brain-damaged state I'd forgotten again what kind of fish he was. Halibut? Hammerhead? I hobbled across the street to his house and rang his bell repeatedly, to no avail. He didn't have a girlfriend that I knew of, he wasn't working nights, and he hadn't said anything about going away for the weekend . . . so where was he?

I went home and thought about calling the police station, but Dave was the only cop I knew. What would I say to some stranger on the phone? The truth was, all I really had on Bonnie was a similar shoe and a similar brick—nothing tying her directly into the murder. Of course, I also had the fact she went nutso on me tonight, but nobody else had witnessed that.

And yeah, I had a motive too, but would it be enough to convince the cops?

This was infuriating. A horrible thought kept running through my head: Bonnie Engels is the murderer.

But who the hell will ever believe me?

I was still the only one who even believed that Penn had been murdered—except for the murderer herself, of course. Bottom line, Penn was a bum, a derelict, a troublemaker, not the kind of guy who'd make number one on the cops' To Do list. I'd need to get more evidence somehow if I ever expected them to reopen his case and nail Bonnie. And what's more, I needed it fast—before those mutant beetles took over my life.

I decided the best thing to do was wait until Dave came home from his movie or barhopping or whatever and get him to help me. First I called the Saratoga Hospital and learned that, yes, a woman named Bonnie Engels with a heavily bleeding arm had just come into the emergency room, and did I wish to speak to her? I didn't, so I hung up the phone.

I'd been to that emergency room a couple of times with my kids, and I knew how long things took there. Once when Gretzky got a piece of a walnut up his nose, we sat there for hours and he eventually sneezed it out before any doctors appeared. So I figured Bonnie would be tied up for a while.

But just in case she somehow made it out of there and headed this way, I grabbed Gretzky's hockey stick to defend myself with. Then I sat in our darkened living room with the curtains open. Planning to pounce on Dave the instant he got home, I watched his driveway across the street and waited.

27

"Daddy! Daddy! Daddy!"

The words kept time with the pounding in my noggin and the throbbing in my foot.

"Daddy, Daddy, Daddy, Daddy!"

Through blurry, half-closed eyes, I could see Gretzky was so excited, he was flapping his arms up and down like a bird. Wait a minute. Where was I? I sat bolt upright in the living room chair. Jeez, I must have fallen asleep.

I looked at my watch. Six forty. I felt like a fool. Sam Spade, even at his drunkest, would never have fallen asleep in the middle of a case, with the crazed murderer almost in his grasp. Was it that delayed concussion syndrome thing again? Maybe I really better check myself back into the hospital.

Now that he was sure I was awake, Gretzky asked me, "Daddy, why were you sleeping with my hockey stick? Do you want to play hockey with me?"

"Gretzky, go to bed," I hissed impatiently. I looked across the street; Dave's car was back in his driveway.

"Daddy—"

"Go back to bed *right now.*" I needed to collect my foggy thoughts and go rap on Dave's door.

Gretzky's lips quivered. He was about to cry. "But, Daddy! I made peepee! Just like a real hockey player!"

God, the kid was such a little sweetheart. I pulled him into the chair with me and we cuddled.

But not for long. Immediately he started agitating again to play hockey. "Sure, and we can use my head for a puck," I said, "because that's how it feels."

He didn't appreciate my attempt at humor. "Real hockey players *always* play hockey after they make peepee," he told me earnestly.

Whoa, I better nip this one in the bud. "Look, I'm not going to play hockey with you every time you go to the bathroom. That's not how it works."

Gretzky was outraged. Oh, the injustice of it all! "But that's what the hockey player said!" Gretzky screamed. "We *have* to play hockey!"

"Be quiet!" I snapped, louder than I meant to, and he started bawling. I felt like bawling, too. I knew exactly what would happen next. Babe Ruth would wake up from the noise, get into bed with Andrea, and start quizzing her about Butch Huskey. Then she wouldn't be able to get back to sleep, and she'd stomp around the house pissed off at me, because it was supposed to be my morning to take care of the kids and let her sleep (we alternate). Didn't any of these people understand I had a murder case to solve? Gretzky's cries were driving me insane. I was getting dizzy again, and I needed coffee—intravenously, if possible. I couldn't face Dave without some coffee first.

"Hockey! Hockey!" Gretzky yelled.

"Coffee! Coffee!" I yelled back, even louder. That shocked him into silence, and he stared at me with wide, frightened eyes. I melted into a worn-out pile of tired, guilty slush. "Honey, I'm sorry, I just really, really, *really* want coffee," I whined, turning into a manipulative three year old myself.

I guess Gretzky could tell I was at the end of my rope, because he said to me, in a suddenly very reasonable tone, "I tell you what. First you can have coffee, then we'll play hockey."

"Thank you. Thank you, Gretzky," I said gratefully, hugging him. Coffee and hockey, then Dave. It was a plan. Dave would probably be more agreeable if I didn't wake him up at 6:45, anyway.

I figured I better get Gretzky and myself out of the house before we had another loud argument and woke up the others. So that's how we ended up at Madeline's at the stroke of seven, just as they were opening up. I peeked in through the window, prepared to go to Uncommon Grounds instead if I saw Marcie. But it looked like Rob was on his own, so Gretzky and I went in. Hopefully Gretzky would get distracted by their books and toys, and it would delay our hockey game even further. "Hey, Rob," I greeted him.

Rob looked up from his coffee grinding, surprised to see me so early on a weekend morning. He turned off the grinder and said, "Hey, my first customers. What's up?"

Gretzky broke in. "Guess what? We went to a hockey game?" Sometimes when he's excited about something, he turns every sentence into a question. "And there was this goalie? And you know how many times he stopped their shots?"

"How many?" Rob asked indulgently.

"Fifty-five million!"

"Wow, that's a lot."

"Fifty-five million trillion infinity!" Gretzky crowed.

"Coffee, please," I put in.

Rob threw me a smile. "I'll make the Ethiopian."

I started to tell him Colombian would be fine, but he'd already turned his back to get the beans. And there's no way he would have heard me anyway above Gretzky, who was singing out, "Fifty-five million trillion infinity infinity zillion thousand!"

Walking gingerly on my twisted ankle, I took Gretzky to the back room, where I sat down and waited for my caffeine while he went to the bookcase and checked out the kids' section. I gazed out the window. The sun was rising, the sky was a gorgeous shade of light blue, and I tried to empty my mind of all my worries. It didn't work.

Rob came up. "Coffee'll be ready in a minute."

I nodded my thanks, and he sat down with me. "Jacob, I want to let you know, we're scheduling The Penn's memorial tribute for Tuesday night. We'll sit around and drink Ethiopian and swap stories about him. How's that sound?"

Sounded great. We could invite Bonnie to come in and tell us the story of how she killed him. I sighed unhappily, and Rob peered at me, his eyes full of gentle concern. "Hey, dude, you look a little spaced this morning."

"Life's a bitch, bro," I told him. "Insanity rules."

"Insanity always rules," Rob agreed.

I wiped some sleep out of my eyes. Maybe if I talked to someone, it would straighten out my fuzzball brain. "I found out what happened," I said in a low voice.

Rob frowned, puzzled. "What do you mean?"

"I know who killed Donald Penn."

Rob stared at me, stunned, and said, "You're kidding."

I shook my head solemnly. "No."

I got a big kick out of Rob's reaction to my success. He was totally blown away, but tried to act Hollywood cool about it. "Man, I don't know what to say. So what are you gonna do?"

Aye, there's the rub. "I'll tell the police. See if they believe me."

Rob nodded thoughtfully. "You have enough evidence?"

Well, by God, that high-heel shoe and that mottled brick ought to be enough to at least get the cops *started.* And hey, if Molly saved the threatening typewritten note that flew through her window with the brick, maybe they'd be able to identify Bonnie's typewriter. Come to think of it, I'd noticed an old IBM Selectric in the Shoeshine and a Smile office.

"I think I do have enough," I said slowly. "I think I can pull this off."

Rob gave a little laugh and shook his head. I got the feeling he didn't really believe me, which pissed me off, but I couldn't say I blamed him. "You're quite a guy, Jacob," Rob said as he stood up. "Let me get you that Ethiopian—on the house."

"And I want milk!" Gretzky squealed from over by the bookcase. Rob nodded and headed for the front room as the kid jumped in my lap with a Curious George book and asked me to read to him. Next to hockey, monkeys are his biggest passion. My eyes weren't quite focusing yet, but reading aloud would require less energy than playing hockey, so I began. " 'Curious George Takes a Job,' " I read. " 'This is George. He lived in the zoo.' "

I was already at the part where Curious George is hiding underneath the elephant's ear when Rob came in with the coffee and milk and put them on the table. I thanked him and kept reading. No doubt Rob was dying to hear my theory about The Penn's death, but I was still irrationally pissed off at him for not believing me, so I decided to make him wait until I finished the book. As I turned the page, I picked up my cup and started to drink, but Gretzky shouted, "I want some!"

"Okay," I said. Yeah, I know three year olds are too young to drink coffee, but he loves a little bit of the stuff in his milk, and I hate to refuse him.

So I poured some coffee into the Great One's milk. I

noticed Rob staring at me, and felt guilty. "I know, I know, I'm raising a coffee addict," I said.

"Yay! Coffee milk!" Gretzky shouted. He put it to his lips, about to guzzle it all down in one gulp, and I turned back to Curious George.

But something wasn't right. I couldn't put my finger on it, but something just wasn't right. I looked back up at Rob.

He was staring at Gretzky. Staring at him, frozen with shock and horror.

What the hell was that all about? Why did Rob feel so strongly about caffeine for three year olds?

And then it hit me.

Oh, no. Oh Lord, no.

No, it can't be.

The coffee milk was already starting to pour down my son's vulnerable throat.

My arm leapt out. It slammed Gretzky's glass away from his mouth.

The glass crashed to the floor and broke, spewing coffee milk all over the place. I desperately hoped that most of the coffee milk was on the floor now—and not inside of Gretzky.

Because that coffee was poisoned.

Rob had killed Penn, and he thought I knew it, so he poisoned my coffee.

I looked at Rob. Rob looked at me. Gretzky started crying.

Then Rob drew a small gun from his pants pocket. My kid stopped crying and stared at it. So did I.

Nothing happened for a moment. Then Rob said, "Hey, Gretzky, you want to go play with the barrel of monkeys? They're in the front room, right by the window."

"Is that a real gun?" Gretzky asked.

"No," Rob said, but gave me a look to make sure I knew he was lying.

"Daddy, why'd you spill my coffee milk?" Gretzky turned to me angrily.

"Sorry, honey, it was the wrong kind of coffee." Rob impatiently waved his gun, a silent message that I better get Gretzky out of there fast. "Hey, why don't you go play with those monkeys in the other room?"

"But you're reading me a book!"

I checked Rob's face. His eyes had narrowed into unreadable slits, and for all I knew he was about to blast us both. I pleaded with my boy. "Honey—"

"No!"

I glanced at Rob again, and this time I had no trouble reading his eyes. Or his gun, which was pointed at me, steady.

"Sweetheart," I said, panicky, "how about if you get the monkeys to play hockey with each other?"

Gretzky's face instantly turned sunny. Monkeys *and* hockey—what a combination. "Okay," he said, and raced to the other room.

I would have heaved a huge sigh of relief if I didn't have a gun barrel in my face. "Now drink your coffee," Rob told me. His voice was ice cold.

"You'll never get away with this," I replied, my voice several octaves higher. I sound like a bad Hollywood movie, I thought to myself, like an actor in someone else's dream.

Rob quickly jolted me back to reality. "Thanks for the tip. Now drink the fucking coffee or I'll shoot you."

"Some choice."

"I'll shoot your boy, too."

"For Christ's sake, Rob, I didn't even know it was you. I thought it was Bonnie."

Rob eyed me in bewilderment, then started laughing. "You're shitting me."

I laughed, too. Who knows, maybe if we shared a little chuckle together, Rob would lighten up. "Hell no, I had Bonnie down cold. I knew she did that second burglary, and she was making death threats against this girl named Molly Otis, so I figured she killed Penn."

Rob abruptly stopped laughing and glowered at me. "So why didn't you just *tell* me? Why'd you have to be so fucking elliptical?"

Elliptical. No one who uses words like "elliptical" would ever actually shoot someone, would they? "Rob, put the gun down already. I can't do anything to you. I don't have any evidence."

Rob gave a you-can't-fool-me look. "Sure, you do. Gretzky drank some of that shit. They'll find it in his blood."

My heart thudded. "You mean, he already drank enough to kill him?!"

Thank God, Rob shook his head no. "But he drank enough so that if I let you go, and you get his blood tested, they'll find it. And they'll find the same stuff in Penn."

This was incredibly aggravating. "Damn it, Rob, why'd you have to *tell* me that? I never would've thought to get his blood tested if you hadn't suggested it."

Rob laughed harshly, then once again stopped abruptly. "Well, let's not cry over spilt milk. Drink up, asshole. And don't try waiting for the cavalry to rescue you. I locked the front door and Madeline doesn't get here 'til eight."

Where was Marcie when I really needed her? If I had known I would die so soon, maybe I'd have had sex with her after all. I grimaced at my coffee and asked, "What's in this anyway?"

"An O.D. of pure metherolamphethamine."

Keep him talking. "What the hell is that?"

"Designer speed. Souvenir from L.A. Very popular among screenwriters." Rob's face twisted into a grin, and his eyes gleamed. "I used it to help me write. And when they autopsy you, they'll figure that's why *you* were using it—to break through that writer's block of yours. Same with Penn, if those idiots ever get around to doing an autopsy on *him.* Your deaths will be attributed to overly pure street drugs. Happens all the time. Smooth, huh?" Without waiting for an answer, he continued, "Don't worry, it'll be painless, just like it was for Penn. No sweat."

"I still don't get it. Why did you kill him?"

"Because he wanted my computer."

"That's a capital offense?"

Rob stepped close to me, and before I knew what was coming he swiped at me with his gun. It crashed into my right ear, and all sorts of police sirens exploded inside me. If only those sirens were real—but they weren't. "Now drink, motherfucker, or your son will regret it." He aimed his gun toward the other room to emphasize his threat.

Gritting my teeth against the pain, I lifted my poisoned cup like I was about to drink it. I needed to think up some good dialogue for myself, and fast. Heck, I'd written enough screenplays, I ought to be able to hit on *something.* But the best I could do was, "Okay, Rob, I'll drink your little concoction, but before I die, I'd like to know why."

Rob looked exasperated, but answered me. "Fucking Penn got turned down for some fucking grant to buy a computer, and then he heard I was trying to sell mine. So he came in here early one morning when I was all alone, and told me I'd better give him my computer for free or else he'd tell Madeline about me having sex with Marcie. I said no, and he gave me three days to change my mind." Rob snorted angrily. "Fuck that, I knew the sonufabitch's reputation. If I said yes, he'd be sucking me dry for the rest of my life. And I'd be standing at the counter there, watching him do it."

"Why didn't you just tell Madeline? Maybe she'd forgive you."

"Yeah, right. Madeline is, like, 1800s. Jane Austen and shit."

I darted a furtive glance at the clock on the wall. *Damn, 7:15 still.* I'd have to hope Madeline came in early—like, way early. "But even if she broke up with you, so what? There's other women. You had your whole life ahead of you."

If I was trying to provoke him even more—which I wasn't—I succeeded. His nostrils flared, his eyes flashed, and his voice turned shrill. "You don't get it, dickhead. If Madeline breaks up with me, my life is *over!*"

"But—"

He slammed me again with the gun, and my head whirled; I was seeing Rob in triplicate now. But it didn't blur the viciousness in his face, which was so close to mine I could smell his coffee breath.

His eyes—all six of them—held mine as he snarled furiously, "I spend *five years* in Hollywood trying to break in, working as a *goddamn waiter* even though I'm a million times smarter than *any* of those airheads. So I give up and come back here, and the best job I can find is minimum wage at some lousy coffee shop." He was so out of control with rage, he was spraying spit all over my face as he talked. "If I don't marry Madeline, I'll be doing this kind of pissant job 'til the day I fucking die."

I snuck another quick glance at the clock: 7:16. Time crawls when you're not having fun. I hoped all the noise Rob was making wouldn't bring Gretzky back in from the other room. "But you could still go to grad school or law school—"

He barked out a sharp angry laugh. "Bullshit, I could never pay back the loans, even if I could get 'em in the first place. There's too many damn lawyers already. And what would I do with a Ph.D.—wipe my ass with it?" He bared his teeth at me. "See, what you jerkoff baby boomers don't get, the Land of Opportunity is deader than disco music. Welcome to the Land of Fucked Up Service Jobs. A rich bitch like Madeline is my only way out!"

7:17. *Shit.* "Hey, I understand it's hard—"

"Yeah, and I understand you checking that clock, but you better check this for a change." He waved the gun in front of my eyes, then pressed the barrel to my forehead.

If ever there was a good time to shit in my pants, this was it. Jesus, what a way to die. Shot in the face by a demented Generation Xer.

My eyes crossed as I watched Rob's finger on the trigger, and his face right behind it. His lips moved. "If I have to shoot you, I will. But I won't shoot Gretzky." I was baffled—was Rob trying to be nice to me?—but he quickly corrected that impression by sneering at me and whispering, "Your son will spend his whole life remembering how his daddy got shot while he was in the next room, playing with monkeys."

I stared at Rob in terror. *This was almost the exact same thing that happened to Donald Penn.* Would Gretzky end up as lonely and miserable as Penn was? My brain went numb, except for some grief-stricken corner that kept thinking two names, over and over: *Penn . . . Gretzky . . . Penn . . . Gretzky . . .*

I don't remember lifting the cup. And I don't remember it reaching my mouth. But I felt myself starting to drink. I felt the bitter coffee trickling between my lips—

"Daddy, Daddy, I made peepee again!" Gretzky shouted, racing in.

Rob, startled, waved his gun away from my forehead for a moment.

The same moment I flung my cup of coffee at his eyes.

He jerked his gun arm toward his eyes, then saw what he was doing and jerked it away. But in the middle of all that jerking, I slammed his arm. The gun fell away from his hand.

Unfortunately it fell closer to Rob than to me. Trying to gain time, I shoved the table in his gut. He gasped, the wind knocked out of him, and went sprawling. But before I could leap around the table and get the gun, he managed to crawl across the floor and reach out his hand.

Out of nowhere, Gretzky swooped down and got to the gun first. He picked it up. "Here," he said, and started to hand it to Rob.

Why'd the kid have to be so goddamn *polite* all of a sudden? *"No! Don't give him the gun!"* I screamed. Gretzky stared at me in confusion, but when Rob grabbed for the gun, he pulled it away just in the nick of time. Pleased with himself, he burst into a huge grin. Then Rob got to his feet, and Gretzky backed up. "Throw it here!" I shouted.

Giggling, Gretzky put his little arm back, getting ready to throw.

Rob put his arms up to block it, getting ready to lunge straight at him.

Then Gretzky feinted a throw. Rob dove to his right.

Gretzky feinted another throw. Rob dove to his left.

"Monkey in the Middle!" Gretzky called out joyfully.

If he didn't throw that frigging thing soon, I'd have a heart attack.

The problem was, Gretzky was into hockey, not baseball. If only that were Babe Ruth throwing the gun, he'd have lobbed it right over Rob's head, no problem. Fathers, here's yet another reason to play catch with your kids.

"Gretzky, throw it already! Throw it high!" I yelled.

Rob couldn't take the waiting anymore either, and lunged forward right as Gretzky finally threw the gun.

Just as I feared, it went low, hitting Rob's knee and then bouncing at his feet. But Gretzky's feinting had made Rob overeager; he couldn't stop his lunge, and it carried him away from the gun. Meanwhile I was lunging too, and it carried me toward the gun.

But not close enough. When I landed on the floor and reached out my arm, the gun was still a foot away and Rob was coming back for it.

Desperately, I slithered forward while Rob scrambled back. His hand stretched out, and so did mine. My fingers grabbed half of the gun just as his fingers grabbed the other half. We both tugged frantically—but he had the handle and I had the barrel, so he had a better grip. I felt it slipping out of my hand.

"Go, Daddy, go!" Gretzky cheered, laughing. His voice must have given me an extra surge of strength, because that's when I gave one more desperate yank and the gun came out of Rob's hand. I quickly aimed it at his face. He stared at me in shock as I stood up slowly, keeping the gun pointed.

"Yay, we won!" Gretzky shouted.

Rob jumped up. "Easy," I said, praying that there wasn't any particular trick to shooting a gun. It seemed like it would be easy, but I'd never done it before. Then all at once Rob ran toward me.

I started to squeeze the trigger.

At the last moment he swerved and ran past me into the front room.

I dashed in there after him. I couldn't let him get hold of a knife or some other kind of weapon. If he tried to, I'd kill him.

Meanwhile Gretzky dashed after me, singing, "We Are the Champions."

Rob was behind the counter, but when he saw me he ducked down out of sight. Shit, now what? I pointed the gun at the spot where I'd last seen his head. But by now he could be anywhere behind there. Gretzky's singing covered any noise Rob might be making. I shifted my aim to the end of the counter, in case he leaped around it with a weapon. I waited, my hand shaking, my finger quivering on the trigger.

Suddenly Rob stood up again in the same spot where he'd ducked down a moment before. I frantically swiveled the gun back at his face. But he didn't seem to be paying me any attention. He was focused on something in his hands.

A small plastic vial. Half filled with some kind of white powder.

Gretzky saw it, too. "Is that candy? Can I have some?" he asked.

But it wasn't candy. It was the poison. Rob opened the vial and raised it to his lips . . .

Good, I thought, *go ahead and die*. He tilted his head back, about to pour the poison down his throat.

Then, for no reason, a phrase from The Penn's preface somehow shot into my head: *"Every man has his clister, his 151 proof, his dreams."*

I still don't quite get it. Why did I suddenly remember those words right then? And why did remembering them give me a wave of compassion for the murderously unhappy young man with broken dreams standing there in front of me?

But that's what happened. It's strange when I think about it, but The Penn's preface, which he labored on for so many pathetic and seemingly pointless years, turned out in the end to have a powerful impact.

That preface saved a man's life.

Because with The Penn's words ringing in my brain, I reached over the counter and wrenched the poison-filled vial away from Rob. He watched in horror while I put the vial safely away in my pocket.

I thought he'd jump out at me from behind the counter and do his best to tear the shit out of me, gun or no gun. Once again I got ready to shoot. But Rob surprised me. He put his head down on the counter. Then he started to weep.

Gretzky was impatient at this latest turn of events. "Can we play hockey now?" he asked me.

I nodded slowly. "Let me just make one phone call first."

This time I remembered the last name. *Mackerel.*

28

The morning sun shone brightly through the window as I carried my java and *Daily Saratogian* to the front table of the coffee shop. Not Madeline's, Uncommon Grounds. I'd been steering clear of Madeline's for the past week, ever since Rob got arrested there.

Rob was still in prison, but I heard on the grapevine he'd be getting out on bail soon. Madeline had broken up with him, but she decided to take the money for the wedding, and spend it on Rob's legal defense instead. A classy lady, that Madeline. There must be someone I could set her up with. Maybe Dave . . .

I wondered what kind of legal strategy Rob's lawyers would dream up. They'd have a tough row to hoe. The D.A.'s office had exhumed Penn's body and found speed in his blood that matched the speed in Rob's vial, so they had Rob cold on Penn's murder.

On the other crimes, they hadn't yet found any evidence proving that Rob burglarized my house that first time, even though I felt sure it was him. But they did find a credit card receipt for some gasoline he bought the night that the Arts Council office, and Penn's apartment, burned down. He got four dollars' worth, the same amount that would fit into a plastic gas container they'd discovered in the trunk of his car, empty. I still didn't know whether Rob's main goal with the arson was to kill me or destroy any of Penn's writings that were in the building.

As I reconstructed it, the reason Rob had talked about setting up a memorial service for Penn was because that made it look like he felt friendly toward the dead man. It would deflect suspicion away from himself, if the cops ever figured out Penn was murdered.

Or maybe Rob was just plain crazy, and that's why he wanted to hold a memorial service for the man he'd murdered. I'd been right that a frustrated artist gone berserk had killed Penn; I'd just been wrong about *which* frustrated artist. Further proof of his craziness was the way he'd watched Penn's funeral from behind the McDonald's sign, out of sick curiosity.

Or maybe he watched the funeral and planned the memorial service because in some way he felt guilty.

In any case, none of these unresolved speculations detracted from the main thing: Rob was stone busted. Unless, of course, his legal eagles came up with something incredibly brilliant. Who knows, maybe they'd make history by inventing a new defense: the Generation X Insanity Defense. Mental derangement caused by the stress of living in a dying civilization.

It was worth a shot. If Rob got a jury of his peers, maybe he'd get off.

More likely, the lawyers would plea bargain and Rob would get sent down for ten to twenty-five, something like that. And then one day, say five years from now, I'd walk into some barren, remote upstate prison to teach a writing class . . . and there in the corner of the room I'd spot a familiar face. And we'd give each other a sad little nod.

But hey, like Yogi Berra and about seven billion other people have said at one time or another, it ain't over 'til it's over. Maybe with all that free time in jail, Rob would end up writing a modern cinema masterpiece. And when they let him out, he'd hit Hollywood and hang out at the Viper Room with Quentin T. and the rest of the guys.

For some reason I put off opening the *Daily Saratogian* for a moment longer, even though there was an article in it I was eager to read. I sipped my coffee and gazed out the window at the people passing by. One of them was Gretchen Lang. She saw me, pursed her lips, and turned away.

It seemed like a lot of people were pursing their lips and turning away from me on the streets of Saratoga these days: Gretchen, Marcie, the mayor, the grant panelists . . . hopefully the bad feelings would ease up in time. Saratoga is too small a place for people to hold grudges.

Already my relationship with Bonnie Engels was improving. She'd approached me three days earlier, while I was sipping coffee at Uncommon Grounds. I'd risen out of my seat, half expecting her to punch me. But instead she wrapped her arms around me in one of her infamous hugs.

This particular hug wasn't as tight as usual, a fact that was explained by the big white bandages on her arm where I'd pitchforked her. She must still be tender there. Though when I say her hug wasn't as tight as usual, I mean she only broke two ribs instead of three.

Her eyes pierced mine as she said, "Jacob, I just want to thank you."

Huh? This woman had a way of bringing out the *Huh?* in me. "For what?"

"For the other night. When you stuck the pitchfork in me."

"Oh." I didn't know what to say. "Well, you're welcome."

"It was so wonderful. You forced me to finally confront my steroid addiction."

I just stood there blinking.

Bonnie took my hand and held it. "Jake, it was awful. It got to where I was giving myself shots in the buttocks three times a day." She put my hand on her ass and squeezed, I guess showing me the spot where the needle went in. "That's why I was acting so weird. I mean, burglarizing people, throwing bricks through windows, trying to kill my dearest friends with pitchforks . . ." She laughed. "That's just not me."

"Glad to hear it." I gently tried to take my hand back, but Bonnie just held it tighter. Her eyes lit up with enthusiasm.

"I'm telling you, Jacob, I've been off the steroids for a week now, and I just feel so great. I'm even boxing better!" She pumped my hand up and down excitedly. "I'm thinking about making an educational video for kids about the dangers of steroids. It would only cost about ten thousand dollars to produce, and the marketing possibilities—I mean, wow!"

I'll spare you the rest of the conversation.

As for myself, and why I was leisurely sipping coffee instead of hunching intensely over my computer while inputting such deathless dialogue as: "Oh my God! It's *them!*" "No! No! *Not the beetles!*" well, here's what happened. First I had fifty-five million trillion infinity infinity zillion thousand (as Gretzky would say) hours of questioning by the cops, during which I managed to leave out such irrelevant details as my various felonies, and the fact that the mayor was a crook and the grant panelists were sleazoids. Not to protect *them*, but to protect Gretchen. There was no way to tell about the mayor and the panelists without telling about her too, and I didn't feel she deserved to have her life ruined.

After that I was questioned by Andrea for another fifty-five million trillion infinity infinity zillion thousand hours, and I was lucky she didn't kill me when she found out all the risks I'd taken. Then I went to bed and slept for another fifty-five million *et cetera* hours, which as I mentioned earlier is not recommended for concussion victims, so kids, don't try this trick at home. I was lucky I didn't get brain damaged—or at least, I don't think I did.

In any case, between one thing and another I never quite got around to sending in that contract. The producers got tired of waiting, and I guess they figured out I wasn't exactly Mr. Gung Ho, so they withdrew their offer and went with another writer—some other flavor-of-the-week guy who'd just written a hot new movie about lesbian zombie serial killers.

Ah, well. I'll miss that 750 K, but bottom line, who cares? Solving Penn's murder—even by mistake—had reminded me there were better things to do with my life than rewriting movies I didn't even give a shit about in the first place. After last week's adventures I felt like a teenager again, like I could do anything: commit B and Es, kick politicians in the balls, hold crazed murderers at bay, all kinds of fun stuff.

Already I'd begun outlining a new movie, not some grade B horror flick, but not the kind of stuff I used to write either. In fact, as you may have guessed, the movie was going to be about Penn's murder. Just for kicks, I was thinking of fictionalizing it so that the main character, the intrepid detective, would be my favorite nonagenarian Presbyterian minister. That way I could get in the scene with the crotchless Minnie Mouse underwear.

I had one more sip of java, then unfolded the newspaper. And there it was: right on page one, above the fold. Judy had kept her promise and treated The Penn well. His preface—actually three of his prefaces, which I'd edited into one—was printed in full, in a large four-column box with a bold black border. Impressive looking. As for content, I flattered myself—and Penn—that between his writing and my editing we'd come up with a damn decent three pages. Better than Joyce, anyway. I skimmed it. "Clister . . . Ethiopian . . . Paula Barbieri . . ."

I smiled. At long last, after thirty years of struggle, Donald Penn was an honest to God *published author.* I read through the preface to make sure there weren't any typos marring his immortality. Amazingly enough, there weren't.

Then I turned to the eulogy I'd written, which ran alongside the preface. Maybe I'd gotten Penn immortality, but he'd done something for me in return: Writing that eulogy had busted my writer's block wide open. Judy had kept my headline: *"A Dead Man's Legacy."* The text began, *"For over thirty years, Donald Penn wandered the streets of our city, drinking Ethiopian coffee wherever he could find it, filling old notebooks and flattened milk cartons with his scribbles, a strange, unkempt, bearded little man, pitied by some, laughed at by others. But now that he is dead, the truth has finally come out: This odd little man was a true literary giant."*

Okay, so I exaggerated a bit.

Somehow I didn't think The Penn would mind.